Forever Faithful

by

Linda LaRoque

Forever Faithful

Published by *L.G. Smith Books*
Cover Art by *Diana Carlile*
http://www.designingdiana.blogspot.com

Publishing History
First Edition, 2008
Digital ISBN 978-0-9979908-0-5
Print ISBN 978-0-9979908-1-2

Published in the United States of America

Chapter One

Johnson Ranch, Texas Hill Country

Gail lay on the bed, a grin stretching her face as she listened to Lucas sing in the shower. She resisted the urge to run into the kitchen and turn on the hot water so she could hear his yelp as the cold stream hit him. Nope, better not this morning. She was taking a week of vacation to do some redecorating and wanted to be in town by nine. Last time she'd done so, he jumped out, chased her down, and pulled her in the shower with him. It would be fun to see her handsome husband run wet and naked through the house again, but... She rolled off the bed and dressed in shorts and a tee shirt.

When Lucas entered the kitchen, Gail lifted slices of crisp bacon onto a paper towel to drain. He caught her around the waist and drew her backside up against him while she poured pancake batter into the old iron skillet atop the stove. His lips nibbled across her neck, making her shiver.

"Mmm, you taste good," he said.

She turned in his arms and put her head on his chest. God, she loved this man. They'd been married four years, known each other a lifetime and the sound of his voice still made her heart lurch. Squeezing his waist, she shoved him back a step, smiled up at him, and teased. "You smell mighty fine to be working with horses all day."

He laughed and started filling their mugs with coffee. "Well, a man never knows when his favorite filly might visit him at the stables."

"So true, but not this morning, I'm afraid." The pancake she handed him covered his plate. He spread butter on it and liberally doused it with maple syrup. When hers was finished, she added a second one for him to the pan and sat down.

"What time do you think you'll be home?"

"In plenty of time to fix lunch. If not, I'll stop and pick up hamburgers at the Dairy Queen." She caught the gleam in his blue eyes and ducked her head to hide her grin. Lucas loved junk food, hamburgers especially.

He devoured his pancake and got up to flip the one in the pan and stood, hip cocked, against the counter waiting for the other side to brown. "Don't cut your shopping short to cook lunch for me. Take your time."

She rose and stacked her plate and cup in the sink.

He added the second pancake to his plate and carried it to the table. "Leave those and get your shower. I'll clean up the kitchen." As she walked out of the room, Gail grinned when she heard him add, "And hey, hon, bring me two burgers for lunch."

~*~

The Johnson Ranch was fifteen miles from Stony Creek, a small town forty miles west of Austin. Gail parked in a metered spot on the town square in front of the bank and checked her makeup and hair in the rearview mirror before shutting off the engine. The hot morning July humidity hit her as she stepped out of the car. Already well into the 80's, the temperature would be over 100 degrees before the day ended. She smoothed the pants of her lime green cropped pantsuit over her hips and looked both ways before crossing the street.

She passed the big glass window of Brown and Guthrie's Accounting Office where she worked and waved to Sue, their receptionist. From behind her desk, Sue grinned and wiggled her fingers in response. The hardware store sat in the adjacent block, so Gail studied the new dresses in the boutique on the corner before moving on to the hardware store. She and Lucas's fourth anniversary happened to be coming up. A new dress would be nice.

By eleven-thirty, Gail's paint purchases were loaded in her car and she started home. Beside her sat a bag of hamburgers. Their scent wafted around her, making her stomach rumble. She'd added fries. Lucas would be in hog heaven.

Gail had lunch on the table when Lucas came in at noon. As he approached her with purpose, his sexy grin melted her innards. He swept her into a deep kiss that left her trembling. Before releasing her, he gave her butt a gentle squeeze. "How'd the shopping go?" he asked as he turned to the sink to wash up.

"Great. Saw Jason. He said Joey is already walking."

"Really? The little bugger can't be that old already." He nuzzled her neck. "Kids sure grow up fast."

"That they do." She pointed to the table.

"Sure is nice having you home during the day, hon. I know you want to work full time, but you know how I feel."

And she did. He wanted her at home, and though she might be happy doing so after they had kids, she needed to work now and gain some experience using the tools she'd toiled for four years to earn. Plus, she needed some independence. Since she contributed to their income, she didn't have to ask for money—could spend when she wanted.

"We don't really need the money. There's a lot to keep you busy around here. Like all that painting and decorating you mentioned."

"I still have time for decorating projects. Sit down and let's eat." They ate quietly for a while, enjoying each other's company.

"When you come home this evening, the bedroom will be a different color. I can't wait to see how it looks with the new spread and stuff I bought last week."

He finished chewing and grinned. "It's not pink, is it?"

"Not pink per se."

He shuddered and his dark brows furrowed. "You're teasing, right?"

"I'm teasing. I think you'll like what I've picked out."

"Whew, thank goodness."

Gail spent the remainder of the afternoon painting the bedroom a sand color and left the baseboards and door trims white. She made the tiger oak four-poster bed with sand colored sheets before smoothing on the tapestry spread with its threads of brown, gold, sand, purple and red. For accessories, she added red and purple throw pillows, coordinating throw rugs, and an old painting she hung above the bed. The scene showed a mare nuzzling her colt. Lucas would be pleased. He loved horses and most of his work on the ranch revolved around breeding them. Two old stuffed chairs sat in front of the window with a footstool between them. She stood back to look at her creation. It was warm and cozy, intimate. Hopefully Lucas would agree.

She'd stepped out of the shower when the phone rang. Towel wrapped around her, she rushed to the bedside table to pick up the receiver. Breathless, she answered. "Hello."

"Hi, hon. It's me. I'm going to be late. The sheriff's office called. Bud needs me, Dad, and your father to meet him at the suspension bridge that crosses Possum Creek."

The bridge and Possum Creek separated Steele land from Johnson land. Though named a creek, in places it was deep and wide enough to be a river. For years the Steele side had been used by both families for picnics and fishing.

"What's wrong?"

"Don't have a clue, sugar. But, it wasn't a friendly invitation, more like a summons. I'll call if I'm going to be very late."

~*~

Lucas drove the half mile from the stables and stopped in front of the main house of the Johnson Ranch. His father and mother had built the hacienda style home in the 1970's and moved out of the house where he and Gail now lived. Big, with five bedrooms, it was more room than his parents needed. Evidently they'd hoped for more children, but they'd never arrived. As a kid, he'd often wondered why.

His father waited on the porch and climbed into the truck as soon as Lucas pulled to a stop. "This is a heck of a note, isn't it?" Randall said as he buckled up. "Can't imagine what's wrong out there now."

"Maybe someone's dumping tires in the water again. No telling what's going on." Lucas pulled away as soon as his father closed the door and spent the next several minutes mulling over what might be going on at the creek.

When they reached the bridge, several county cars lined the culvert in the shade of the trees. A narrow dirt road led into a common place for folks to pull off the road and park their cars to go fishing. The sandy area was flat with an eight foot drop down to the water. Over the years, a trail had been cut through the brush that led downstream closer to the bank.

Bud Sharp, Stone County Sheriff, met them as they climbed out of the truck. He pumped their hands. Bud looked like he'd lost some weight. His belly didn't hang as far over his belt as it used to and his khaki pants sagged in the butt. Lucas knew his wife worried about his cholesterol level and had him on a diet. "Randall, Lucas, thanks for coming. Sam got here a few minutes ago."

Randall spoke up. "Sure thing, Bud. What's the problem?"

Bud walked with them to the deep drop. "Look real close down there. See anything?"

Lucas strained to find something unusual in the dark water. The sun slipped from behind a cloud, and he saw sunlight glance off glass in the water. "Damn, it looks like a car down there."

He glanced back at Bud.

"Yep, it's a car all right. Got a wrecker coming to drag it out." Bud looked between Lucas and his father.

"Got any idea whose it could be?"

Lucas shook his head as his father spoke. "I don't have a clue. How about you, son?"

"No idea at all. Has anybody been able to make out the model?"

Before Bud could answer, a wrecker from Billy's Towing Service in Stony Creek pulled in, and Bud hustled over to show Billy where to park.

Billy, wearing his usual overalls, joined them and looked down into the water. "Ooo wee, how you reckon that got down there, Lucas?"

"Don't have an inkling. This hasn't become an addition to your wrecking yard, has it?"

On occasion teenagers pulled under the trees here to work on their cars. Once last fall, Lucas called Billy out to pick up a motor someone left sitting on the cliff edge. Looked like they'd tried to push it over into the creek, but ran out of steam.

Billy laughed and slapped Lucas on the back. "Real funny, Lucas." He shook hands with Randall. "How ya doing, Mr. Johnson?"

"Good, how about yourself?"

"Fine and dandy."

Lucas glanced over at Billy's wrecker, parked to the side of the clearing. Billy noticed and shrugged. "Bud says to wait. He's got a diver coming all the way from Austin to check the area before we start hauling her out. Probably nothing, but if it's a crime scene, don't wanna destroy any evidence."

A crime scene? Hell's bells, a crime hadn't occurred around Possum Creek in forever—since his high school years. A bunch of kids got drunk, a brawl started, and before the party ended, a boy almost drowned. Sam Steele had been sitting on his front porch and heard the distant screams carried on the night air. Bud's daddy was sheriff back then and seems about half the senior class landed in jail. Thank goodness he'd been out of town that weekend.

Lucas walked over to sit on a stump beside Sam Steele. It had been just over a week since he and Gail had last seen her father. "Hey, Sam, know anyone missing a car in these parts?"

"No, son, sure don't. Could be someone disposed of an old junker. You know how trashy some folks can be. Like dumping all those tires down there." He shook his head in disgust.

Nodding in agreement, Lucas scanned the area around them. Some people bore no respect for others, much less the land. This was a beautiful spot. Huge oak trees lined the creek. Rock cliffs, covered with stubby trees, brush, and grasses, rose behind them. Running along the cliff, a path had been cleared through the thick brush and was easily passable if one watched where they put their feet. It gradually sloped downhill to the creek bed lined with sand and river rock. There the water grew shallow enough to fish and swim.

Lucas looked at his father-in-law. Though only in his early fifties, the man looked older. His face was sun-browned and wrinkled, especially around the eyes and mouth. Working outdoors aged a man, especially one with Sam's pale coloring and blond hair. His wife leaving him probably hadn't helped. But when his blue eyes lit with humor or anger, the man looked ten years younger.

"Hey, how about coming to dinner tomorrow night? You haven't been over in a while. Gail's been

8

painting and will want you to see all the frou-frou she's added to the house."

Sam grinned and nodded. "I'll be there."

They heard the approaching roar of a motorcycle. A young man riding a Harley, towing a small trailer, drove in and parked to the side out of the way. Bud walked over to meet him. The biker removed his black helmet to reveal a buzz haircut. He sported a Hawaiian shirt, shorts, and what looked like combat boots. Lucas and Sam, along with the other men, moved closer so they could hear. "Hi, Sheriff, I'm Tom Wilson. Hear you need a diver."

"Sure do, son." He looked the kid up and down. His outfit didn't exactly encourage confidence. "You sure you're qualified to do this?"

Tom pulled his wallet from his hip pocket, flipped it open to his badge, and held it out to Bud. Bud glanced at it and nodded.

"Okay. Anything you need, let us know."

The diver unloaded equipment from the trailer and small rear trunk, and then started pulling on a wet suit. Billy backed the truck as close to the creek edge as possible and waited. Air tank and face mask in place, carrying an underwater light and fins, Tom eased down the steep bank. He sat down, put on his fins, and disappeared into the dark depths of the water. Approximately ten men peered around the truck trying to see.

They could see beams of light under the water, but not much else. They all waited expectantly for him to surface and say something, but he remained below.

Finally he surfaced, removed his mouthpiece, and called out to Bud. Bud leaned over the edge in anticipation.

"Sheriff, the windows and doors are shut with no broken glass. It's a 1978 Olds Cutlass, can't tell the color." He lifted his goggles. "Two bodies in the front."

Chapter Two

The phone rang at seven. It was Lucas.

"Looks like we'll be here late. There's a car underwater and it's got two bodies in it. Bud had dispatch contact the coroner's office. A forensics team just arrived from Austin and another diver went down with a fella named Tom Wilson."

She gasped. "Do they have any idea who it might be?"

"If Bud knows, he's not saying."

She could hear voices in the background and Bud's booming voice. "Hurry the hell up. It's getting dark out here."

"That water is so murky, how can they see anything?"

"They've got lights. And I can see camera flashes radiate from beneath the water."

"I'll hold dinner until you get here."

"No, you go on and eat. I'll pop a plate in the microwave when I get home."

Gail hung up the phone and plopped down on the sofa, feet pulled up under her. Two bodies, the thought gave her the willies. Good grief, who could they be? As far as she knew, no one around here had been reported missing. The fact didn't mean anything, though. They could be from anywhere.

She ate, fixed Lucas a plate, and put the leftovers

in the refrigerator. Though tempted to begin painting the living room, she hated to get started and not have time to finish. She cleaned the bathroom and put out the new towels she'd bought with scented candles to match. Left with nothing else to do, she turned on the television, flipped through the channels, and then turned it off. Nothing was on worth watching.

A "woof" sounded at the back door. She let Chief, Lucas's German shepherd, in the kitchen. He trotted to his bowls and she added dry food to the empty one and freshened his water. She received a nudge on her leg and a lick on the foot in thanks. "You're welcome."

Gail sighed. She was bored all by herself. If she went on to bed, Lucas wouldn't be able to see how pretty the bedroom looked with the new spread and all. She looked around the room and her eyes stopped at her wedding portrait hanging above the fireplace. They'd waited four years before marrying. Her father wanted her to get a college degree, meet other men before settling down at eighteen. He didn't want her to commit to a life of ranching, tire of it, and then leave like her mother. Lucas didn't want to wait, but agreed out of respect for her father. She'd gotten her education, crammed five years of study into four, but never dated anyone other than Lucas while in Houston.

Her eyes lit on the floor-to-ceiling bookcase covering the wall to the left of the fireplace. Lucas had a bunch of Elmer Kelton's western novels standing neatly on one row. She thumbed through them, selected *The Pumpkin Rollers*, and snuggled down on the sofa to read. Chief settled at her feet, yawned, and laid his head on his paws.

She was grinning at the story's description of

farmers-turned-cowmen when she heard the sound of Lucas's truck. Chief's head lifted, he stood and stretched before trotting to the carport door. Gail looked at the clock. It was after nine. Lucas came in and bent to greet his faithful friend.

"Hello, boy, you protect the home front while I'm gone?" Lucas teased Chief as the dog danced around him. "Good boy!"

He kissed Gail. "Hi, sugar. Boy, am I bushed. And hungry."

"Take a quick shower and I'll get your supper ready."

Lucas yelled from the bedroom. "Wow, hon, looks great in here."

She joined him in the middle of the room as he looked around. "Like it okay?"

He wrapped his arm around her shoulders and pulled her close. "I love it. You did a great job. What color is the paint?"

"Mohave sand."

"Nice." He released her and strode into the bathroom.

Gail sat at the table while he ate, listening to Lucas's every word. Chief lay at his feet. "Town is going to be in an uproar tomorrow. Press will be here from Austin, maybe some of the other big cities, too."

"Do they have any idea who the bodies are or whether or not it was an accident?"

"Bud's not saying anything, but he was grim all night, so I suspect he knows something he wasn't telling. There was no identification on the bodies, so it may take a while to learn their identities. Shouldn't take him long though to find out who the car belongs to, which will be a strong lead as to who the man is. Maybe the woman, too."

How terrible for someone's family. "Maybe Bud can distribute pictures for identification."

Lucas laid his fork down. "Did I not tell you? The bodies have been there a long time. There's nothing left but bones and some clothing."

Gail shivered. "God, all this time someone has been down there? But, the creek's not very deep. How could it hide a car?" She got up to refill both their glasses of tea.

"Seems there's a deep hole there just off the bank. It's probably twenty feet deep by forty feet wide, though not in an exact square or circle. Don't have a clue what could have gouged it out."

She thought back. "Seems I remember Daddy saying he used to go swimming there as a kid. Did he have any idea it was there?"

"No, don't think so. My daddy used to swim there, too." He grinned. "I think our two old men used the place to go skinny-dipping and then walk up the creek and fish." Lucas finished off his supper and pushed his plate back. "Bud asked everyone there and neither my or your dad stepped forward with any information, so I assume they didn't know the hole existed."

The phone rang and Gail went to pick up the wall extension by the back door. "Hi, Daddy. We were just talking about you and Randall skinny-dipping in your youth."

"That we did, girl," said Sam. "You fix Lucas a nice supper?"

"Of course I did. He's cutting a slice of cake as we speak."

"Tell him to enjoy his cake, because in about twenty years, he'll have acid reflux if he eats this late in the evening."

"I'll tell him." Had he eaten tonight? He was all alone now. "Daddy, what did you eat tonight?"

"Ruth left a plate for me in the oven. Don't you be worrying about me. I get plenty to eat."

"Well, you know you're always welcome here. Everything okay over there? You just call to chat?"

"Wanted to know how you're taking the news about the bodies down at the creek. You okay, baby girl?"

"Why, sure, Daddy, I'm fine. It's terribly sad, but...you don't think it's someone we know, do you?"

His hoarse voice rasped in the phone. "No, no, don't have a clue who it could be. It's just, you know, you're still my little one, even though you're a married woman now."

"Well, I'm fine. Quit your worrying and cut down on your smoking. Your voice is hoarser tonight."

Sam coughed. "Got a touch of the allergies, that's all."

Allergies, my foot. "Please, Daddy, try to cut down." She worried about him. He smoked too much and had a persistent cough. Somehow she'd see he got in to see Doc Smith in the next week or two.

"Okay, I will, I promise. Tell Lucas if he or Randall hears anything to let me know, and I'll do likewise."

Gail hung up the phone. "Daddy thought I might be upset. He worries about me too much."

Lucas snagged her around the waist and pulled her onto his lap. "I guess that's a daddy thing. I'll probably be the same way someday." He fed her a bite of cake.

She chewed and thought how cute Lucas would be with a little girl tagging along with him at the stables. Wouldn't it be wonderful if she missed her period next week?

"You want some milk or coffee with your dessert?" She tried to get up, but he held tight.

"Nah, tea is good."

"Daddy said to tell you to enjoy the cake because in twenty years you'll have acid reflux when you eat this late."

Lucas frowned. "Boy, he's just full of exciting news."

The phone rang again. Gail answered, and handed it to Lucas. "It's your daddy."

As he listened, Lucas's smile turned into a frown. He hung up the phone and turned to Gail. "The forensics team found evidence the two people were shot—murdered. And the woman was still alive when she drowned."

~*~

Lucas felt whipped. His shoulders ached and, if he didn't eat soon, he'd fall over in a faint. He'd ridden fence all day and didn't make it home for lunch. The wind had blown continuously, his eyes stung, and he wore a layer of grit. He pulled his truck into the carport and groaned as he eased his tired body from the cab. The tantalizing smell of roast beef and fresh yeast rolls assaulted him and his stomach growled with anticipation. His grin of appreciation faded. Shoot, he'd forgotten to tell Gail her dad was coming for dinner.

She met him in the short hall directly off the carport with a kiss and leaned in to hug him. He stepped back and threw up his hands.

"Whoa, babe, I'm filthy." Dang he felt guilty. "Honey, I'm sorry I forgot to tell you something."

Her body stiffened. "What?"

"I invited your daddy over to eat tonight."

"Oh, is that all?" She kissed him again and patted his cheek. "You sweet man, I cooked plenty."

Sighing with relief, he followed her into the kitchen, walked past the alcove holding the washer and dryer into their bedroom located directly behind the carport. As he pulled off his boots, he yelled, "I'm going to shower." The carpet felt good against his sore feet.

He heard her, "okay," just before he closed the bathroom door. A moan escaped him as the hot water hit his shoulders and back. Leaning against the stall wall, he let the warmth wash over him and ease the tension in his muscles.

The water cooled for a minute, and he froze waiting for a blast of cold to hit him. When in a playful mood, Gail loved to give him a shock in the shower by turning on the hot water in the kitchen. He sighed with relief as the stream stayed hot.

When he stepped from the bathroom, he heard Sam's voice in the living room. He quickly pulled on clean cut-offs, a tee shirt, and stepped into a worn-out pair of sandals. On his way out the door, he ran a hand through his damp hair. Their living area was separated from the kitchen by a half wall. Sam and Gail stood by the bookshelves, looking at a photo album and laughing quietly.

"Hey, Sam, glad you could make it." Lucas put his arm around Gail's shoulder and pulled her close. She melted against his side and laid her hand on his chest.

"Gail says you forgot to tell her you'd invited me."

"Yeah, I did." He looked down at his wife. "Guess I need to brush up on my husbandly duties."

Gail hugged him. "It's all right."

Sam snorted. "Lucky you've got a forgiving wife. Some women would've thrown a tantrum."

With a chuckle, she said, "Now that'd be a sight. Anyway, you're my dad and don't need an invitation." She took his hand and looped her other arm through Lucas's. "Come on, you two. Supper is on the table."

As Lucas held Gail's chair, his hands slid down her arms in a caress and he planted a kiss on her cheek. "Mmmmmm. Roast beef, one of my favorites."

Sam chuckled. "Happens to be one of mine, too."

Conversation grew lively as they ate. The town was on its ear because of all the media in Stony Creek and the rumors flying around. Folks had to fight crowds to buy groceries and eat in the cafe.

"I talked to Dad earlier," Lucas said. "The car belonged to a traveling salesman named Lamar Jacobs of Houston. Mr. and Mrs. Jacobs had recently divorced and he told his ex-wife he intended to leave Texas to start a new life." He paused for a drink of tea. "She had the impression he'd met a woman somewhere around Austin and would pick her up on his way to Canada. The last time Mrs. Jacobs talked to her ex-husband was in June of 1982. The fact he'd not contacted her or his son in the past twenty-some odd years wasn't a mystery to her as Lamar never took his marriage or parenthood seriously."

Sam speared another piece of roast beef and coated it with thick gravy. "I was in town today and news vans from Austin, Houston, and San Antonio were parked around the square. Stopped by On the Square Cafe for a cup of coffee. Lola said she'd had to hire an extra cook and waitress to feed the horde of news people. The motels are full and some of the town's citizens are cashing in on the booming business and rented out rooms."

Chuckling, Sam added, "This town hasn't had anything this exciting happen since 1935 when Homer Poage shot Jimmy Wilson in the leg for getting his daughter Susie pregnant. The next day, leg bandaged and pale faced, Jimmy married Susie in front of old Judge Snyder at the courthouse."

Gail laughed. "Daddy, you weren't even born back then."

Sam grinned, making his blue eyes dance. "Maybe not, young lady, but my old man was around and he loved to tell the story."

"Yeah, I remember Granddaddy Johnson telling it a time or two," Lucas said. Lucas wondered how long it would take to identify the bodies. He knew the remains had been sent to the forensics lab in Dallas. Speculation as to their identities would be the favorite topic of folks around the county for months to come.

Sam spoke up. "I don't see how they'll ever be able to identify those bodies unless they've got some clues to go on."

"Don't you ever watch those forensics shows on television?" Gail asked. "A killer always leaves clues."

"Yeah, Sam, it just takes longer sometimes to find those clues. Of course, they can use Lamar Jacobs's son's DNA to help identify him. Unless someone comes forward, it'll be harder to identify the woman."

Gail started clearing the table. Lucas went to the refrigerator for the leftover cake. He set it on the table and turned back to the cabinet for dessert plates. Gail poured them a cup of coffee from the pot she'd had ready to start brewing when they sat down.

Sam rubbed his hands together in glee. "I was sure hoping there'd be some chocolate cake left." The older man's brow furrowed. "Guess I better make sure I take an antacid before I go to bed."

"Daddy, you act like you don't ever get sweets. Ruth cooks for you all the time. She's an excellent cook and the woman dotes on you. I can't imagine why you're so excited about left over cake."

"Yeah, but she's been on a health kick. Wants me to eat frozen yogurt and crap like that."

Gail's face paled. "Why, have you been sick?"

Lucas could feel the concern animating from her body. She looked at Lucas in accusation. He shook his head. Hell, he didn't know anything.

"Nope." Sam shifted in his seat. Gail continued to stare at him. "Oh, all right, my cholesterol's high and Doc Smith wants me to lower it some, but he gave me some pills, so I don't know why the old bat keeps trying to make me eat stuff I don't like."

Lucas had to bite his cheek to keep from laughing. He could just imagine what Ruth had been serving Sam. One day he'd met her at the grocery store and her cart had been full of green vegetables, fish, and chicken. No beef whatsoever. For a Texas cattle rancher raised on beef, that was a hard pill to swallow.

Gail looked at her daddy through narrowed eyes. "Are you telling me everything?"

Sam nodded and went back to his cake.

"Daddy?"

Lucas watched as she studied her father. Yes, his brown leathery complexion was paler than normal, but not much. The man's wide shoulders didn't seem to hold as much muscle as he remembered. He'd lost some weight, but if Ruth had him on a diet that was to be expected.

Sam dropped his fork and sat back. "Ah, hell, it was just a tiny little pain one day. Ruth got all excited and made a mountain out of a mole hill."

"Where was this pain?" Lucas asked. *Please don't let it be a heart pain.*

Sam glared at Gail, but she wasn't giving an inch.

He muttered, "All right, it was a chest pain. Are you satisfied?"

"Not particularly. I imagine Doc Smith had some other orders for you other than to watch what you ate. He said to stop smoking, too, didn't he, Daddy?"

"Hell, yes, but I've tried and can't do it. I'm like every other smoker—I've quit a thousand times and here I sit dying for a cigarette right now."

Gail met Lucas's eyes. He squeezed her hand.

"Well, could you try harder, Daddy? Please. I'd like for your grandchild to know you."

Lucas thought that might be just the incentive Sam needed to finally kick the habit. If only Gail were pregnant now.

"Are you pregnant?" Sam cocked an eyebrow and grinned. Lucas's heart lurched to his throat in hope.

She threw up her hands and choked out. "No, I'm not pregnant. But I hope to be someday."

Sam coughed and cleared his throat. "Nothing would make me happier than to be a grandpa."

Gail covered his hand. "Please, Daddy, try to cut down on your smoking."

He gripped it in his big palm. "I'll do my best, honey. I promise."

Chapter Three

Sam knew he was as mean as a grizzly bear, but he couldn't help it. He wanted to quit smoking, but dammit, the trying was killing him. Doc Smith gave him some pills to take the edge off his nerves, they made him want to sleep all the time. The nicotine gum made him want to puke. The patch worked okay, but it didn't comfort him after meals like a good smoke did.

He sat on the front porch and looked out on the oak trees in the fading evening light. How many times had he sat here and enjoyed the view while remembering the joys of raising his baby girl, and the pain of his wife leaving him? Too many to count.

July had been a scorching month and two weeks into August the heat hadn't let up. The scrub brush and grass across the county were dry and could ignite in an instant. They needed rain something fierce.

With a sigh, he heaved his weight from the rocking chair. Better get to bed. He had to be in Austin by nine o'clock in the morning to see the lung specialist Doc Smith was sending him to. Probably a waste of both their time. He'd hear the same speech Doc gave him, "You gotta quit smoking, Sam. You're one step away from lung cancer." Yeah, yeah, he was trying, dammit. Doc had the gall to say his lungs resembled a large lump of coal.

~*~

Monday morning, the first week in September, the Possum Creek murders were the talk of the office. Gail tried to concentrate on work, but finally gave up and joined the others in the break room where Sue held the floor. The phone rang out front. The young receptionist appeared not to hear it as she entertained her audience.

"The man's been identified as Lamar Jacobs. The woman's identity is still a mystery." She took a swig of her diet soda and continued. "A wallet with driver's license, credit cards, and *five thousand dollars* in cash was found in the trunk of Lamar's car."

"What about the woman?" Ron, the firm's senior partner, asked. "Anything on her?"

Sue was on a roll. "Can you imagine having that much money in cash?"

Ron snapped his fingers in front of her face. "Earth to Sue. What about the woman?"

"Oh, right. Nada, not a thing was found—no purse or jewelry. They did find a gun in the creek bottom."

According to Alex, who'd heard it from one of Bud's deputies, forensics had determined both victims were shot in the head with a .38 caliber handgun. Scuttlebutt was Lamar died instantly, but the woman's wound wasn't fatal. She most likely passed out from the pain and blood loss, and the shooter thought she was dead. Shortly after the car hit the water, the woman revived and struggled to get out of the car and probably drowned.

Gail wondered how on earth they could know such a thing. She shuddered. Most likely the gruesome details would come out later. The poor woman. Gail couldn't imagine anything worse than being trapped and drowning, unless it was being caught in a fire and unable to escape. The horrors that went through the mind were unthinkable.

~*~

At the end of September, Gail breathed a sigh of relief as the television vans moved out of town. By October, life in Stony Creek had returned to normal. Occasionally the subject of the Possum Creek murders arose, but it didn't create the fervor it had in July. Most folks believed it a mystery that would remain unsolved. By the first week of November, gossip had turned to courting issues. The new widower, Judge Spooner, was squiring Hattie Bloomberg around town each weekend. She'd been a widow for over ten years. Bets were placed at the cafe as to when the wedding would take place.

Fall turned into winter and before they knew it, Christmas was upon them. Christmas dinner with Lucas's folks and her father was a joyful affair. They stuffed on turkey and cornbread dressing, opened gifts, and shared memories of Christmases past. Gail considered her life near perfect. Only one thing was missing—a baby.

~*~

Gail drove away from town in the Lexus she and Lucas had bought for her to drive to work. As she pulled onto the county road leading to the ranch, she marveled at the beauty of the wildflowers lining the two-lane highway. The bluebonnets weren't as thick this spring due to the lack of rain in March, but they still made for a colorful landscape. Interspersed among them and adding contrast were red Indian blankets. The field behind their house was full of wildflowers, and as the sun set in the evenings, their aroma carried on the breeze. Lucas's truck was in the carport when she pulled in.

The smell of frying steak reached her before she opened the door from the carport. Chief met her in the hall, wiggling from head to tail, tongue lolling from his mouth. She reached down and scratched his ears.

"Hey, boy, smells like someone is cooking your favorite dinner."

The dog 'woofed' his appreciation and trotted alongside her, his nails clicking against the wood floor.

Lucas caught her around the waist and kissed her. "Mmm, you taste good." He swatted her on the rear. "Hurry up, dinner will be on the table in ten minutes."

Dressed in soft, faded jeans and a sweatshirt, she slid her feet into comfortable lined moccasins and joined Lucas at the table.

When they finished eating, they curled up on the sofa to watch television. Both enjoyed the new forensics shows and watched them when they could. With two skeletons discovered almost in their backyard, the methods of new investigative techniques were even more enticing. Gail relaxed in the crook of his arm, her head on his shoulder. Both his arms were around her and she stroked his hands.

"I started my period today." She could feel Lucas still and knew he was disappointed. Each month she got so excited, especially if a day or two late, only to have her hope squashed. She felt his lips against her hair and his warm breath against her ear.

He squeezed her gently. "I'm sorry, baby. I know you're upset, but it'll happen when we least expect it. We're doing our part. We've got to relax and let nature make it happen."

She knew he was right, but it was such a disappointment every month. Her body wasn't cooperating and she took each failure personally. "Maybe I should see a doctor. I could be sterile or something."

God, what a horrible thought. Adoption was an option, but she wanted to carry Lucas's child in her body, nurse it at her breast. She tried to swallow the lump in her throat.

Lucas rubbed her arms. "You are not sterile. Look at Sandra and her husband. It took them four years to have their first baby."

Yes, it did, but Sandra could have been taking the pill. Plus, she and Lucas had been married almost five years. "I guess."

"Hey, why don't we take the horses down to the gorge and have a picnic tomorrow? Afterward we can ride over to your daddy's for a visit."

She'd wanted to go through some of the stuff in the attic where she'd grown up. It'd be best now before it started getting hot. Last summer she'd tried, but the heat drove her back downstairs. Plus the activity would take her mind off of not being pregnant. "I'd like that. I suppose you want fried chicken."

"Well, the only time you fix it is when we have a picnic, so I most certainly do."

She poked his flat belly with her index finger. "Just trying to keep you healthy, slim, and sexy."

And she didn't want him to develop heart disease like her father, her either, for that matter. Sure, he worked hard and needed more calories, but there had to be a limit.

He looked down at his waist, brow wrinkled. "Hey,

I haven't gained an ounce since we've married." He slapped his hard abdomen. "That's pure muscle, baby."

Gail shook her head. "You are such a little boy when it comes to your food."

"Darn right. Gotta' be or I might starve to death." Lucas shut off the television and let Chief out for a minute. Gail took a frying chicken out of the freezer and sat it in the refrigerator to thaw. As she checked the pantry for what she'd need in the morning, she heard Lucas in the bathroom getting ready for bed. She snapped out the kitchen light and closed the lid on the washer on her way to their bedroom. Lucas was turning back the bedcovers as she went into the bathroom to brush her teeth. When she came out, Lucas was asleep. She slid in beside him. He automatically reached out, gathering her against him. The rise and fall of his chest against her back lulled her to sleep.

~*~

The following morning, after breakfast, Gail started fixing lunch. Lucas went to the stables to check on a couple of sick horses and rode back on Grayboy, with Junebug on a lead rope. The sun shone out, but the air felt crisp as they left the house. They rode across level ground covered with wildflowers. Gail would never tire of seeing them growing among the scattered boulders, scrub brush, and prickly pear cactus. In the shade of the occasional live oak tree, their color appeared deeper, adding contrast to the carpeted ground. In the gorge, the slight breeze didn't reach them, but it was still chilly. They built a small fire and spread their quilt against a large boulder.

This place brought back lots of old memories. Gail smiled as she unpacked their lunch. "Do you remember the day you taught me how to build a camp fire?"

He chuckled. "How could I forget? You used almost an entire box of matches. That's when I decided you'd better learn to use flint or two sticks because you'd freeze to death if you had to depend on matches."

"Do you remember the time when I was eight and you were thirteen and Daddy let me camp out here with you?" It was one of Gail's favorite memories. "We fished and cooked our dinner over the fire."

"I remember you didn't like cleaning the fish." He took another chicken leg from the basket. "They were such puny little things anyway, not much meat on them. Good thing Mom packed us food to carry along."

She watched as he ate the chicken, licking his fingers as he did so. His hands were large and strong, yet could be tender and gentle. She'd always loved his hands, even when he'd been a boy and they'd hinted at the strength they'd one day possess.

"That was also the first time you let me shoot your twenty-two rifle."

They'd spread their sleeping bags on either side of the fire. Lucas's dog, another German shepherd named Tonto, found a spot between them. Gail hadn't been afraid of the dark or sleeping under the stars, not with Lucas. Even at eight, Lucas had been her hero and her best friend. She felt as safe as if she'd been with her father.

"You weren't a bad shot, for a girl." He laughed and then sobered, deep in thought.

"What are you thinking about?"

He looked up. "I was remembering your dad. That night after you'd fallen asleep, I'd barely dosed off when I heard something. Tonto's ears stood straight up, but whoever was out there wasn't a threat or he'd have been bristling. I got my rifle and went to investigate. Your daddy stepped out of the shadows."

Gail was stunned. "Why?"

"He came to see if I would look after you properly. Evidently he was satisfied because he patted me on the shoulder and left."

She shook her head. She knew her daddy was protective, but to sneak up on them in the middle of the night. Geez, it's a good thing she never knew. She'd have been so embarrassed. When she'd asked to go the next time, he'd agreed without any argument. It hadn't been long after that Lucas started camping out with his buddies, and she hadn't been included. For a while he let her tag along with them fishing, but after one of his friends teased her, making her cry, she'd been excluded. The boy received a busted lip.

"Your daddy was right to check up on you. Sure, he'd known me all my life, but that didn't guarantee I was responsible and could take care of you."

Gail nodded. "I guess you're right."

Full, they stretched out. Lucas cradled her head on his shoulder. She put her arm around his waist and snuggled against his side. He rolled to face her and kissed her—his lips were warm, comfortable, nourishing. Her childhood memories of Lucas were special. They'd been friends long before becoming lovers. The warmth of the fire and sunshine lulled them to sleep.

When Gail woke, Lucas was propped up on his elbow, watching her. He grinned. "Did you know you snore?"

"I do not...oh you brute! You're teasing me—

again." She poked him in the belly.

He stood and pulled her to her feet. "Better get on over to your dad's. I bet Ruth has a fresh cake we need to sample."

Gail laughed. "If she does, I bet Daddy's not willing to share."

They found Sam in his rocker on the front porch. He scrambled to put out his cigarette and waved his arms to dissipate the smoke. Lucas laughed at the older man's attempt to deceive.

"Daddy, you can relax. I caught a whiff of smoke a mile back. You're busted."

Sam cleared his throat. "It's only my second of the day."

Ruth, dressed in her ever-faithful jeans, stepped out on the porch. Large-hipped, but not fat, she looked good in pants for a woman her age. Her pink tee shirt hugged small breasts, the color enhancing the silver blond hair. It swayed against her chin as she talked.

"He's lying, Gail. I've given up trying to keep count."

Ruth had been Sam's housekeeper for as long as Gail could remember and the only mother figure, other than Lucas's mother, in her life.

"None of your business, woman."

Ruth ignored him and hugged Gail, then turned to Lucas. "How are ya, Lucas?"

"Good, Ruth. You happen to have any coffee made? I'm dying for a cup."

Gail smiled as Lucas put his arm around the older woman and walked with her inside.

"Don't give him any of my chocolate cake," Sam barked.

"Daddy, you're terrible." Gail looked at the circles under her father's eyes and noticed he'd lost weight. "I'm worried about you. Are you sick?"

"Of course I'm not sick. Just that woman is driving me crazy. She's on me all the time about working too much, eatin' this or that—nag, nag, nag. Heck, I work so I don't have to listen to her harp."

"You could fire her, you know."

"I suppose."

Gail knew that would never happen. In truth, he cared deeply about the woman, or at least she thought so, and again she wondered why her father never married Ruth or some other woman. "Daddy, I know you love Ruth and she loves you. How come you've never remarried?"

Sam blushed to the roots of his blond gray hair. He coughed and sputtered. Gail pounded on his back, then sat back down and waited. He wasn't getting out of it this time.

"I'm still married to your mother."

Gail was stunned. "But why? You've not seen or heard from her in twenty-five years. Why haven't you filed for desertion?"

Her father didn't respond. He leaned back in his rocker and set it in motion. Surely he wasn't hanging on to the idea she still might come home.

"I don't know." He started coughing again and struggled to catch his breath. Gail looked down at his hands as they gripped the rocker arms. She'd not noticed before how gnarled they'd become. "I guess I kept waiting for her to come back for you." His chin rose in defiance. "Not that I'd let her take you, mind you, but I hoped she'd change her mind and want to stay. We'd be happy again." He shrugged and looked at her. "It was easier to believe my daydreams than face reality."

He continued to rock. "One time, I considered remarrying. Even talked to a lawyer about divorcing your mother. But, the lady wouldn't marry me, so..." He shrugged. "Figured it for the best."

Sadness washed over her. "Daddy—"

"Look what I found." Lucas stepped out onto the porch, carrying a tray loaded with slices of cake and coffee cups. With his hip, he held the screen door so Ruth could come through carrying forks and the coffee pot. When he glanced at Gail, he said, "Uh, oh, did I interrupt something?"

"Not a thing, son. Put that food down." Sam moved his ashtray from the table to the porch floor.

Gail sighed and nodded to Lucas. He mouthed a silent and solemn sorry, and sat the tray on the table beside Sam's chair. Sam reached for the biggest slice of cake. Before he could lift it, Ruth reached out and swatted his hand with a fork. "That's Lucas's slice. You get one of those smaller pieces."

"Ouch, woman, that hurt."

She snorted. "You know you have to watch what you eat. Be grateful I'm letting you have another piece. You've already had one today."

Mumbling, "bossy women," Sam picked up a plate with a smaller piece and started eating.

Ruth's cake was delicious. It happened to be the same recipe Gail used, but for some reason, tasted more moist. Maybe she just needed more practice.

"Daddy, if it's all right with you, Lucas and I are going to look around in the attic today. It stayed too hot last summer and I'd like to see some of the old pieces up there."

Sam nodded and finished chewing. "Take whatever you want." He stood and walked into the house.

Ruth started collecting plates. Gail and Lucas rose to help her and they carried everything into the house.

Gail loved the old house she'd grown up in. It wasn't elegant like Lucas's home, but comfortable and homey. A farmhouse with clapboard siding and gabled windows upstairs, the huge kitchen ran the length of the back of the house. The ranch itself was also smaller. Sam had two ranch hands and Ruth cooked for them, plus took care of the house and Gail when she'd been a child. Of course, during the summer she'd shared in the chores and helped prepare the meals, cleaned house, and worked outdoors.

In the attic, Gail found an old library table that would look nice in their living room. Lucas used the corner of a sheet to wipe it clean and then sneezed as dust flew. He rubbed his nose. "I bet this is 100 years old. Wonder why your daddy hasn't had it downstairs."

"I don't know. We'll ask him about it before we take it. Look at this old washstand." It was white, the wood split in places and the paint peeling. "Wouldn't it look good in the kitchen?"

"It's busted. Looks like trash to me."

"I can fix it." She glanced around. "Sure wish I could find some old glassware. One of these days I'd like to have a china cabinet and start collecting a few pieces."

Gail spotted an old suitcase stacked under some boxes in the corner. It was one of those hard sided cases in turquoise. She pulled it free and flipped the catch.

Inside old pictures were scattered on top of a woman's clothes. She rummaged around and her hand closed on a book. It appeared to be a diary. Gail opened it to the first page. *The Diary of June Sayer Steele, June 1980.* Her heart thumped with excitement.

"Lucas, look what I found." She held the diary up for him to see. "It's Mama's." Tears stung her eyes. She knew very little about her mother. Now she had a chance to learn something about her—to read a slice of her life.

Excitement rushed through her like a surge of electricity. She flipped the journal open to an entry in the middle.

I feel as though I'm drowning. The heat, the work, the boredom are eating away at my soul. God help me, I'm dying out here on this...

Gail's heart thundered in her chest. Disappointment and apprehension assailed her, making her gasp for breath.

Lucas's arm came around her. "You okay, hon?"

She slammed the book closed and buried it under the clothing in the suitcase. "Yeah, just a little over excited." She flipped the catch on the suitcase. Maybe later she'd be ready to face her mother's thoughts.

Chapter Four

Gail stepped inside On the Square Cafe and breathed a sigh of relief as the cool air washed over her. It was 90 degrees outside and the humidity in the 80's. Built in the 1950's, the diner's owner kept the decorating theme authentic. Red and white Formica tables with chrome legs and red vinyl stools and bench seats contrasted nicely with the black and white square floor tiles. Booths still sported the old wall jukeboxes. She looked around the crowded room and located her best friend from high school sitting alone at a back booth. Smiling, she slid into the empty seat.

"Sandra, it's good to see you." As usual, Sandra was a bundle of sunshine.

"Hey, girlfriend, thought you'd never make time to meet me for lunch." Her bright blue eyes twinkled with happiness and her blond pageboy bounced as she talked. "I ordered our favorites. Hope that's okay."

"You mean hamburgers with fries?" At Sandra's nod, Gail shrugged. "Well, why not? One on occasion won't kill us."

Their food arrived and they were quiet for a few minutes.

Gail put her burger down and wiped her mouth on her napkin. She cleared her throat. "How long did it take you to get pregnant with Rose? I mean, I don't want to be too personal, but did it take a while when you decided you wanted a baby?"

Sandra's face clouded with concern. She covered Gail's hand with her own. "Oh, honey, how long have you been trying?"

"Since the day we got married. It'll be five years the end of May."

Sandra quirked an eyebrow and grinned. "And I suppose you get plenty of exposure?"

Gail giggled. "Oh, yeah, it's not for lack of trying." She sobered, instantly finding it hard to meet her friend's eyes. "Do you think I should see a fertility specialist?"

"No, no, not yet." Sandra squeezed her hand. "It's not uncommon for it to take several years, even longer in some cases. When do you have your yearly checkup?"

"Next month, with a doctor in Austin." Thank goodness she had that to look forward to. Hopefully she'd get some answers.

"Ask for his advice. And try not to worry. From what I've read, stress can have an effect on conception."

Gail glanced up to see Alex Guthrie walking toward them. His blue eyes sparkled with curiosity when he stopped at their booth. In his navy jacket, gray slacks, and Gucci loafers, he looked like he'd stepped out of GQ magazine.

"Hello, ladies, having a good lunch?" Alex's gaze took in every aspect of Sandra's appearance and then turned to Gail.

"Hi, Alex, have you met Sandra Rivers? She's married to Ted Rivers. We all went to high school together."

Alex extended his hand. "No, I've not had the pleasure, though I do know your husband from high school. He graduated several years behind me." He took Sandra's hand and held it for a minute. Gail froze, afraid he'd bend at the waist and kiss it. "I'm pleased to meet you."

Sandra nodded and reclaimed her hand. "Likewise."

He fixed Gail with a smile and winked. "As usual, you're looking lovely, my dear."

Heat infused her face. She resisted the urge to slap the smirk off his face. "I've told you not to call me that. To you, I'm Gail or Mrs. Johnson."

With a laugh, he said, "Now, now, don't be so stuffy. I assure you I mean it most respectfully."

Sandra gaped at the exchange between them, and Gail wanted to disappear.

Someone on the other side of the room called his name. A glimpse of annoyance streaked across his face as he turned and waved. "Excuse me, ladies, nice to see you."

Sandra's gaze followed Alex as he walked away. "Wow, girlfriend, he's a real hunk." She coughed into her hand. "I think he's got the hots for you, my friend."

"God, he comes on to every woman he meets. He's bad enough at the office, but I can't believe he'd be so offensive in public. You'd think at his age he'd be married. He's the perpetual playboy."

Gail couldn't completely relax around Alex, partly due to Lucas's warnings. To be honest, the main reason was the primitive sexuality he exuded. Having known only one man sexually, her husband, she felt at a disadvantage and knew her attraction was in part due to curiosity. And dammit, if she wasn't mistaken, the man knew it confused her. Though he was nothing but courteous, she'd begun to suspect his accidental little touches and endearments were deliberate. Today's outrageous behavior was proof.

The man had his choice of any number of women, why would he be interested in her? He'd not be adding her to his long list of conquests. She looked at her watch. "This has been fun, but I better get back to work. Let's meet at least once a month from now on."

~*~

"Lucas, I need to attend a conference in Chicago weekend after next."

He stopped chewing and swallowed. "Do you have to go?"

"No, I don't have to, but I'd like to. It's an opportunity to meet some people in the business, make some contacts." She took a sip of her tea and wiped at the condensation ring on the table with her paper napkin.

"You know when we have kids those contacts won't be important."

When—an issue she struggled with constantly. Yes, then she'd want to be home full time. Until that time arrived, she needed to make the most of her career opportunities.

"Lucas, contacts are always useful in business. Sure, when the kids are born, I want to stay home with them, but I'll probably go back to work when they're older." She poured them more iced tea and returned the pitcher to the refrigerator. "And the conference conducts workshops on the latest in computer technology. I want to stay current in my field."

She sat back down, propped her elbow on the table, her chin cupped in her hand. "Is it a problem? Do you have something planned that weekend?"

"No, it's not a problem, but I don't like the idea of you going off without me."

"Hey, why don't you come along? I'm sure you can find something to do during the day while I'm in meetings, and we can see the city at night." It could be a mini-vacation for them.

He brightened at the idea. "Hmm, that's a thought." Then he frowned and shook his head. "Darn, I can't leave. We've got two mares about to foal about that time. I need to be here."

"Why can't Tom take care of them?"

"His nephew is graduating from college that Saturday, and he'll be out of town."

"Well, shoot."

"You go ahead and go, hon. I'll make the next one. Who all is going anyway?"

"As far as I know, just me and Alex. Ron hasn't made up his mind." She hoped the older partner could make the trip. She had no desire to go off with Alex, but she was a professional and this trip was important to her.

His jaw went rigid, expression mulish. "I don't think it's proper for you and Alex to go off on a trip together—it doesn't look right."

Gail almost laughed, and then realized he was serious. Her face heated. "Doesn't look right to whom?" She stood up and put her plate in the sink. "What you really mean is you don't trust me, isn't it?"

"Shi…no, that's not what I mean." He raked his fingers through his hair and sighed. "I trust you, but I sure as hell don't trust Alex Guthrie. He's a womanizer, and everyone in town knows it. Alex is notorious for his affairs, and he doesn't limit himself to single women. How he woos them into bed, I don't have a clue. I've heard rumors about alcohol and preying on their need for attention circulated. He's destroyed at least one marriage in Stony Creek." He hit the table with his fist. "By God, Gail, if he touches you, I won't think twice about beating him to death."

Gail blanched at his vehemence, but pursed her lips in defiance. After all, she was a grown woman.

Lucas cleared his throat. "I don't like it, but it's your decision. I don't want people thinking my wife is one of his conquests."

Gail sighed. "Lucas, I work with the man every day. Don't you think I know what kind of man he is? Yes, he's a womanizer and flirts with almost every woman he sees, but he's not going to hit on me, one of his business associates." At least she hoped not. After his behavior at the cafe last week, she couldn't be sure. If he did and got physical, she could take care of herself. Her roommate in college had talked her into taking martial arts. It was time well spent.

He cleared his throat. "I don't like it, but it's your decision."

Gail nodded as he went back to eating. A slight frown wrinkled his brow. She admired the strong tanned hand holding his fork. With the other, he lifted the glass of tea and drank thirstily. His gold wedding band winked at her. He sat his glass down, and she reached for his hand and twined their fingers together. The frown on his forehead relaxed and he smiled, blue eyes twinkling.

~*~

Friday morning Lucas drove Gail into town to meet Alex. Parked in front of the office building, he got out of his car as they drove up. Lucas transferred Gail's bags, slammed the trunk close, and pulled her into his arms. He whispered against her hair. "You be careful, my love. Call me when your plane lands."

Her arms slipped under his and clutched his shoulder blades. "I will." She leaned back to see his face. "I'm going to miss you."

"You better. I'll miss you, too."

He kissed her hungrily. The intensity startled her and she tried to pull back, but Lucas deepened the kiss until he felt her respond. She clung to him, forgetting they had an audience. Alex coughed. Lucas broke the kiss and winked down at his wife.

Her face flushed. She mouthed, "You devil!"

He laughed and turned to Alex. His voice deadly serious, he said, "Take care of my wife."

Alex saluted. "Understood, man, understood."

He'd spent a good deal of the previous afternoon brooding about Gail's trip. Lucas knew he was being a bit unreasonable, but something nagged at his memory. A few weeks ago he'd dreamed about a dark-headed woman sneaking down to the creek at night to meet a man. With her hair and beautiful skin glowing in the moonlight, he'd thought of Gail, but this woman was more buxom and wore bright red lipstick and gold hoop earrings. When he dreamed of the woman again, flashes of childhood memory burst in his head. Could the woman be June Steele, Gail's mother? Was it possible she'd been cheating on Gail's father when she left town all those years ago? He didn't think Gail would cheat on him, but the dream unsettled him, put doubts in his mind about her true nature.

He snorted and shook his head to clear his mind. His wife was the most honest woman he'd ever known, and the most beautiful. She resembled his memory of her mother, but her eyes were dark blue, her long dark hair straight, not curly. He'd been her first lover and by God, he'd be her only.

Gail was aware of the threat; she deserved his trust.

~*~

Tired from the trip, the site of Lucas's truck parked in front of the courthouse cheered her when she and Alex drove up. It had been a productive trip, but she was glad to be home. She'd missed Lucas more than she thought possible.

Gail didn't wait for Lucas to open her door. She jumped from the car and ran toward his open arms. His large body enfolded hers, blocking the cool night air and warming her.

Alex turned his back on their reunion and opened the trunk. "Got her back safe and sound as promised, old man."

Lucas released her and slapped him on the back. "I appreciate it, Alex."

Gail took her cosmetic bag while Lucas lifted her wheeled garment bag to the pavement. "Thanks for driving, Alex. See you in the morning."

"We won't be expected until noon so sleep in tomorrow."

"Great!" She wouldn't complain about getting to sleep in a little later.

Lucas took her elbow and steered her to the passenger side of his truck. He tossed her suitcases in the bed and turned to her. Gail felt the door handle against her back as Lucas brought his body in contact with hers. She ignored the jab of the metal as his heat quickly enfolded her.

He dropped his head and brushed his lips across her cheek. She stood on her toes and circled his neck with her arms as he molded her body to his. "Oh, baby, I missed you something fierce." His lips took hers in a possessive kiss, his mouth teasing and stroking.

A car burned rubber as it left the stop sign. Cat calls and whistles echoed around the square. Then someone shouted, "Hey, man, get a room."

Gail absorbed the vibrations as Lucas's big body shook with laughter. He squeezed her waist. "I'm glad you're home."

He opened the door for her and ran around to the other side to get in. She shared details of her trip as he drove.

"Did Alex hit on you?" Gail thought he was teasing, but when she noticed his grip on the steering wheel she knew otherwise.

"No, he did not." Gail hated to lie, to keep anything from Lucas, but felt no need to make an issue of Alex's flirting. Her boss had made it quite evident he desired her, and to be honest, her body had responded to his attempted embrace. But, she'd let him know his advances were not welcome, and if they persisted, she'd be unable to work with him. He'd apologized and been a perfect gentleman the remainder of the trip.

"Did he ever try to come into your room?"

Gail screeched. "Of course not." She crossed her arms over her chest as she stared at Lucas, willing him to look at her. This was a side of her husband she'd never seen. God, she hoped he couldn't tell she wasn't being honest with him. They'd promised to always be truthful, but in this case, it happened to be for his own good. He continued to stare out the front window. "Lucas, I don't appreciate the inquisition. If you don't trust me, we've got some serious issues. I—"

"Gail, honey…" He reached for her hand. She jerked away. "I'm sorry. I trust you, but dammit I don't trust him." She didn't respond and turned to look out the window. "All right, I'm an…a…"

"Yes, you are," she sputtered.

"You don't even know what I intended to say."

"Well, you don't want to know what word I'd use to fill in the blank."

"That bad, huh?" He chuckled.

She snorted and refused to look at him.

"Forgive me? Please?"

"Don't question me like a child again, Lucas. I'm a grown woman and am not too stupid to know what's going on around me. I realize the man is attracted to me or something, and I'm not exactly comfortable around him, but he's never been anything other than a gentleman. If I can't handle a situation, I'll ask for help."

Lucas growled low in his throat. Gail started in surprise as he pounded the steering wheel with his fist. Then he took a deep breath and muttered. "Okay. Now dammit, give me your hand."

She did and he raised it to his lips. They rode in silence for a minute.

"So, you feel the trip was worthwhile?" Lucas watched her with his brow furrowed.

"Yes, I do. One of the major software companies

gave demos on a new program Alex plans to buy. I'm ahead of the game having seen it already."

Lucas nodded. "Good, glad you got something out of it."

"I'd like to buy a computer to use at home. There may be a time when I want to work after hours, plus I'd like to be able to surf the net on occasion."

"Sure, get what you want. Then I can do some of the ranch book work at home rather than going up to office at the big house."

"I'll start looking next week."

He stroked her knuckles with the pad of his thumb. "We need to run by and see your dad tonight."

Gail didn't like the lines of worry wrinkling his brow or the tenseness of his jaw. Her heart lurched. "What's wrong? He's not sick, is he? It's those damned cigarettes, isn't it?"

"No, hon, he's not sick. He's fine." He sighed deeply and rubbed the back of his neck. "I don't know how to tell you this other than just spit it out."

Dread inched up her spine and made her scalp tingle.

"Forensics in Austin determined the gun found at the bottom of Possum Creek is the pistol used to murder the two people in the car."

"So, what does that have to do with Daddy?"

"The serial number matches up with a .38 registered to your daddy. He bought it twenty-five years ago."

"But..." She shook her head.

"Your daddy hasn't seen the gun in over twenty years. He wasn't sure when it disappeared, but in September, after your mother left, he noticed it was gone."

Gail couldn't breathe. Blood thundered in her ears and she was shaking. "That doesn't mean anything. Someone probably stole the gun. And just because it's the same caliber doesn't prove that gun killed those people. Why would he want to kill someone he didn't even know?"

"Honey, I'm so sorry, but…they think the woman is…might be your mother."

A strangled wail tore from her throat. "Nooo, not so, I know it's not so."

Lucas lifted her hair and stroked her neck. "Baby, it's going to be all right."

She nodded. "I need to see Daddy."

When they reached Sam's, Gail was out of the truck and running up to the porch before he could open her door. She charged into the house without knocking.

"Daddy, where are you?"

"In here, baby girl."

~*~

Lucas closed the door and followed Gail into the kitchen. Sam stood up and took his daughter in his arms. She was crying now. Sam patted her back, not awkwardly as some men would do, but like a pro, someone who'd done so often. Lucas smiled at the close relationship between father and daughter. He hoped one day he'd share a close bond with a child of his and Gail's. He hoped never to have to comfort her over something like this.

"Everything is going to be okay, Gail. Don't worry. Sit down here and let me pour you and Lucas a cup of coffee." Gail sat and Lucas took the chair beside her while Sam located cups. He poured them each a mug full of coffee and set them on the table. "Now, how was your trip?"

"Good, but I don't want to talk about it." Her face twisted. "What if they try to pin those murders on you, Daddy?"

"Hey, now, don't go borrowing trouble. We don't know any such thing." Sam patted her hand. His face was even more drawn and tired looking than usual. For the first time, Lucas wondered if the man's health wasn't worse than what he'd let on.

Sam cleared his throat. His voice was hoarse. "I guess Lucas told you they think the woman in the car might be your mother." He curled his fingers around his cup as if warming them.

Her eyes a startling blue against her pale skin, Gail squeezed her Daddy's arm. "Yes, he did. What do you think?"

"I don't rightly know. It could be possible." His face looked tortured. He dropped his head and stared at his cup. His voice cracked. "I'd...I'd hoped never to have to tell you this, but I suspected your mother was seeing another man."

Again that vision of June Steele in a man's arms popped into Lucas's mind. Where had he seen them, and when? He shook the mental image away.

Gail gasped and covered her mouth with her hand.

"The day June left, she dropped you at Ruth's sister's house for the day." He looked up and smiled sadly. "You loved to play with Ruth's nieces and nephews. When I got home, Ruth handed me the note." Sam's hand shook as he lifted his coffee to his lips and took a drink. He swallowed and set the cup back down. "She said she couldn't stand living so isolated anymore and when she got on her feet she'd be back for you."

He looked at Gail and smiled through trembling lips. "I picked you up, took you to Lucas's mother, and went looking for her. Drove to her daddy's and sister's, everywhere I could think of she might have gone, but didn't find her."

Lucas remembered the time well. He'd been enthralled with the baby girl, for a while at least. The memory made him smile.

"I was gone several days, but when I held you in my arms, I knew I'd never let her take you from me. I saw a lawyer the next day." He shrugged. "But, your mother never came back."

Tears glittered in Gail's eyes and she nodded.

Sam looked solemn. "One more thing, honey. Bud wants you to stop by the clinic tomorrow and let them draw some blood for DNA testing."

Chapter Five

Gail sat in a chair, similar to the ones in high school, with her arm flat on the attached top. Susie, Doctor Smith's nurse, tied a rubber band around her upper arm. "Squeeze and make a fist for me, Gail." The nurse poked around with her finger in the crook of her arm, looking for a vein. "Just a little stick, now."

The sheriff leaned against the doorframe, arms folded across his chest. Big and burly, Bud was an intimidating figure. Gail had known the man her entire life. Though she respected him and his authority, he was like a big old teddy bear to her.

"Sorry to have to ask you to do this, Gail. But, we've got to know."

Concerned, his forehead rippled with frown lines. She also needed to know if the woman was her mother. It just ticked her off to be told to report for blood work, not having a say in the matter.

"I understand, Bud, but you understand this. My father did not kill those two people in that car."

The sheriff straightened and frowned down at her. "Nobody said he did, young woman. Now don't you make matters worse by making a to-do out of this."

Gail snorted. "That's easy for you to say. It's not your father we're talking about here." She looked at the blood-filled vials lined up on the counter. "Susie, leave me a little, would you?"

Susie chuckled and loosened the band around her arm. "Last one." She pressed a cotton ball where the needle entered her flesh and slid the needle out. Then she took a piece of tape and secured the cotton in place.

Gail rolled the sleeve of her blue silk blouse down and fastened the button. "Thanks, Susie. When will you have the results?"

Susie looked to Bud.

"It usually takes six to eight weeks, not a day or two like they show on those forensic shows on television." He nodded to Gail. "I'll let you know something soon as I do. Thanks for coming in."

Gail couldn't speak only nodded. She didn't mean to be rude and tried to smile, but the situation unnerved her. It felt unreal.

Bud must have recognized her struggle because he patted her on the back. "It's all gonna be okay, Gail. The woman could be someone else entirely, but if it's your mama, you want to know and give her a proper burial."

Shocked at the realization, she'd not thought about making funeral arrangements. Of course she hadn't, she hadn't believed until now the body could be her mother's. She stammered. "Yes, you're right." Giving him a wobbly smile, she left the clinic.

Of course, the entire town knew about the gun and by noon they knew she'd stopped to give a blood sample. The gossip lines were buzzing and Gail could imagine the speculation and theories being bandied about. To avoid questions, she remained in the office during lunch. Alex insisted on picking up lunch for her and sat in her office to keep her company while she ate. He didn't quiz her, but kept the conversation on company business. His thoughtfulness surprised her.

She was grateful to get home. Lucas was there and had started dinner. He had spaghetti on to boil and a pot of sauce simmering. A nice salad sat on the table ready to toss with dressing.

Without saying a word, she laid her head against his back and hugged him. He turned and wrapped her in his arms.

"Bad day, love?"

"Yeah, I'm the big item of gossip right now."

He rubbed her back in slow, soothing circles. "It'll blow over. Soon it'll be something else."

"I know."

~*~

The first Tuesday in June, Gail took off work and drove in to Austin for her doctor's appointment. The weather already hot, she dressed casually in the lime green sundress Lucas loved for her to wear. Barelegged, she wore soft, tan sandals with gaudy stones in bright colors across the toe straps. In Doctor Lane's examination room, she sat on the heated table in her lovely paper top with her lower half covered with a paper sheet when Doctor Lane walked in. As usual, she smiled and shook Gail's hand.

"How are you today?"

Gail wanted to blurt out her misery, but answered, "Fine."

After the exam, Doctor Lane helped her sit up. "Now, everything looks and feels normal. Of course you'll be hearing on the results of your Pap smear and blood work. Are you having any problems?"

When Gail started relaying her doubts and fears, the words tumbled from her mouth in a torrent. Before she knew it, she was crying and Dr. Lane stroked her shoulder in comfort.

"Gail, I don't see a thing to keep you from getting pregnant. Your uterus isn't tilted, your ovaries feel healthy, and I see no sign of disease. Things can be going on we can't see, so I'll schedule you for some tests. Check with my nurse on the way out and she'll set the appointments up for you. When I get the results, I'll call you." She stood and shook Gail's hand.

"Thank you, doctor."

"You're welcome." She patted Gail on the back. "You'll be back in here pregnant before you know it. Try not to worry."

~*~

"What'd the doctor have to say?"

"She didn't think anything was wrong, but to be on the safe side, scheduled me for some tests. They couldn't set them all up on the same day, so I need to go back next week and stay overnight. Do you think you could come with me?"

His brow furrowed in thought. "Sure, I'll work things out with Tom. He can get Pete or Chuck to cover for me. It'll be nice for us to get away for a couple of days."

"She also said…" Gail couldn't resist a giggle as she winked. "I'm to enjoy my husband, go places, have fun, and not think about getting pregnant."

Lucas nodded. "Dr. Lane sounds like a smart lady." I like the idea of getting out more. Seems with me being older, we missed out on dating, dancing. Maybe we should take off one weekend and go to a B&B. We need to make up for lost time before we have a family."

Gail looked up in surprise. "That's what the doctor

said, though not in those exact words. I'd love to go dancing."

He stood up and turned on the radio. "Until Friday night, my dear, our dance floor will be..." He stomped his heels making Chief bark. "...the kitchen tiles."

She laughed as he pulled her from her chair and swung her in the two-step to George Straits' "All My Exes Live in Texas". Lucas threw back his head and sang along with George. When Chief started howling, he looked offended, but laughed and lunged for the dog.

"Why, you mangy old hound, what do you know about music?"

Chief dodged his hand and took off at a run with Lucas on his heels, both slipping and sliding when they hit the wood floor in the living room. Their game of chase was pretty much a nightly ritual though they usually confined it to the yard.

The phone rang and Gail rushed to pick it up. She giggled into the phone and tried to stop laughing. "Hel...tee hee...lo."

"Gail? It's Tom. I'm at the barn."

She couldn't stop laughing. "Yeah...sorry, Tom...so funny."

"Sounds like a party going on over there, or a dog attack."

"Lucas and Chief are playing."

Tom snorted. "Tell that boy to stop messing around and get over here. We've got a sick mare about to foal."

Gail sobered. "He'll be right there." She hung up and relayed Tom's message to Lucas.

He headed for the door, then stopped and drew her into his arms. Against her cheek, he whispered, "Sorry to have to leave the dance, sugar. You be ready for our dance date Friday night, you hear?" His lips claimed hers in a promising kiss.

"I will." She walked to the carport with him. "I'll leave a lamp on for you."

Drat, they'd been having so much fun. She cleaned up the kitchen, fed Chief, and looked around for something to do. Her eyes lit on the library table they'd brought from her dad's. Lucas had cleaned it and the wood had deepened in color. She went into the spare bedroom and looked at the washstand she'd been fixing. One of the doors hung by one hinge, but she'd located a replacement for the missing one. The drawer needed a new bottom as did the cabinet itself. She'd need to use the power saw to cut boards, so would wait until the weekend when she could set up outside.

The suitcase she'd brought home had been stuffed in the closet. She'd been anxious to read the diary the day she'd found it in the attic, but her mother's words had been so despondent, she'd been terrified to continue. Did her mother really love her or would her written words reveal some terrible truths she didn't want to know? Whatever it said, the diary would reveal the truth. Gail wanted to read the entries alone. Tonight was the first time Lucas had been called away since she'd brought it home. Her heart was ready to withstand whatever her mother's words revealed.

Gail opened the suitcase and stared at the contents, thinking. It held a few changes of clothes, the pictures, and the diary. For the first time, she wondered why the suitcase hadn't been unpacked. Most people did so as soon as they returned home. And why were the pictures and diary in it? She was surprised her mother hadn't taken the diary with her when she left. Maybe she'd packed two suitcases and decided to leave this one behind. Unease settled over her. Something wasn't right.

She carried the diary and pictures with her into the living room and sat down on the sofa. The pictures were color, but didn't have the vibrancy of more modern photos. In one, her mother and father stood side-by-side and smiled for the camera. They were outside the house she'd grown up in. The trees and grass were green and the irises in the front flowerbed in bloom so it had to be sometime in the spring. Later in the summer, the grass would've been drier and the flowers without blooms. She turned the picture over. It was marked *May 28th, 1980—our wedding day.*

Gail looked through the other pictures. One showed a very big and pregnant June. Sam had his hand on her massive belly and grinned for the camera. Another photo was of Gail in the hospital, minutes after birth, and there were several of her with each of her parents. The last two were of a six-month old Gail and one where she looked close to a year old.

She put the pictures on the coffee table and opened the diary.

June 1, 1980. Last week Sam Steele and I got married. It was sooner than we'd planned, but I'm pregnant. Sam is excited about the baby and bought this diary so I could write my thoughts. He's such a sweet man and I love him so. Next week I'll be eighteen. Sam's twenty-five and was furious when he discovered I wasn't twenty like I'd told him. Daddy had to sign for us to get a license. Then he left without a backwards glance. His lack of feeling still smarts.

With the diary open in her lap, she thought how sad

to learn her grandfather wasn't a caring man. When a child, Gail had painted a picture in her mind of what her mother looked like. Sam had only shared one picture of June with her, and when she'd turned twelve, he'd let her keep the picture in her bedroom. Her mother's hair was dark like Gail's, but in the picture she wore it curly. Dark brown eyes were heavily made up with shadow and black mascara. Her red lipstick matched the red dress she wore. June was a beautiful woman, one to draw a man's attention. Gail, also dressed in red, sat in her mother's lap and smiled happily for the camera. For the thousandth time, Gail wondered what had happened between her parents and where her mother was today. Was she the woman in the submerged car? A shudder traveled up her spine. She hoped it wasn't a foreboding of what they'd learn in the future.

Gail read through the entries describing June's growing belly, doctor's appointments, and the first time Gail moved. She smiled at her mother's enthusiasm that her baby appeared healthy. There were also entries about boring ranch life, constant work, and little time for fun. It seems before they'd married, Sam had taken her out on Friday and Saturday nights and to church on Sunday. Now, except for church, they stayed home.

September 10, 1980. A woman started work today. Sam hired someone to help me around the house. He's such a sweet man. Ella is a couple of years older than me and is rather bossy, but I don't mind as long as I have help.

The following entries made reference to a friendship growing between June and Ella, though at times June hinted at being jealous of Ella. Over what, she didn't say. June described church socials, the baby shower she'd been given, and a trip to Austin to purchase a baby bed.

January 9, 1981. Oh, my gosh, my water broke. I was mopping the kitchen floor and I felt it trickle down my legs into my shoes. Eek! Doctor Smith said to wait until my pains are at least ten minutes apart before coming in. Sam is beside himself, pacing the floor and timing my contractions. He's going to be such a wonderful daddy.

Gail smiled as she imagined Lucas pacing and timing contractions. As he did when stressed, he'd rake his hands through his sandy brown hair and it would be sticking up all over. One of these days it would be their turn. She was lucky to be loved by a man like Lucas. He was faithful and gentle, and would be a good father. His tall, muscular body and wicked smile just added fuel to the feelings he initiated in her heart and body. Each evening when he walked from the bathroom to the bed, her eyes ran over his hard chest sprinkled with brown hair, his lean waist, and long legs, and her body clenched with anticipation. He was a beautiful man and his loving made her toes curl.

January 11, 1981. Today we brought our beautiful baby girl home from the hospital. She was born yesterday morning at nine fifteen a.m. When she finally arrived, Sam looked like he'd been pole-axed. For nine months we tried to get ready, but the minute we saw her, we realized we weren't prepared at all. Until she was placed in our arms, we had no idea what a miracle birth was or how wondrous God's work. Thank you, Lord Jesus, for our miracle.

Tears ran down Gail's cheeks and dropped onto her

blouse. She'd not known if her mother believed in God. Her father did and saw to it that she did, too. And her mother had loved and wanted her. The knowledge spread like warm butter through her body. For years she'd wondered why her mother had left. She'd fluctuated between hatred for the woman who'd hurt her father and idol worship. With her mother's picture, she'd daydreamed different scenarios of the day her mother would return for her. A famous movie star now, June Steele would give up Hollywood to be with her daughter and husband again. Gail may never know the reason her mother left, but now she knew it wasn't because June didn't love her daughter.

February 1, 1981. Though I've come to love and depend on Ruth Ella, the woman can get on my nerves sometimes. You'd think Gail was her baby, not mine. She's always telling me how to take care of my baby. Today, I'm sorry to say, I hurt her feelings, but she'd criticized me one too many times.

Gail gasped. Ruth Ella? The woman Daddy hired to help her mama was Ruth? Caught between morose and somber thoughts and the glory her mother loved her, a nagging suspicion hit Gail—why hadn't Ruth ever mentioned knowing her mother?

Chapter Six

"Lucas! Over here."

Lucas held his hand above his eyes to deflect the bouncing lights as he peered through the gyrating bodies on the dance floor at Bubba's Boogie Bar. Robert and Jason stood, waving at them from across the room.

He pointed to his friends. "There they are, hon."

With his arm around her shoulders, they maneuvered through the dancers toward a round table in the far corner. As usual the room was full. Vintage neon signs and clocks advertising brands of beer covered the walls, while rotating spotlights pulsed with the beat of the country-western music. Lucas couldn't resist the rhythm, and with his arm around Gail's waist, danced her across the room to their friends.

"Hey, guys, it's good to see you." Robert and Jason shook his hand and hugged Gail. "Hey, keep your dirty paws off my wife," he said teasingly as he moved down the line to kiss Cheryl and Patty's cheeks.

"Well, ditto, hoss," Robert said as he knocked Lucas's hat askew. Lucas yanked it off and feinted a punch to Robert's middle. Gail smiled at the playful banter.

The three men were inseparable in high school and college. All three had been good-looking and popular. Robert was of medium height and stocky with brown hair and eyes. Jason appeared to be the clown of the group. Of course, she'd been in high school during their college years and she hadn't seen them much until she and Lucas married. She'd become fond of the men and their wives.

Robert's wife, Cheryl, had been homecoming queen Gail's freshman year and Patty, Jason's wife, had been in the queen's court and a cheerleader. To them, Gail had been a little known sophomore and below their notice. Gail stood behind their chairs and gave them each a hug. Lucas held her chair and she slid into it.

Cheryl spoke up, voice raised to be heard above the band. "It's about time you two got here." She flipped a long strand of auburn hair back from her face. Complexion beautiful, she wore just enough makeup to enhance her dark eyes and full lips, without looking overdone. "The guys thought you two love birds might be otherwise occupied and were about to barge in on you." Her blue eyes lit with good humor as she grinned mischievously.

Patty, petite with short blond hair, laughed and added. "Another catastrophe avoided." Her blue eyes flashed to her husband and she hugged his arm.

Jason, thin and lanky with red-blond hair, added, "We're tired of seeing this old boy lookin' love struck this long after his wedding. Makes us normal guys look bad."

"Bull! You guys don't need any help in that department," Lucas said. He slapped Jason on the back. "Anyway, I've seen you mooning over Patty like a sick calf often enough to know how the land lays." He winked at Patty and Jason's face mirrored his hair. Everyone at the table roared with laughter, and giggling, Patty gave her husband a sympathetic hug.

Lucas signaled for a waitress and turned to her. "What would you like to drink?"

"I'll have a light beer."

He ordered two beers and they settled in to talk while the band took a break and they could hear each other.

Cheryl tucked another loose strand of hair behind her ear and fiddled with her earring. "How're things going at Brown and Guthrie Accounting, Gail?"

"Good. It's challenging work and never boring. Though on pretty days I long to be working in the fresh air at the ranch."

Lucas looked at her with surprise. "I never knew you felt that way."

Gail shrugged. "It's nice I can help out on the weekends if I want." She looked at Cheryl and Patty. "How about you, Cheryl, ready to quit work and have the family you guys talk about?"

"Not on your life. I've seen how hard Patty works staying at home with three kids. I think I'll hold off a couple more years." She leaned into Robert and he put his arm around her. "Maybe by then Robert will be the county's district attorney, instead of the assistant, and I can work part-time."

Patty laughed. "You're smart to wait. It seems I work from daylight to dark. I long for the day I'll get to go to the bathroom by myself."

Her remark brought another round of laughter. Still grinning, Jason stroked Patty's hair. "They are a handful, for sure," he said, squeezing his wife's shoulders. "You do a heck of a job, sweetheart."

Patty blushed prettily. "Why, Jason, that's the

sweetest compliment you've ever given me."

The band hit a chord and then started a country waltz. Talk would be impossible for a while. Lucas pulled Gail onto the dance floor. He was a good dancer and twirled her around without missing a step. "Have I told you how fetching you look in those tight jeans, sugar?"

"At least three times, darlin'."

"Good. I want to make sure you know how much I appreciate your womanly attributes."

She rolled her eyes. "You are something else, mister."

He laughed and pulled her closer.

"You didn't happen to see what I had on underneath this outfit tonight, did you?" She'd put on the red teddy from Victoria's Secret he'd drooled over earlier in the week.

His Adam's apple bobbed up and down as he swallowed. He cleared his throat. "No, I didn't. Are you going to tell me?"

"No, I'll wait and tell you later."

The dance ended and they walked back to their table. Lucas leaned in and whispered in her ear, "Tease." She just grinned.

A tall stately blonde approached their table. Gail couldn't help staring. She wore skin-tight black jeans and a black sweater cut low to emphasize her abundant boobs. When she noticed Gail, her shiny lips, coated in blood red lipstick, turned from smiling to pouty. Gail expected fangs to pop out at any minute and blood to drip from her mouth.

Lucas sat with his back to the woman but Gail sat sideways and watched her. Hateful glances for Gail radiating from her eyes, she bounced seductively closer. Uncomfortable looks passed between Robert and Jason and they squirmed in their seats. The woman stopped behind Lucas's chair, hand propped on her slim hip. Robert cleared his throat and tried to signal Lucas with an arched eyebrow and nod. Lucas finally got the hint and swiveled on the seat of his chair.

His shoulders tensed.

"Lucas, darling, where have you been?"

Her voice was deep and raspy—sexy. Gail sniffed. Caused by smoking if her nose was accurate.

He smiled at Gail, stood and turned to face the woman.

"Tabitha, what a surprise, it's been a long time. I heard you were living in Reno." He dropped a polite kiss on her cheek.

Gail stiffened at the gesture, heat infusing her face.

"Yes, that's true, darling." She tilted her head, and lips puckering, mewed, "Surely you can do better than that after I've been away so long?"

"Afraid not, I'm a married man now." He laid his hand on Gail's shoulder. "Have you met my wife? Gail, this is Tabitha Mason, an old friend."

Gail knew her face and neck must be beet red. At least the lights were low. "Hello, Tabitha, it's good to meet you."

Tabitha studied her and nodded. "Yeah, you, too." Then she looked at Lucas. "So, it's true, you waited for this child to grow up and married her."

Cheryl gasped and Patty sputtered at the woman's rudeness. Lucas leaned down to cup Gail's cheek and brushed a soft kiss across her lips. "I'll be right back, hon."

He turned and took the woman's arm in a firm grip. "As everyone can see, Tabitha, she's a grown woman now. Let me escort you back to your table." Gail watched as he walked her away from them.

Well, well, how good a friend was Tabitha? Gail knew Lucas had been with women while in college, but she didn't want to know who they were. And did they just meet and dance or was there more to the relationship? *What do you think, Gail? He's a man with a healthy sex drive.* His senior year, when they'd started dating, she felt sure he'd been faithful, but it still hurt to think of him with other women.

"Don't give her a second thought, Gail," Jason said. "She chased Lucas for years, but he was never interested."

Gail took a sip of her beer. "Don't worry about it. I do hope though there won't be a lot of Tabithas crawling out of the woodwork." She watched the two couples exchange worried glances and her stomach twisted.

Lucas didn't sit down when he returned. He took her hand and led her back to the dance floor. He pulled her close and whispered in her ear. "I'm sorry, babe. She never meant anything to me."

Gail tilted her head back so she could see his face. "What's that supposed to mean, Lucas? Did you just dance with her or were you intimate with her?" His face flushed darkly and she put her head on his shoulder so she wouldn't have to see the truth in his eyes.

"Hell, you know I wasn't a monk before we got together."

Yes, she knew it, and due to her limited experience with other men, having the issue surface made her feel inadequate. "What was that kiss all about?"

"Lord, Gail, we were friends at one time. It was only a friendly peck on the cheek," he said through gritted teeth.

"Fine. I'm glad to know the boundaries here. Let's see, it's okay to kiss old friends, whether they were past lovers or whatever." She tossed her head to sling hair out of her face. "In my case, since I don't have any past lovers, I'll have to reserve my friendly pecks for old boyfriends."

"Dammit, Gail, you're making an issue out of something so…"

The music stopped. When they returned to the table, she grabbed her purse. "Excuse me, I'm headed for the ladies room." Without waiting for an answer, she turned and walked to the restrooms located near the entrance.

~*~

Mad, yet disgusted with himself, Lucas plopped down in the chair and drained his beer. The atmosphere was tense. Jason and Robert shot him sympathetic glances, but not the two women. Cheryl slapped him on the arm.

"What were you thinking kissing Tabitha? Are you stupid, or what?"

"I guess. Hell, I don't know what I was thinking."

He looked up to see Gail leave the ladies room. She started their way and then, big smile on her face, detoured. Where the hell was she going? She stopped at a table with two couples, put her arm around a man's shoulders, and bent down to…to…her back was to him, but hell it looked like she'd kissed him on the cheek. Blood rushed to his face and he lurched out of the chair.

Jason and Robert each held an arm before he took two steps.

"Sit down, man, before you make a fool of yourself," Jason said.

Lucas gasped for air, relaxed his clenched fists, then nodded and sat down, his eyes never leaving his wife. She straightened, turned and moved toward them. Not for the first time, he noticed the looks of appreciation she received from the other men in the room. He was proud she was beautiful, but tonight their approval fed the fire in his gut.

Gail slid into her chair. "Sorry I took so long. I saw—"

Cheryl blurted out. "Hey, what are you two doing tomorrow night?"

Gail shrugged and looked at Lucas. He growled, "I don't know. What'd you have in mind?"

"We're getting together at our house for supper and to play forty-two." Cheryl looked at Gail. "Do you know the game?"

"No self-respecting Texan doesn't know how to play forty-two. I'd love to come." She looked at Lucas.

He nodded. "Fine."

She knew he was mad and didn't care. With a smile, she patted his cheek. He grabbed her hand.

"Who'd you stop to talk to?"

She pointed to the table where she'd stopped. "You mean over there?"

"Hell, yes, you know what I'm talking about."

"Oh, Alex Guthrie and some of his friends. I was surprised to see him here. Doesn't fit his image, but he's dressed in jeans and I have to admit he didn't look half bad."

Lucas couldn't cover the deadly tone in his voice. His words came out in a growl. "You kissed Alex?"

"I did not. I wanted to tell him something and had to bend down and yell in his ear to be heard above the noise."

Lucas relaxed slightly. "Couldn't it have waited until Monday?"

She shrugged. "No, not really and I wanted to meet his date. He stopped by the table one day when Sandra and I were having lunch and she asked about him. She thinks he's good looking and we wondered why he wasn't married."

"Sandra's a married woman with a child. Why should she care?" He struggled to keep from strangling her as he waited for her explanation.

"Just because she's married doesn't mean she doesn't notice someone's good looks." Her lips twitched. Why she wanted to laugh at his discomfort.

"That's right, boys," Patty said. "You can't tell us you don't notice when a woman is good-looking because we do and watch to see your reaction. The thing is women notice beautiful women and good-looking men—one with envy and the other with appreciation." Patty's eyes sparkled with mischief and all three women laughed in agreement.

"Anyway," said Gail, "we had lunch together today to discuss a client and I wanted to know what Alex had learned this afternoon after meeting with the man."

"You had lunch with Alex?"

"Yes, we talk business over lunch on occasion. I thought you knew."

"Hell, no, I didn't know." He hit the table with his fist. "Now I know why I catch people looking at me and whispering."

Cheryl held her hand up. "Hey, now, if they're gossiping about them having lunch together, they're just plain stupid. Professional women do have lunch dates with men and vice versa. It's part of having a career."

Robert looked at Lucas with sympathy. "You'll get used to it, old man. It was hard for me to handle at first, too, but you have to trust your wife." He circled Cheryl's shoulders with his arm and kissed her on the temple. She smiled up at him. "I occasionally have dinner engagements with women, too, and Cheryl understands."

Lucas muttered, "I don't like it one bit." He tugged on Gail's hand, pulling her from her chair. "Let's dance."

It was a slow number and his arm locked around her waist like a vise. "Why didn't you tell me, Gail? I knew you took clients to lunch sometimes, but not about the lunches with Alex."

She pulled back and raised her chin. "I'm your wife, not your child, and don't feel I need to give you an accounting of what I do every day."

"Dammit, you know how I feel about Alex."

"Yes, I do, so why should I have told you knowing you'd only get upset?" She sighed. "Maybe I should have told you, but it's business, not a date. You need to get past your jealousy or it's going to cause a rift in our relationship or have a negative effect on my career."

He pulled her closer. "I can't help being jealous, but I'll try to curb it."

"Thank you."

"I don't trust the man." He tightened his grip on

her waist and growled in her ear. "No more little scenes like tonight, okay? You were yanking my chain, weren't you?"

She giggled. "Yes, dear. Doesn't feel good, does it?"

~*~

The music ended and they'd almost reached the table when the band started "Cotton Eyed Joe". Jason pulled Patty to her feet. "Come on, honey, let's boogie." Laughing they all joined the couple on the dance floor. When the song ended, they fell into their chairs.

"Whew, that was fun," Robert said. "I believe I've worked up an appetite. Nachos, anyone?" The other two men voiced their agreement.

Lucas nuzzled her neck sending a delicious shiver down her back. "Nachos okay with you or do you want something else?"

"Nachos are fine, but I'd like a cup of coffee." She'd only had two beers, but didn't want anymore.

"Good idea. Think I'll have coffee too and some water."

Gail leaned into the cradle of his shoulder. He hugged her close and whispered, "I love you."

"I love you, too."

Three orders of nachos, six cups of coffee, and waters arrived. Gail turned loose of the hurt she'd felt earlier, determined it wouldn't spoil their night out together. When their plates were empty and their coffee cups refilled, talk turned to the unidentified woman found in Possum Creek. All eyes looked at Gail with apprehension.

"It's all right. I can't say I'm comfortable with the

topic, but I would like to know the latest information."

Robert served Stone County as assistant DA and felt frustrated they didn't have more evidence to go on. He looked at Gail. "If she's not identified as your mother, we'll be back to square one. Guess we could have everyone in the county line up and give a blood test to see if we could match DNA."

Cheryl was also a lawyer in private practice with two other lawyers. "What makes you think it's someone from around here? We've not had any missing people in the last twenty-five years that I know of."

"You're right because I checked. We have several couples who split up and one or other of the spouses left town." Robert shot Gail a concerned glance.

"Don't walk on egg shells around me, Robert. I know my mother left Daddy in June of 1982 to never return. How many other spouses ran out on their families?"

"Five that I've been able to come up with. Three were women your mother's age and the other two were men in their thirties." He shook his head. "No telling how many others are out there. But none of these people were reported missing. Their spouses knew they were leaving and didn't suspect foul play."

Five people? The number seemed a lot for this area. She wasn't sure how wide an area Stone County covered. Daddy had looked for Mama hoping he could talk her into coming back home, but he'd not been able to find her. "Mama left a note, but Daddy never heard from her again. What about the others?"

"Don't know," Robert said. "I've been trying to get Bud to talk with each of them. Hopefully he'll get to it next week. He's so busy I may end up having to do it myself."

Jason pushed back his chair and turned to his wife. "We better get home or we'll be paying the babysitter overtime. See you guys tomorrow night."

They all walked to the parking lot together and honked and waved as they pulled away from the bar. If Gail didn't know better she'd think they were still teenagers. Lucas reached for her hand. "Did you have a good time?"

"A great time."

As they pulled up to the house, the automatic floodlight came on. Chief greeted them in the carport, wiggling and jumping. "Have you kept the home-front safe, boy?" Chief barked. "Good dog. Run take care of business." The dog ran into the bushes and a short time later, Gail heard him bark at the door. Lucas let him in.

She went into the bathroom to brush her teeth and wash her face. When she came out, Lucas sat in one of the old stuffed chairs with one boot off. In the process of removing the other one, he looked up and froze when he saw her in the red teddy she'd bought at Victoria's Secret.

"My God, you're beautiful."

She smiled and struck a pose for him. "Thank you. I assume you like the teddy."

He groaned. "Like it? I love it. Come here."

Eyes never leaving his, she walked into his arms. He laid his face against her stomach, and she ran her fingers through his hair. They held tight and caressed each other. "We better get to bed." She pulled back and turned to her lingerie drawer to get a gown.

"Please, wear the teddy to bed tonight."

"All right."

Their loving tender, Lucas made her body hum with pleasure, and cry out again and again. She gloried in his touch, but it hurt to know he'd touched other women the way he touched her. She didn't doubt his love or that Tabitha was a part of the past. *So, get over it, Gail.* Her feelings were petty. She had no right to be jealous of the women he'd known before her.

~*~

Gail went online and booked a hotel room for the following week. Making arrangements to be off two days wasn't a problem, though she might have to work extra hours to catch up when she returned.

They left early Tuesday morning for Gail's 11:00 a.m. appointment. By three o'clock p.m. they were finished for the day. At the hotel, they swam then showered and went to a nice restaurant. Later they drove down to Sixth Street and found a place to dance. It was the most fun they'd had since their honeymoon.

By noon the next day, they were on their way home. They were in Gail's Lexus and she leaned back in the plush seat and relaxed. She was glad the tests were over and they'd know something soon.

Lucas squeezed her hand. "Tired?"

"A little, but I had so much fun last night."

He grinned. "You do like to dance."

"Yes, I do, and I don't think I'm alone in that department."

He chuckled. "No, you're not." Lucas put both hands on the wheel and concentrated on the congested traffic. It seemed the freeways in Austin were perpetually under construction. When they were out of town and the highway less crowded, he asked. "When did Dr. Lane say we'd hear back on the tests?"

"She said a couple of days, so I figure we'll hear by Monday."

"Does she have your office number and cell?"

"Yes, she won't have any trouble getting me. I gave her your cell also."

He nodded. "Did she say what our options would be if the test were all normal?"

Gail sat up straighter. He was trying to be nonchalant, but she could see his worry. "She said if they found nothing to prevent me from conceiving, she'd recommend you get checked out."

Lucas nodded, but Gail saw him chewing the inside of his mouth.

He cleared his throat. "Did she happen to say what type of tests they'd do?"

"The first thing they'd do is a sperm count."

Lucas shot her a desperate look. "Uh, did she happen to say how they do this test?"

Gail had to cough to keep from laughing. "They take some of your sperm and put it under a microscope and count how many sperm per something or another. I forget what she called it."

He shuddered. "I don't think I want to know how they collect this sperm."

Chapter Seven

"We're having wine with our dinner this evening, *Madam*. And French bread."

"Mmm, sounds good."

The wine was perfect with the Italian food and helped Gail to relax. After dinner, they sat on the sofa to finish off the bottle and read more of June's diary.

March 10, 1981. Gail is two months old today. We had our checkup with Doctor Smith and he said our baby girl is doing just fine. She smiles and coos. It tickles Sam to death. He's crazy about our baby.

March 29, 1981. Darn Ruth Ella's hide. I got Gail all prettied up in her red dress. She's so beautiful in red with all her dark hair. I wish we could figure out how to make it lay down. It sticks up all over the place.

Lucas laughed. "I do remember that about you. Even when you were around two, your hair still looked ragged."

She poked him in the belly. "Well, thank goodness it's manageable now."

"Yeah and so pretty." Lucas ran his fingers through it as they read.

I came in from getting myself dressed and there she lay in her crib in the blue dress. Ella always likes for Gail to wear that one because she picked it out. When I asked her about it, she said Gail spit up on the red one. Ooooh, she makes me mad. I looked at the red dress and there wasn't a mark on it.

They read through similar accounts of Gail growing and learning to crawl. Of weekend trips to Possum Creek to swim and for picnics and drives in the country. In November, some of June's discontent started to become evident.

November 12, 1981. I am so tired today. Ella and I have cooked three meals for the hands and washed and dried dishes and then there was the ironing and housework. It's the same old thing day in and day out. I love Sam but we don't ever go out anymore. I'm sick of staying home. My only joy is Gail. She grows sweeter every day.

Chief stood up, his ears pointing to the ceiling. He looked at Lucas. "Have we got company, boy?"

Chief gave a low, "Woof."

Gail pushed up off the sofa and put the diary on the bookshelf with Lucas's collection. "Who can that be? It's after eight o'clock."

"I don't know, maybe Mom and Dad." Lucas opened the front door as car lights switched off outside. "Looks like Ruth's car."

Gail joined him at the door. "That's odd." She often came over, usually earlier in the evening.

Ruth stepped onto the walk, bearing a cake carrier. Lucas held the door open for her. "Oh, boy, I hope that's what I think it is." He took the cake from her and balanced it on one hand.

Ruth laughed. "It's kind of hard to disguise."

Lucas hugged the older woman. "I love you, Ruth."

"Yeah, right, you love my chocolate cake."

He grinned. "That, too."

Ruth blushed prettily at his teasing. Her blond hair

appeared almost gray now, yet she remained a nice-looking woman. He'd never understood why Sam hadn't married her. Tonight she looked trim in a casual blue pantsuit.

"Come on in the kitchen, Ruth. Let me put on a fresh pot of coffee." Gail started the coffee while Lucas grabbed cake plates and forks. "Have a seat."

Ruth sat down and looked around the room. "You've done a good job in here. I love this wall color. What's it called?"

Lucas spoke up. "It's called cappuccino and cream."

"It's calming and really sets off your dishes and accessories."

Gail smiled as Lucas put his arm around her. "She's a good decorator. We'll show you the rest of the house after we eat."

"Good, I've been wanting to see what all you'd done since I was here the last time."

They concentrated on their cake and coffee for a minute.

"Gail, Sam said you found your mother's diary."

"Yes, I did. We were reading it when you drove up."

Ruth glanced into the living room. "Really?"

"Yes, and it's been wonderful learning how my mother felt about me."

Ruth looked surprised. "Why, she loved you, child. Didn't you know that?"

Why would Ruth think she knew that? Her mother was rarely, if ever, mentioned around her. "How could I? Daddy didn't talk about her unless I asked specific questions."

"Oh dear me, I'm sorry." She shook her head in dismay. "You mean all these years you've wondered?"

Gail nodded. "Yeah."

The older woman looked uncomfortable. Gail rushed to change the subject. "By the way, I didn't know you and mother were friends."

"Honey, I just always thought everybody knew."

"You never mentioned her to me or said anything."

Ruth frowned and poked at her plate. "No, I never quite knew how to mention your mother to you. Your father never talked about her, and I figured he didn't want me to either."

Gail nodded. "That's understandable."

Ruth laughed. "As to being friends, we got along most of the time. Sometimes we mixed like oil and vinegar."

Lucas poured them more coffee. "Yeah, we could tell. She thought you interfered with Gail." He grinned. "Especially the way June dressed her."

"We fussed about some of the stupidest stuff." She covered Gail's hand with hers. "But, I sure didn't realize you doubted your mother loved you. I'm so sorry."

She squeezed Ruth's hand. "It's not your fault or Daddy's either. He tried to reassure me, but you know how kids can be." She shrugged. "Let's take our coffee in the living room." Gail and Ruth left the kitchen while Lucas loaded their plates and forks in the dishwasher.

~*~

Lucas listened to their chatter as Gail took Ruth through the house. "Oh this is a nice color. It almost looks like Mexican clay tile." He was proud of what she'd done. Their home looked as good as those in

Gail's home design magazines. He sat down in the club chair so the ladies could have the sofa when they returned to the living room.

"Is that the old suitcase you found the diary in?"

"Yes, but Daddy thought you'd put it there."

"No, I hadn't seen it. I always assumed she took it with her when she left. As a matter of fact, I can't imagine her leaving it behind."

Chief sat unmoving in the hall as Gail and Ruth stood in the guest bedroom. He followed Ruth's every movement. Lucas grinned at the silly mutt. *Wonder why he is so enthralled with the woman.* When they sat on the sofa, Chief stationed himself between them. Ruth acted slightly afraid of Chief. Which was odd, she'd never shown fear of him before.

"He won't hurt you, Ruth. For some reason tonight he's checking you out."

She gave a nervous laugh. "Oh, I see. Wonder why."

He shrugged. "Who knows what goes on in his head?"

"Chief," said Gail. The dog looked at Gail. She reached down and scratched his neck. "You're such a good dog. What's got into you tonight?"

Ruth put out her hand. "Hi, Chief, come here, boy."

Chief stood to sniff her hand, then sat back down on his haunches.

They sat back and drank their coffee. Ruth looked around the room. Her eyes lit on the bookshelves. "Whose book collection?"

"Mine," said Lucas. "I love westerns. Do you read?"

"Me? No, never sat still long enough." She stood up and walked to Gail's wedding picture hung above the mantel. "Oh dear me, girl, this is just beautiful. The smaller one your daddy has just doesn't do you the justice this one does."

Lucas joined her in front of the portrait. He loved the smile on his wife's face as she held onto an old wood column. The contrast between the stateliness of the badly needing paint church and the flawless beauty of his wife made the picture much more striking.

Ruth looked at her watch. "Well, I better get home. It's almost ten o'clock."

Lucas put his arms around Ruth's shoulders. "Surprise us like this again. Anytime, you hear?"

She chuckled. "You'd think you never got sweets, Lucas, and I know Gail bakes for you."

"A man can never have too many sweets."

Ruth hugged Gail. "Bye, hon."

"Thanks for coming, Ruth. We enjoyed your visit."

Lucas and Gail stood and watched as Ruth got in her car and drove off. Chief had his head between their legs, watching also. When she was gone, Chief turned and walked back into the den. He sniffed the sofa where Ruth had sat and the floor where her shoes had been.

Gail looked at him in question. Lucas shrugged. "I don't have a clue. I've never seen him act this way before."

~*~

Gail hadn't been at her desk more than thirty minutes when her phone rang. "Brown and Guthrie, Gail Johnson speaking."

"Gail, this is Dr. Lane. Your tests all came back normal. There is absolutely no reason why you can't get pregnant. But remember, the mind can do strange things to the body. If you're worried and tense, that alone could keep you from conceiving. Do you understand?"

"Yes, I do."

"Now, encourage that husband of yours to get in for testing as soon as possible. I know men are hesitant about this, but the sooner he's tested, if something is wrong, the sooner we can get it corrected. Call my office and my nurse will give you the name of some doctors your husband might want to see."

"I'll do that, Dr. Lane. Thank you."

Gail hung up the phone. Her entire body smiled, if such a thing was possible. Nothing appeared to be wrong with her. How would Lucas take the news? She knew he'd be happy she was fine, but he hadn't looked excited about going through tests. He wanted a child as much as she did though, so he'd do it. She called Dr. Lane's office back, spoke to her nurse, and jotted down the names of three doctors in the Austin area.

She beat Lucas home that evening. He called and said he'd be late getting in so she prolonged starting dinner. She and Chief walked down to the stables to see him working with a colt.

"Hi, hon, come see this baby." Lucas worked in the stall with the colt and her mother. He saw Chief and said, "Stay, Chief." Chief sat on his haunches and whined.

Lucas brought the colt closer to the stall door. The mare snorted, stamped her foot, and started toward him. "It's all right, mama, I won't let anybody hurt your baby." He stroked the mare's neck and she relaxed.

"Oh, Lucas, she's a beauty." The colt was brown like her mother, but had a blaze of white on her forehead. Lucas nudged the colt closer and Gail reached through the bars and stroked her neck. "So sweet."

"Yeah, she is. It's amazing, isn't it? I never get tired of seeing these new lives. Each one is different."

Lucas leaned over the stall door and kissed her. "How was your day?"

"Good. I heard from Dr. Lane this afternoon."

He froze and looked at her expectantly, anxious to hear her news.

"She said all the tests returned normal. There's no physical reason I can't conceive."

He nodded. "Good, I'm glad. Guess that means I'm the culprit."

"Not necessarily. Remember, I said physical reason. It could be psychological. But she did recommend some doctors for you to see."

He went back to working with the colt.

"I'll see you at supper. About seven okay?"

"Yeah, fine, I'll be there."

Gail turned and left the stable. "Come on, Chief, let's head home."

On the way back from the stables, Gail stopped by the garden behind the big house and picked some of her mother-in-law Sharon's tomatoes. They were ripe and juicy. It was nice out so she decided to grill steaks. She put potatoes in the oven to bake and made a salad.

She heard Lucas's truck pull into the carport. Chief met him at the door and barked to welcome him home. He headed straight for the bathroom to shower. She tapped on the door. "I'm throwing steaks on the grill."

"Okay, I'll be right out."

~*~

Lucas found Gail on the patio wearing shorts and a

halter-top. She'd gotten a little tan and looked good enough to eat. He joined her at the grill and kissed her neck. "Mmm, you look delicious."

"Well, thank you, darlin'." She turned and kissed him on the lips. "Would you like a beer with your dinner?"

"Nah, tea will be good. Here, let me finish the steaks for you." She handed him the tongs and went inside. A few minutes later she returned with two glasses of ice and a pitcher of tea.

"I think we'll eat out here. Does that sound all right?"

"Yeah, be great."

Gail held their plates while he put the steaks on them. He shook his head when he looked at hers. "That is the puniest little piece of meat I've ever seen."

She looked at his large steak. "Yeah, well, that's all I can eat. If I start eating like you do, I'll be as big as the barn."

He snorted. "A little weight wouldn't hurt you."

"Are you saying I'm skinny?"

"No, ma'am, I'm not." He held up his hands. "You're perfect just like you are." Jeepers, he better learn to keep his mouth shut about this weight issue. He took a big bite of steak. "Perfect!"

Gail took a big bite of salad and chewed. "Your mama grows mighty fine tomatoes."

"You been stealing from her garden again?"

"You bet. I do every chance I get."

Lucas laughed. It tickled his mother for Gail to visit her garden. Tom and his wife did, too. Sharon always planted too much, but with the help of everyone on the ranch, her crops didn't go to waste.

Finished eating, they held hands and looked out onto the land sprawled before them. Their backyard backed up against a barbed wire fence that enclosed cattle. At present the pasture happened to be empty. It was filled with wildflowers of red and yellow. They added texture and color growing among the cactus and scrub brush that covered groupings of large boulders spaced here and there. The boulders were too big to try to remove so they remained and added interest to the grassland. Someone had planted honeysuckle along the fence and their yellow blooms emitted a sweet odor that carried on the slight intermittent breeze. When the mosquitoes started biting, they gathered their plates and glasses and went inside.

The dishes didn't take long to wash and put away. They went to bed early. Before supper, Lucas had found the doctors names on his desk and put the list in his wallet. He'd make an appointment, but not right away. It was something he needed to get prepared for in his mind. The possibility he might be sterile hurt and depressed him. Surely he wasn't one of those insecure men who'd feel emasculated if he was sterile. He prayed he wasn't.

He turned to his wife and pulled her close. "I'm glad you're all right. If I'm sterile, we'll still find a way to have a baby. I promise."

"Oh, Lucas, please don't be overly worried about this now. If for some reason we can't have a baby, we can adopt. There are lots of kids out there who need a home." She rubbed his back. "You know I've heard of couples who adopt a baby and in a few months find out they're pregnant."

"I've heard that too." *Lord, please don't let me be*

sterile. He'd love an adopted child as much as if it resulted from their bodies, but he also wanted to see Gail grow big with their child, watch her nurse it at her breast, see both their features on its little face. Was that petty and small on his part? Probably, but he couldn't help it.

~*~

It was the first week in July when Bud stopped by her office.

Her door was usually open and when he closed it behind him, she knew the news wasn't good. "Gail, can you talk a minute?"

Gail's breath caught in her throat and it took a minute to be able to speak. She stood and walked around to meet him. "Yes...I can."

He coughed and cleared his throat. "I'm sorry to tell you this, but the remains of the woman found in the car in Possum Creek have been positively identified as your mother. The match is almost perfect. There is no room for doubt." He was quiet for a minute, waiting for her to say something. Her throat wouldn't cooperate. "Uh, I'm driving out to notify your Dad. He'll want to get her remains released from the morgue for burial." He laid a big hand on her shoulder. "He's going to need you, honey."

Lips trembling, she nodded. "Thank you for letting me know, Bud." She closed the door behind him. Her mother. Someone had murdered her mother with her father's pistol. Now all hope of ever knowing her vanished. She dropped her head to her hands. *Oh, Mama, why did you have to leave?* There was no time for what ifs. Everyone would believe her father did it. But he didn't. She knew he didn't.

Tears filled her eyes. *I've got to get out of here.* She gathered her things and stopped by the receptionist's desk. "Sue, I'm leaving for the day. If anyone calls for me, tell them I'll return their call in the morning."

Sue looked worried, but didn't ask questions. "Yes, I will."

Gail called Lucas on his cell phone and then drove straight to her father's. Lucas beat her there and was in the kitchen with her father when she arrived.

"Daddy, are you all right?" Sam stood and hugged her.

"I'm fine."

Gail could see he wasn't. He'd been crying and his leathered face bore lines of despair.

"I just can't see why anyone would want to kill June and that man. It doesn't make sense."

Ruth washed dishes, but stopped periodically to wipe tears off her cheek. She sniffed. "Maybe it was that man's wife. She followed him and then did it."

He shook his head. "How would she have known the water was so deep there? Not being from around here, she wouldn't."

Ruth shrugged. "You never know about folks. She might have just taken a chance the water was deep and got lucky."

"Do you know of anyone around here who knew about that deep spot, Sam?" Lucas asked.

Sam thought for several minutes. "I don't ever remember anyone mentioning it. I sure didn't know. Don't think Randall knew either."

Gail covered her mouth and moaned. "Oh, God."

Lucas took her hand. "What's wrong, honey?"

She choked on a sob. "Mama was alive when that car hit the water. She came to while water seeped into the car to drown her and fought to get out." Tears rolled down her cheeks. "It must have been horrifying to be trapped and unable to do anything."

Sam choked out a groan. "You don't know that for a fact."

"Yes...yes, I do. Robert stopped by the office a few days ago and said forensics had found torn fingernails and the vinyl around the door handle possessed deep gouges." Also the woman wasn't wearing a seat belt and the man was.

A blood-curdling wail startled them. They looked up to see Ruth, face ashen, turn and rush from the room. "Oh, goodness, I forgot Ruth loved her, too."

Her father got up. "I'll see to her."

Lucas tugged on her hand. "Come here, baby." He settled her on his lap and pulled her head to his shoulder. "It's a terrible thing, a terrible way to die, but you can't change anything, Gail."

She sniffed. "I know." She'd never known her mother and then to learn she'd been murdered and suffered terribly before she died was bitter medicine indeed.

"We'll see she gets a nice funeral. You and your daddy probably need to go to the funeral home tomorrow and make arrangements."

"Yes, you're right. I'd forgotten about that part."

"I'll go with you."

They heard the front door open and close. Sam came back in the kitchen and sat down. "I sent Ruth home. She and June were close. Oh, they fussed a bunch, but they loved each other."

Gail emitted a tearful giggle. "You should read Mama's diary. Seems like they were at odds all the time."

Sam grinned. "Never could figure out why June didn't want to get rid of Ruth and find someone else. She always harped about her. Let me say one word though, and she jumped down my throat."

The weight of what lay ahead pressed down on her heart. She covered her father's hand with hers. "Daddy, we need to see about funeral arrangements. Do you feel up to going tomorrow?"

He nodded. "Might as well get it over with."

"I'll take off then. Lucas said he'd come with us."

Sam looked at him. "I appreciate that, son."

"Anything I can do, Sam, you just let me know."

They all jumped when the phone rang. It was on the fourth ring when Sam picked it up. "Hello."

"Yeah, Bud, what do you need?"

Sam studied the toe of his boot while he listened. "I understand. You don't have to explain yourself to me. You're just doing your job."

Sam glanced at Gail. "What time? Gail and I need to be at the funeral home sometime to make arrangements."

He nodded a couple of times. "Okay, I'll call you when I find out what time they can see us."

Sam said goodbye and hung up the phone.

"What did he want, Daddy?"

"He needs me to come in for questioning about the murder of your mother and that man."

Chapter Eight

Faulkner's Funeral Home sat on the outskirts of town. Their appointment was for eleven o'clock a.m. Lucas and Gail pulled into the parking lot just as Sam got out of his truck. He stopped to wait for them before going inside the gracious colonial building with its tall columns and wide veranda.

Ed Faulkner met them inside and shook hands with Sam. "Sorry to see you here under these circumstances, Sam." He directed them to his office. When they were all seated, he said. "Do you have some idea of what you want?"

Sam looked at his daughter. "Gail and I discussed it last night and decided to have a quiet grave-side service."

Ed nodded and filled out some forms. By noon, all the arrangements had been made, and they drove into town to eat.

The On the Square Café was full and noisy. When they walked in, all talk ceased and heads turned in their direction. Sam's face reddened and anger heated Lucas's own. He clapped Sam on the shoulder and directed him to a corner booth. "Just ignore them, Sam. You know how gossipy this town is."

"Yeah, Daddy." Gail took his arm and slid into one side of the booth, pulling him in beside her.

Sam wiped his brow. "It's only natural for them to

be curious."

Lucas bit out the words loud enough for them to echo around the room. "Yeah, but there's such a thing as good manners, too." He allowed his gaze to sweep the crowd. Heads turned back to their food. Some looked ashamed to be gawking, others defiant.

"Lucas, I'm hungry for a hamburger and fries today." Gail gave him a crooked grin.

"Really? Sounds great to me. How about you, Sam?"

"I thought she didn't let you eat hamburgers, Lucas."

"Oh, she relents on occasion."

"Hamburger for me, too, then."

Gail kept the conversation light during lunch. Talk turned to the new colts in their stable. They had three, and they were all beauties. "I think the bay mare is the prettiest, Daddy. Sweet, with beautiful lines, she holds her head like a princess." Just like Gail did. Lucas watched her animated face in profile—the long graceful neck, high cheekbones, and patrician nose. Every time he looked at her, he thanked the Lord again for blessing him with this beautiful woman. He smiled. He'd decided the colt would be hers if Gail wanted her. Her comment cinched it. Junebug had a few more good years, but it would be nice for Gail to have a colt to train to take her place.

Sam chuckled and winked at Lucas. "She always did enjoy the colts." He grabbed the check. "My treat today. You guys come on by the house. I need to talk to you about some things."

Gail looked startled and Lucas shrugged. He didn't have a clue what *things* Sam had on his mind.

Sam was in his rocker on the porch when they drove up. Gail sat in the one beside him. Lucas perched his hip on the porch rail and leaned back against the post.

"What's on your mind, Daddy?"

He cleared his throat. "I think it's time I signed the ranch over to you, honey."

Gail froze, expression confused. "Why?"

He shrugged. "It's time I retired, don't feel as good as I used to."

Gail's eyes filled with worry, and she touched his arm. "Daddy?"

"Ah, hell, I've got lung cancer. Start treatments next week."

"Why...why didn't you tell us?" Gail's eyes filled with tears, and she covered her trembling lips with her hand.

Voice gruff, he blustered. "Now don't start bawlin'. I'll be all right, just sick for a while."

Gail clutched his arm. "Come stay with us so I can take care of you."

Sam patted her hand. "No, baby, you've got a job and a husband. Besides, Ruth will take care of me."

"But, she's not family." Gail brushed a tear away. "I could do a lot of my work at home."

"No. I want to stay at home and Ruth is almost family." Sam looked at Lucas. "If you want to run some cattle on my place, get Gail to take you around and locate the tanks." He grinned. "Guess that'd be foolish as you two probably covered every inch of our land when she was a kid."

"Yeah, Sam, we did. I think I know it well enough to make plans. Are you sure this is what you want to do?"

Sam nodded.

"What about money, Sam? Do you have enough for your needs?"

Sam studied Lucas's face and smiled ruefully. "Gail chose well when she set her cap for you, Lucas." He remained quiet a minute and then took a deep breath. "I'm fine on money, son, but I thank you for asking."

Lucas's chest tightened. Sam looked sicker than he'd let on, and he was probably trying to ease the blow for Gail. "You ever need anything, let us know. And Gail's invitation to live with us stands."

~*~

Later that afternoon, Sam drove into town to the sheriff's office. The deputy on duty called Bud on the phone and he came right out. He shook Sam's hand. "Thanks for coming in, Sam. I know this is a hard time for you. I'm mighty sorry about June."

Sam nodded, and voice gruff, said, "It's good to know at last what happened to her." Bud motioned to a chair. He sat down and shook his head. "I didn't kill her and Lamar Jacobs, Bud. I hope to God you find who did and make them pay."

Bud sat behind his desk, the rolling office chair creaking as he settled his bulk in it. "This is mighty awkward, Sam, but with the murder weapon being your gun, you're one of my top suspects."

Sam snorted. "Who else you got on your list?"

"I'm not at liberty to share that with you, Sam."

"I expect not. What do you want to know?"

Bud pulled a yellow legal pad in front of him and started writing. "I need a full accounting of your whereabouts on the day June left."

He gave the names of the two men who'd been working for him at the time. They'd been mending fence that day and taken sack lunches to keep from taking the time to return to the house for lunch. Ruth had met him at the back door when he'd come home, June's note in her hand. He'd never forget one minute of that evening and the week that followed. Gail was at Ruth's sisters. He'd picked her up and gone to the Johnsons'. Randall was away overnight, but Sharon had seen his distress and held him as he'd sobbed out his grief. She'd offered to take care of Gail while he looked for his wife. He'd been gone two days and returned without a clue of where June had gone.

When Sam left the sheriff's office, the sun was making its way toward the horizon. He felt tired to the bone and hungry. At least Bud hadn't thrown him behind bars—yet. After he crossed the bridge across Possum Creek, he pulled off into the small clearing where the Cutlass had been pulled from the water. He killed the engine on his truck and rolled down the windows. Staring out, without seeing, he wondered again for at least the thousandth time. But this time his question was different. *Oh, Junie, who did this to you?*

~*~

The following day, cars lined the narrow roads that wove through Stony Creek's cemetery. Most were friends of Sam and Gail, none of June's family attended. The casket was covered with a large arrangement of white lilies. Their sweet scent wrapped around the mourners. Sprays and baskets of flowers hugged the casket stand and lined the outside of the partitioned area. Under a green tent with Brother Bailey officiating, June Steele was laid to rest.

Sharon and Randall Johnson had the immediate family back to their house for an informal dinner. Lucas kissed his mother's cheek. "Mmmmmm, my favorite chicken ranch casserole. Thanks, Mom."

"You're welcome, son." She turned to the others. "Come grab a plate and help yourself. I've got tea, wine, or beer."

"Beer for me," said Sam.

"And me," added Randall.

Gail dished up a serving of the casserole and added salad and bread to her plate. She walked to the refrigerator for the tea. "What do you want to drink, Lucas?"

"I'll take tea." He took the glass from her hand and pressed a sweet kiss on her lips. "Thank you, hon."

She nodded toward the patio. "You want to eat outside?"

Lucas looked toward the dining room where his parents sat with Sam and raised his voice so they'd hear him. "We're going out to the patio."

"Fine," said Sharon.

The table sat under a tree. A breeze flowed across the water in the pool, cooling the air before it brushed their skin. Gail picked at her food. She looked up, her eyes large with pain. "Daddy's not telling us everything, is he? His cancer is bad."

Lucas wanted to fold her in his arms, but she held herself stiffly, wanting the truth, not comfort. He leaned back in his chair. "No, I don't think so. He's trying to candy coat it for us."

Tears pooled in Gail's eyes. "I've never known my mother, and now I'm going to lose my father."

Lucas took her hand and pulled her over onto his lap. He forced her head to his shoulder and cuddled her close. "Honey, you don't know he's going to die." He closed his eyes and prayed his words weren't a lie. "With treatment, he could live a number of years yet."

"I know, but I'm so scared. He must think he's going to die if he's giving up ranching. What will he do with himself all day?"

Lucas had been wondering, too. Sam was an active man and though he'd aged in the last couple of years, he wouldn't be able to stand inactivity for very long. "I don't know, hon, but we'll find things to keep him busy."

She kissed his neck. "I don't know what I'd do if I didn't have you, Lucas. You're my rock."

"I'll always be here for you, baby, always."

~*~

Sunday morning, Lucas and Gail lingered over breakfast and read the Austin paper. Lucas turned his section around so Gail could see it. "Look, Shaffer Farms right outside of Austin is having a three day auction starting next Monday." He read, "Thoroughbred horses will be placed on the bidding block for three consecutive days. Day one of the auction is reserved for interested parties to study the mares and stallions up for sale."

Gail poured them another cup of coffee. "Are you interested? Do you need more breeding stock?"

"Yeah, I could use another good mare, and I'm always on the lookout for a perfect stud."

She sat down. "You think you might go, then?"

Lucas studied the ad. He didn't want to be away during Sam's illness, but he wouldn't be going far and could get home at a moment's notice. Ruth was available to take Sam to Austin and Sam wouldn't hear of Gail taking off, or allow Lucas to leave the ranch and make the drive. So he might as well plan to go. He tapped the pencil he'd marked the ad with against the table. It would be an opportunity to take care of some other business also.

"Yeah, I think I will." He reached for her hand. "Will you be all right here by yourself?"

"Of course."

"Good. Let's hurry or we'll be late for church."

As usual, the church overflowed with parishioners. Lucas's folks were already there in the customary pew. Sam sat across the aisle from them. Gail and Lucas slid into the pew behind him. Gail placed her hand on his shoulder.

"How you feeling this morning, Daddy?"

Sam patted her hand. "I'm fine. Quit fussing over me." Gail flinched at his harsh words, but she didn't say anything. Lucas saw the hurt on her face and squeezed her shoulder.

Brother Bailey stepped up to the pulpit. "Today our lesson is a reminder of God's words on gossip and slander." He looked out at his congregation over his reading glasses. A few people squirmed in their seats and cast anxious glances in Sam's direction.

"Turn in your Bibles to Proverbs, Chapter 18, verses 6-8 and follow along. *A fool's mouth is his undoing, and his lips are a snare to his soul. The words of a gossip are like choice morsels; they go down to a man's inmost parts.* Gossip is one of the devil's tools. He loves for us to sin against God and put our souls in jeopardy." Brother Bailey took off his glasses and surveyed his flock. Some members hung their heads.

He shoved his glasses back on. "Now turn to Chapter 7 of Matthew, verses 1-2. *Do not judge, or you too will be judged. For in the same way you judge others, you will be judged and with the measure you use, it will be a measure to you.*" He closed the Bible, removed his glasses and put them in his pocket. "Don't fall into Satan's trap. He loves for us to sin, and remember, in God's eyes, one sin is as great as another. And the Lord doesn't discriminate."

His sermon continued for thirty minutes. A talented man, he reprimanded his worshippers, showed them the path to forgiveness, and then lifted their hearts. Lucas didn't doubt many would be on their knees tonight repenting, but by morning they'd have forgotten their promises and find something else to gossip about.

~*~

On a Monday in the middle of July, Lucas kissed Gail good-bye, grabbed his duffle bag, and got in his truck. He felt guilty as hell. Yes, he would go to the auction, but he had another errand in Austin he'd kept from Gail. They were supposed to tell each other everything, but…

Lucas checked into a motel on the outskirts of town then located Dr. Jamison's office. His appointment was for 3:00 p.m. The waiting room overflowed with men of various ages who were dressed in a variety of styles from boots and jeans, to work uniforms, to designer suits. When called into the examination room, Dr. Jamison's nurse had him strip and put on a hospital gown. He felt naked and vulnerable. It took all his willpower not to struggle into his clothes and rush back into the hot, humid Austin heat.

"Ah, hell, I can't do this." Lucas jumped off the table and reached for his jeans. The door opened, and a middle-aged man entered the room. Lucas froze.

"Thinking about taking flight?"

Lucas flushed and nodded.

Dr. Jamison held out his hand. "Mr. Johnson, I'm Dr. Jamison. I know this is uncomfortable for you, but it's necessary if we're to get to the reason why your wife hasn't conceived." He sat down on the round stool and dropped a clipboard on the small desk. "Make up your mind now what it's going to be. You going or staying?"

Lucas thought of how badly he and Gail wanted children, released his breath, and sat his jeans back on the chair. "Okay, let's get it over with."

Dr. Jamison gave him a complete physical and told him to get dressed. He returned with a bottle with a number and Lucas Johnson written on it. "My nurse will direct you to a private room where you can collect a sperm sample."

Lucas thought he'd die of humiliation when the nurse appeared and led him to a room, but she was matter-of-fact and he remembered she probably did this many times every day.

"If you need them, there are magazines and videos in the drawers and a bathroom behind that door. Leave your sample on the shelf above the sink. Stop at the receptionist's desk on your way out and make an appointment for two days from now." She left, locking the door behind her.

Back in his truck, driving from the hospital district, Lucas heaved a sigh of relief. Thank goodness that's over. Now, if he could get through the next two days before he got the results. He'd had this appointment several weeks but been unable to tell Gail why he needed to go to Austin. The horse auction was the perfect excuse. She would have wanted to be with him. He couldn't share the experience right now. It showed his weakness, he knew, but he couldn't seem to get past it. Dr. Jamison's nurse had told Lucas to abstain from sex for several days before the test so the results would be more conclusive. He'd tried but his desire for Gail spoiled his good intentions. She had only to look at him and his body hummed with longing.

Guilt nudged at his conscious. He should've told her about the doctor appointment but didn't want her to worry and fret. Plus, he knew she'd be anxious to hear the results, and he wasn't sure he'd be as ready to share them.

He felt almost giddy with relief the test part was over as he drove toward Shaffer farms.

Pickups and trailers lined both sides of the road leading into the nicely maintained stable area. Lucas parked where he could easily turn around and walked up the caliche road. He registered, took a catalogue and climbed up on the bleachers to sit down and wait for the handlers to put the horses through their paces. In the pamphlet, he marked several mares with pedigrees of interest and one stallion.

All of the horses were fine examples of horseflesh, but the two he'd selected earlier were still the ones he wanted to bid on. The stallion drew a lot of interest. If Lucas wanted to purchase him, the price would be high. He drove back to the motel, showered, and went out to find something to eat. After a large steak and a couple of beers, he returned to the motel and called Gail. She answered on the third ring.

"Hey, hon, how are you?"

"I'm fine. I miss you, though. Went over to see Daddy and took supper."

"How was he?"

"Pretty sick. He couldn't eat much. I wanted to spend the night, but he wouldn't let me."

"Gail, don't let his gruffness hurt you. It's hard for him to admit he's sick and needs you. Just call him in the morning to set your mind at ease."

"Did you see some horses you want to buy?"

"Two pretty little mares and one stallion. Doubt I'll buy the stallion. Bids will probably go too high."

"Where are you staying?"

Lucas gave her the address and phone number and they said goodnight. "I love you, sweetheart."

"You, too, love."

Lucas ate breakfast at Denny's and arrived at Shaffer Farms before 8:00 a.m. Bidding would start at 9:00. He wanted to take another look at the horses and make sure he hadn't missed a special animal. The stallion walked up to the fence and snorted at him. He was beautiful with a strong neck and sleek lines. Lucas chuckled when the chestnut butted him in the chest. "Sorry fella', didn't think to bring treats with me."

"Here you go, son, give him a couple of these."

Lucas looked down at an older man with a badge reading "Shaffer Farms, Ben Shaffer, owner." He held out his hand. "Lucas Johnson, Mr. Shaffer."

Mr. Shaffer shook it. "Call me Ben, young man." He held out a couple of peppermint candies. "These are Dancer's favorites."

Lucas took them. "Thanks." The stallion took them

from his hand, chewed twice, and swallowed. Then he proceeded to sniff and nibble on Lucas's shirt pocket.

Ben laughed. "He's a greedy son-of-a-gun."

"He looks like good breeding material. Why are you selling him?"

"I'm retiring. Have cancer and none of my kids are interested in keeping the farm running. Want to sell the place and let developers build condominiums out here." The old man's good spirits faded, and he suddenly looked tired.

"I'm sorry—about the cancer and the developers. Thought about selling it yourself to someone who might want to continue your tradition here?"

His eyes twinkled. "That'd show 'um, wouldn't it?" He shook his head. "I don't know if anyone would be interested." He scratched his chin and then grinned. "I'll talk to my lawyer and see what he says." He slapped Lucas on the back. "Buy this animal, even if the price goes up to $30,000.00. He's worth every penny. And he likes you." Ben tipped his hat and walked away.

Lucas left the farm the proud owner of two mares and the stallion. Ben's crew would deliver them next week. Ben invited him back for dinner that evening, and Lucas took him up on the offer. His housekeeper, Sarah, served a pot roast with potatoes, carrots, a salad, and hot rolls.

"Ma'am, that was a fine meal. Thank you."

Sarah's face was flushed from the kitchen heat, and sprigs of her damp gray hair curled around her plump face. "You're welcome, son. Love to see a healthy eater."

Ben snorted. "You'd see one every night if you'd

serve me meals like this." He nodded toward Sarah. "She's got me on some screwy diet."

"I do not. The doctor has you on a heart healthy diet."

Sarah cut Lucas a large slice of apple pie and a smaller one for Ben.

"Hey, woman, that ain't fair."

Sarah waved her knife in the direction of Ben's dessert plate. "Shut up, you old bear, and eat your pie or I'll take it away from you."

Ben pulled the small piece closer and started eating.

Sarah turned to Lucas. "If you want another piece of pie, stick your head in the kitchen, and I'll get you one."

"Thank you, Sarah, but this is enough." He patted his belly. "Have to keep my trim figure for my wife."

She patted him on the shoulder. "You do that, son. Keep your woman happy."

"I do my best."

"I just bet you do." She chuckled on the way out the door.

"She's a character. Been with you long?"

Ben shoved his empty plate back. "Too long. Thinks she's the boss and not me."

"Maybe it's time you married her. She loves you, you know."

"Yeah, I know, but I'm a sick old man. She deserves someone healthy, not a worn out old cowboy."

Sarah bustled back in and started grabbing plates. Mouth tense, she muttered, "Maybe she has the right to decide for herself what she wants."

Lucas laughed as Ben sputtered and tried to come

back with a comment. He pushed his chair back. "I better get back to the motel. Thank you both for the fine dinner."

Ben stood up and walked him to the door. "Thanks for coming. I enjoyed your company. Gets lonely around here with no young folks to talk to."

They shook hands. Lucas put on his hat. "If you decide to put your farm up for sale, give me a call and I'll put out the word in Stone County."

"I'll give it some thought. May take you up on your offer to come see your place and meet that pretty wife of yours."

"We'd like that."

The following morning, Lucas sat before the desk in Dr. Jamison's office. The doctor looked through his file, then took off his glasses and looked up. "You're in fine health, Mr. Johnson, but you do have an extremely low sperm count."

Lucas strode from the doctor's building into the heat and made his way toward his truck. Doctor Jamison's words echoed in his head. "I'm sorry, but it would probably be a miracle for you to ever father a child, but—" He'd been unable to let the man finish. Air, he had to get outdoors where he could breathe. The doctor's call followed him out the door. "Mr. Johnson, please…"

Chapter Nine

Gail drove into the carport. Chief lay curled up by the door, a book at his feet. What on earth? She got out of her car and Chief stood up, staggered, and then waited for her to approach him. He usually bounded up for a good scratch.

"What've you got here, fella'?" She bent down to pick up the book. It was June's diary. The cloth cover bore dirt and teeth marks. "Shame on you, Chief. You know better than to bother things in the house."

Chief's ears flattened and then she noticed the hair around his neck and head stood on end. He was either hurting, anxious, or both.

"What's the matter, boy?"

She reached out and touched his head. He whined and drew back. Her heart thundered in her chest. She looked around and noticed what appeared to be blood stains on the cement floor. They weren't large, just small spots and a smear or two. She bent down and examined Chief. Thankfully, she didn't see any wounds, but felt a couple of knots. Someone had hit him. Fury ripped through her.

"Did someone hurt you, boy?"

He "woofed," nudged the diary, and stepped unsteadily up onto the step that led inside. The door was unlocked. Her anger dissolved and fear inched up her spine. Someone had been in the house.

She shoved the door open and Chief stepped in first. He turned and waited for her to follow. With the diary in her hand, she followed him through the house. It looked undisturbed but small things, like the way the cushions on the sofa and chair were fluffed, caught her eye. Chief sniffed and walked from the coffee table to the bookshelves and then to the sofa. He followed a trail on the carpet and went into the office. At the closet door, he barked and nudged the suitcase.

The suitcase and the diary? Oh, Lord, what was going on here?

~*~

Lucas drove without seeing. Trees, hills, and buildings flew by in a haze. After leaving Dr. Jamison's office building, he'd driven to the motel and checked out. He'd considered staying another day, but didn't have an excuse. He didn't want to go home and face Gail. If only he could erase the past three days and pretend none of this had happened, he would. It wouldn't change anything though. He'd never watch his child grow in Gail's body, never look in his child's face and see his features reflected there. God, it hurt. He never dreamed it could hurt this bad. Who was he kidding? Never in his wildest imagination did he believe he and Gail couldn't have children.

His cell phone rang. It was Gail. He ignored it and each ring stabbed at his heart. Tears filled his eyes and dropped onto his cheeks. He hit the steering wheel with his fist. *Why me, Lord? Why?*

He pulled his truck into the parking lot of a beer joint out in the middle of nowhere. It was a weekday and just four o'clock, but the place was already packed. Lucas found a booth and ordered a beer. The cool liquid felt good going down his throat. He rolled the bottle across his forehead and the cold eased his headache for just a minute.

The jukebox blared out a country western tune and couples drifted to the dance floor. He watched their feet slide across the scarred wood. Lucas looked up to see a pretty blonde watching him. She smiled and arched an eyebrow. He shook his head, held up his hand, and wiggled his ring finger. The woman gave him a pouting smile and turned away.

His cell phone rang again and he turned it off to let voice mail pick up. *Not yet, I can't talk just yet.* He ordered another beer and munched on peanuts while he waited. The blonde found a dance partner and boogied by giving him an "aren't you sorry?" grin.

~*~

Lucas had started his third beer when his cell phone beeped, indicating he had a message. It appeared impossible to completely shut the damned thing up. He wanted to ignore it but dialed in to see who'd called. It was from Gail. Dammit, did she have to be so clinging? He listened.

"Lucas, someone's been in the house. Bud's here now. Why haven't you answered your phone? Where the hell are you?"

Fear clutched his chest and guilt robbed him of breath. *You sorry sack of shit. You sit here drowning your sorrows in beer and ignoring pleas for help from your wife—the woman you swore to love and cherish always.* Lucas had never felt so ashamed.

In his truck, he called Gail. "Honey, I got your message, are you all right?"

"Lucas? My, God, where have you been? Why

didn't you answer your phone?"

His stomach roiled. "I'm sorry, baby. I'll explain when I get home. Are you okay?"

"I'm fine. Someone went through the house looking for something. When I got home, Chief met me at the door. Mother's diary was at his feet. It has teeth marks on it and blood. I checked Chief and he has a knot on his head, but no bleeding wounds." She paused. "Where are you, Lucas?"

"I'm about ten miles out of town. I should be there in twenty to thirty minutes. I love you, Gail." Lucas ended the call and concentrated on getting home. Who would want June's diary?

Bud's patrol car stood out front when Lucas arrived. Gail met him at the door and flew into his arms. He held her tight, grateful she hadn't walked in on the intruder and been hurt, feeling guilt for his earlier selfish feelings. Then he felt warmth against his leg and looked down. He released Gail, squatted, and gently ran his hand over Chief's head feeling a small lump.

"Good dog, Chief. I'm proud of you, boy." He ruffled the hair around Chief's neck and pulled him closer for a hug.

He stood to find Gail watching, a smile on her face. "Whoever it was, Chief wasn't about to let them leave with anything of ours." She reached down and grasped a handful of hair on each side of Chief's face and put hers close to his. His ears pricked up, ready for her words. "I think you deserve a special treat tonight, don't you?"

Chief backed up and, with a twitch, "woofed."

Gail laughed. "Steak it is, boy."

Bud called from the other room. "Lucas, you and Gail come on in here."

They were in the office where Bud watched as one of his deputies dusted the suitcase for prints. "Going to need your fingerprints so we can eliminate them from the fresh ones we found." He held the diary in a large zip lock bag. "We'll be able to get more prints from this and compare blood samples. They won't be worth anything without suspects to compare them with. I'd like to see if the blood on the book matches the spots on the drive though." Bud removed a handkerchief from his back pocket and wiped his brow. "Got some good fingerprints, so if we can match 'em, we won't need anything else."

Lucas rubbed the tendons in the back of his neck. "How'd they get in the house, Bud?"

Bud hitched up his pants and rested his right hand on the butt of his pistol. "Didn't break in, that's for sure." He turned to Gail. "You sure you locked the door this morning?"

"Positive, Sheriff. After living in the city, it's a hard habit to break."

"Anyone else have a key besides you two?"

"Just Mom and Dad," Lucas said. "I can't think of anyone else."

"I gave one to Daddy, Lucas, in case we were gone and he needed in."

Lucas put his arm around Gail's shoulders. "I don't think my folks even know about the diary, and when Sam was here, he didn't seem interested in it."

Gail nodded. "Anyway, Daddy's been sick. I can't imagine him driving over here when he could call and ask for the diary if he wanted it."

Bud studied them both and shook his head. "Regardless, this doesn't look good for Sam, Gail. If we find his fresh fingerprints on it, I'll have to take him in, sick or not."

"Daddy did not come into this house to take something and, he did not kill my mother." Gail's voice edged on hysteria.

"I'm not saying he did. But, I have to look at every angle. What do you think, Lucas? Would Chief have bitten either of your parents?"

Lucas couldn't imagine the dog biting one of his folks, even if they were trying to steal their furniture. And Sam had been around Chief since the dog was a pup. Chief felt at ease around him. "No, I can't. Whoever came in, Chief probably knew them, but it was someone he didn't trust."

Pete closed his kit and stood up. "I've got three sets of fresh prints on the suitcase, Bud, and a couple of old smeared ones. Only got one set on the bookshelves." He turned to Gail. "When's the last time you dusted, Ma'am?"

"Why, it was just two days ago. Lucas wasn't home and I got bored and started cleaning."

Pete nodded. "Figured it hadn't been long ago. Y'all come into the kitchen and I'll take your prints for comparison."

Gail and Lucas watched as Bud carried the suitcase and diary to his car and locked them in the trunk. He turned back before getting into the driver's seat. "I'll let you know something as soon as we get a match of the prints."

Lucas waved. "Appreciate it, Bud."

After they left, Lucas helped Gail dust and get rid

of the black powder covering most of the tabletops and bookshelves. Lucas took three steaks from the freezer to grill. Rather than wait for potatoes to bake, Gail opened a can of ranch style beans and made a salad. When the dishes were clean, they took their coffee back outside. The smell of charcoal and grilled meat hung on the air. Chief prowled the yard and, after taking care of business, curled up at their feet.

Gail broke the silence. Her voice was wary and carried a tinge of hurt. "Why were you gone so long, Lucas? I thought you finished buying the horses yesterday. Why didn't you come on home?"

Lucas couldn't answer for a minute. His heart was lodged in his throat, threatening to choke him. He glanced at Gail to see tears glittering in her eyes. *Oh, God, I've hurt her by being selfish and now I'm going to inflict more pain with my news.*

His voice was hoarse. "I saw a doctor Monday and had to return for test results this morning." Gail's hands clenched in her lap and she wouldn't look at him. "It was wrong of me not to tell you, to not ask you to go with me, but I was so damned scared."

"Of what, Lucas? Did you think I'd love you any less if we couldn't have children? I loved you enough to share my fears with you. Why couldn't you love me as much?"

"Dammit, that's not fair, Gail. You know how much I love you." He sat forward and dropped his head into his hands. "It wasn't you I doubted, but me."

His heart ached and his pride was destroyed, and he was angry. "I feel less than a man. I can't father a child. My sperm count is so low Dr. Jamison said it would be a miracle for me to father a child." His voice cracked. "I'll never feel my child growing inside you, Gail."

She sat in his lap and pulled his head to her breasts. "Oh, Lucas, we can adopt a child and make it our own."

"It's not the same." He rubbed her belly, imagining it large with child.

"No, it's not, but we can make it better by loving a child who needs us." She stroked his hair. "Why did you ignore my calls today and where were you?"

He groaned. "I wasn't ready to face you yet. I stopped at a beer joint on the highway and was on my third beer when I got your voice message."

She didn't say anything and Lucas felt even worse. It was a selfish, childish thing to do. "I'm sorry. It won't happen again." He nuzzled her neck with his lips.

That night, Gail turned in his arms and loved him with a passion that shocked and delighted him. He'd been gone four days, yet it felt more like four weeks their hunger was so great.

Cradled in his arms, voice slurred with sleep, Gail murmured, "Don't shut me out again."

He smiled and kissed her forehead. "I won't."

"And remember, miracles...can happen," she whispered.

~*~

Saturday afternoon, a horse trailer with Shaffer Farms on the side drove up to the stables. Lucas was expecting the horses but surprised when Ben himself climbed from the cab.

He walked over to greet the older man. "Hey, it's good to see you, Ben."

Ben stretched the kinks out of his legs and shook Lucas's hand. "Thought this would be a good time to take you up on that offer of a visit."

Lucas slapped him on the shoulder. "I know why you're here. You came to see if I'd bragged about my pretty wife. Come on and meet her. She's admiring her new colt."

When they entered the stable, Gail looked up from the bay colt and smiled. "I've decided on her name, Lucas. I'm calling her Butterscotch." She walked toward them.

Ben stopped. "I'll be darn, she's as pretty as you said." He cocked an eyebrow at Lucas. "She can't be sweet though. The good-looking ones are usually mean."

Lucas threw back his head and laughed. "Ben, this woman is a sweetheart and can cook too."

Gail reached Lucas's side and slid an arm around his waist. "What's going on over here? Sir, is Lucas telling tall tales?"

"Honey, this is Ben Shaffer of Shaffer Farms. Ben, my wife Gail."

She extended her hand. "Good to meet you, Ben. Lucas was impressed with your operation."

"You, too, young woman."

Gail linked her arm through Ben's. "Come see the colt Lucas gave me. Her name is Butterscotch." They stopped in front of the stall holding the colt and her mother. The colt neared the door and nudged Gail affectionately.

Ben looked over the mare and her colt. "Good looking stock, Lucas. The mare and Dancer will make fine looking colts."

"My thoughts exactly." He was proud of his animals and anxious to get the new horses bedded down. "Let's unload Dancer and the mares."

When the horses were unloaded, Lucas said, "Come on up to the house, Ben. You're staying for supper, aren't you?"

"Well, I hoped you'd invite me."

After supper, Lucas helped Gail clear the table. "I'm glad you decided to spend the night. We've got lots to talk about."

He turned to Gail. "Are you sure it's all right with you, Ma'am."

"Of course, it is," she said while putting glasses in the dishwasher. She turned. "I'm glad you can stay. I want you to meet my father. He's been sick and your company will do him good."

On the drive over, Lucas explained to Ben his folks were in Houston visiting one of his mother's sisters and wouldn't be back for a week. Laughing, he added. "Otherwise, you'd have to extend your trip to stay and meet them. Dad would enjoy hearing about your horses."

Sam met them at the door. "This is a mighty fine surprise." He shook Ben and Lucas's hands and kissed Gail. "Ooh, wee, my baby girl brought her daddy an apple pie. Now that is a surprise."

Gail laughed. "Just don't count on it being a habit."

Ben looked at Sam in sympathy. "They got you on a diet, do they?"

"Hell, yes. Between Gail and Ruth, I don't get a decent morsel to eat." He turned and they followed him into the room.

"Daddy, it's not that bad." She turned to Ben. "What he means is he doesn't get to pig out on fatty foods."

Sam snorted. "Same difference."

The men sat down around the big kitchen table. Gail sat pie and coffee in front of the men and joined them.

Lucas watched as she sipped her coffee and looked around the room as they talked. Her eyes lit on the dish drainer stacked full of dishes and a dirty skillet sat on the stove. He wondered if Ruth was getting sloppy with her housekeeping. Maybe caring for Sam and the house was getting to be too much for her.

"Daddy, did Ruth come today?"

"No, she's been sick. Her cat bit her on the foot and she got a bad infection. Has to keep it elevated above her heart until the infection goes away."

"Goodness, I've heard animal bites can be bad, but didn't know they could get that bad."

"Cat bites are especially dangerous," said Ben. "Their teeth are long so the wound is deeper. Perfect growing place for bacterial infections."

Sam nodded. "Yep, that's exactly what she said. She's got it all wrapped up and hobbling around. I told her to stay home all next week and take care of herself."

"When did all this happen?"

"Oh, Thursday or Friday, I guess. Just know she called this morning. I didn't even know the woman had a cat." He shook his head.

Gail studied her father, her brow wrinkled with worry. Lucas said, "How about I take you to Austin for your treatment Thursday then." Gail's smile read relief.

Sam's chin shot up. "That's not necessary. I can drive myself."

Gail's face looked as mulish as her daddy's. "You'll do no such thing. You'll either let Lucas drive you or I'll take off and take you myself."

Sam hit the table with his fist. "Dammit, Gail, I'm a grown man, not a child."

Gail's face fell. Her lips trembled but she managed to utter, "Excuse me." She shoved her chair back and left the room.

Sam dropped his head into his hands. "Shit! I'm sorry. You can take me, Lucas. I don't want her going, 'cause it's worse than I've let on."

Lucas grasped Sam's arm and cleared his throat. "We both know that, Sam. I don't know how, but we felt you weren't telling us everything."

"I'll be lucky if I survive the surgery."

Ben spoke up. "Excuse me for sticking my nose in your business, but your daughter is a strong young woman. She'll handle whatever you tell her. Don't shut her out. For both your sakes."

Sam nodded and looked toward the stairs. Pain wrinkled his brow. Lucas assumed she'd gone to her room.

"Let me go up and talk to her."

Lucas knocked on the door. "Gail?" He went in without waiting for a reply. Gail lay on her back on the bed, her arm thrown over her eyes. He lay down and she rolled toward him. "He's hurting, baby, that's why he's such a grumpy old bear."

She sniffed. "I know." Her body shuddered.

"Why don't you stay here tonight and talk. Ben and I'll pick you up in the morning and go in to town for breakfast."

She nodded. "Thank you, Lucas."

~*~

Sam watched Gail see Lucas and Ben to the door

and kiss Lucas goodbye. It was strange watching your daughter kiss a man. Where had his baby gone? Seemed only yesterday he'd brushed her long dark hair, plaited it, and tied a ribbon on the end of each pigtail. He could still see that snaggle-toothed grin. The thought of leaving her and never seeing his grandchildren left a physical ache in his heart.

Gail closed the door and walked into the living room where he sat on the sofa. He patted the cushion next to him. When she sat down, Sam put his arm around her shoulders and hugged her. She dropped her head to his chest and cried.

"I'm sorry, baby."

"I can't bear to lose you, Daddy. What'll I do when you're gone?"

He stroked her hair as he'd done when she was a child and came to him with one kind of hurt or another. "You've got Lucas now. That's my only comfort. I know he'll always be there for you. And someday you'll have a house full of babies to keep you busy."

Sam was startled when she cried harder. "We...can't have...children. Lucas is...sterile."

He patted her back and whispered words of comfort. What a shame. Life wasn't fair. Some women, like his Junie, could get knocked up the first time they had sex. Others took years to conceive.

"Honey, there are lots of babies out there that need parents. You'll adopt and in time you'll not remember they weren't born of your body because they were born of your heart."

"Oh, Daddy, that's the sweetest thing I've ever heard." She blew her nose and sniffed. "Very poetic."

Sam snorted and Gail giggled.

Voice shaky, she asked, "Daddy, do you have very long?"

He closed his eyes and prayed for strength. "No, baby, I don't, six months at the most."

Chapter Ten

Thursday evening, Gail, along with Ron, his wife Ellen, and Alex drove to Austin to catch their flight to California for another conference. At the airport, Ron commented on her lack of enthusiasm. "Gail, you don't have to go. We understand you're going through a lot right now." They sat in the lounge and waited for their flight. He squeezed her hand. "You need to be home to take care of your daddy."

They would receive additional training on the new software system the firm had purchased and she needed the instruction. She dropped her head to his shoulder for a second, then straightened. This man reminded her so much of her father. "I appreciate it, Ron, but Lucas will take good care of Daddy."

"Good man, your husband."

Gail smiled. "Yes, he is."

Their conversation helped lift her mood, yet the weekend dragged by and she did have some difficulty paying attention to the speakers. It wasn't until Saturday evening at dinner that she was able to relax. They all ate dinner together. Ron and Ellen left the dining room around nine, but she and Alex continued to peruse the brochures with computer hardware and software the company intended to purchase to upgrade their business. When the waiter asked for the third time if they'd like anything else, Alex suggested they go to the bar.

They located a padded booth with enough light to read by. "How's this?"

Gail slid across the soft leather seat. "It's fine."

He slid in beside her and they spread the pamphlets between them. "What'll you have to drink?"

She'd had several glasses of wine with dinner. "I probably should have coffee."

"Ah, come on, have a drink with me. I don't want to drink alone." He picked up the drink menu and flipped through it. "Try something you've not tasted before. How about an apple martini?"

She looked at the listed ingredients. "Mmm, sounds good. And it's made with vodka instead of gin. I can't stand the taste of gin."

Their drinks came, and as they talked, they made a final decision on the system they wanted.

"Can the company afford to spend that much money at one time?" Gail knew they made a good profit every year, but the cost amounted to more than what they'd originally decided on.

Alex took a sip of his Scotch and water. "Ron doesn't want to go over our set figure, but I think once he realizes the system is expandable, he'll agree."

Gail nodded. "It'll save money in the long run."

He studied his drink a minute and then looked at her. "You're doing a good job for us, Gail. If we decided to open the business up to another partner, would you be interested?"

She was totally taken off guard. "I ...gee, I don't know what to say. I mean, yeah, I think I would."

"Ron wanted me to see how you felt about it. Nothing's been decided yet and it would require a financial investment on your part." Gail felt flattered and pleased. Of course she worked hard and made the company money, but part ownership wasn't something she'd thought would ever happen. Daddy would be so proud. Would Lucas be proud too, or would he feel threatened because she'd be permanently invested in her career?

As they talked about the possibilities, one drink turned into three. Alex was funny and entertaining. She'd never seen this side of him. Before she knew it, they were up dancing and she was laughing at his outrageous behavior. She didn't feel drunk, so when Alex suggested one more drink before heading upstairs, she agreed. Alex was good company, and she'd not had this much fun in a good while.

As they got up to leave, Gail stumbled and Alex caught her around the waist. "Whoa, maybe you shouldn't have had that last martini after all."

She giggled. "I'm fine, just been sitting too long and my legs are shaky." When the elevator rushed upward, her knees buckled and Alex tightened his grip on her waist. She threw her arms around his neck. "Oops, I guess…I'm a little…drunk."

~*~

Her body was plastered against his and Alex could feel every line and curve. He buried his face in her hair. Body throbbing, voice gruff, he laughed shakily. "Hang on to my neck, I'll get you to your room."

"Okay." He felt her lips at his throat. She nuzzled. "Mmm, you smell good."

Swallowing loudly, Alex groaned. "You're drunk, Gail."

"Uh huh…drunk." She sighed deeply and sniffed.

"My Daddy's dying." Her words ended on a sob. The elevator door opened, and he tried to maneuver her into the hallway. He finally gave up and lifted her into his arms. People backed away to give him space with his weeping cargo.

At the door to her room, he set her on her feet and held her upright with his body. He rifled through her handbag looking for her door key. By the time he got her to the bed, she was sobbing in earnest. He bent to lay her down, but she refused to turn lose. "Don't leave me, please."

How he'd longed to hear those words from her. So what if she was drunk? Passions inflamed, he stretched out beside her on the large bed. She turned in his arms and he held her as she cried. He felt her kiss on his throat, her lips moving over his jaw to his mouth. Heat engulfing him, he took her mouth and took control. His body burned for this woman and when she didn't push him away, his lips broke from hers and traveled down her neck to brush the globes of her breasts above her rounded neckline. She groaned and arched into him.

"Oh, God, Gail…"

Mindless with the need to touch her, taste her, he unzipped her dress and tugged it to her waist. Her breasts were pale white in the darkened room, the lacy bra only enhancing their beauty. He cupped them in his hands and bent to tease a nipple through the lace.

She jerked and cried out. "Lucas, oh God, Lucas…"

~*~

Pounding woke her. She cried out when she realized the noise was in her head. When she turned to look at the clock, it increased in intensity and her stomach roiled in reaction. Throwing back the cover, she ran to the bathroom and emptied her stomach. Groaning from the weakness of her limbs and the pain in her head, she leaned on the lavatory and rinsed her mouth and face. It wasn't until she sat on the toilet to empty her bladder, she noticed her state of undress. She didn't have on a gown. The only time she slept nude was after she and Lucas had sex. Memories of the previous evening filtered back through her aching brain. Horror hit her in a wave and she bit her fist to keep her moans from alerting the people in the room next door.

Two hours, six cups of coffee, four aspirins, and a hot shower later, she managed to meet Alex and the Browns downstairs for their ride to the airport. She wore sunshades to cover her swollen eyes.

On the plane, Alex touched her hand. "Are you all right?"

She yanked it away. "No." Her lips trembled. "What exactly happened last night?"

He leaned his head back against the seat. "Nothing you didn't want to, sweetheart."

~*~

Gail was bone-tired when they got back to town Sunday afternoon. Her headache had improved, but her stomach still rolled, especially when she thought about her indiscretion the night before. God, what had she been thinking? She hadn't. She'd been flattered with Alex's proposal, relaxed by the alcohol, and having a good time. Then the full effects of the booze hit her, she'd remembered her father's health, and become a blubbering drunk, grasping for any comfort she could find. The last thing she remembered was getting up from the table to go upstairs. If not for Alex, she'd have fallen on her face. The rest remained a blur. Shame washed over her with a wave of nausea. If Lucas found out, he'd never forgive her.

As prearranged, Lucas met her in town. Sick with guilt and remorse, she could only cling to Lucas and didn't offer her mouth for his kiss. "Are you okay, hon?"

"Don't feel good, nauseated and my head hurts something fierce." At least it wasn't a complete lie.

He massaged her neck. "You want to go home then. I bet your daddy has something around the house to eat. He'll understand."

She pulled back. "No, I'll be okay. I need to see him." They picked up supper to take out to Sam. Ruth was still sick, but Tom's wife filled in until she got back.

Sam relaxed in his recliner when they arrived. Gail kissed him, concern about the paleness of his skin taking precedence over her own misery. "How do you feel, Daddy?"

"Not too good. Seeing you makes me feel better." Sam patted her back.

Gail could only pick at her burger, but what little she got down helped her stomach. After dinner, they sat around the living room, feet propped up on the coffee table, and sipped from their mugs of coffee.

Sam broke the silence. "My surgery is scheduled for next Thursday."

Gail froze with her cup in mid-air. "So soon?"

"I want you both to know my will is with Jeff Taylor in town. A couple of months ago I went in to the funeral home, picked out my casket, music and everything, so you wouldn't have to go through that ordeal."

"Daddy!"

"Don't carry on, now. I wanted to have the plans taken care of. I'll be buried beside your mother."

Gail's insides started to shake and her dinner rose into her throat. Her sins last night and now this. Her eyes filled with tears and threatened to overflow. "Excuse me." She made a mad dash for the bathroom before she disgraced herself in front of them.

Both men took in her wan appearance when she returned, but neither questioned her. She sighed with relief. With a cough to steady her quivering voice, she asked, "Is Ruth going to be here during the day next week to take care of you?"

"Yes, she offered to stay during the night, too, but I said I'd be fine on my own."

"You will not. What if you get sick during the night? Daddy, you're having major surgery. I—"

"Why don't we spend the night over here next week until you're better?" said Lucas. "Gail won't be able to rest unless you've got someone with you and we're the most logical choice."

Sam threw up his hands, then wagged a finger at Gail. "Oh, hell, all right. But don't you be smothering me."

"We won't, Daddy."

"Good."

Gail stood up and took their cups into the kitchen. "We better go. I've got the day off tomorrow, but Lucas will be up early."

Sam stood. Gail struggled not to weep at her father's appearance. In the last few months he'd aged at least ten years. Pale and thin, his flesh sagged on his bones. Just getting up and walking to the door took a lot of effort. *My Daddy, the man who's always been here for me is going to die. Oh, God, I can't bear to lose him.* Her throat constricted, cutting off speech. She hugged him bye and went outside without saying anything.

On the trip home, Lucas reached over and squeezed her hand. She sobbed herself to sleep that night in his arms. Though she knew he sensed something more than her father's illness was bothering her, he let it go. He just held her close and stroked her back.

~*~

Since Sam had to be at the hospital at 6:00 a.m. on Thursday, they drove in to Austin on Wednesday night and stayed at a motel. By 8:00 they were rolling him into surgery.

Lucas watched Gail pace back and forth in the waiting room. They'd been waiting for two hours. A nurse had come out several minutes earlier and said the surgery was taking longer than they'd expected, but Sam was doing fine. She hadn't eaten any breakfast, so after the nurse left, he went to the cafeteria and brought back coffee and breakfast burritos.

Gail shook her head. "I'm not hungry, Lucas."

"I know you're not, sugar, yet if you don't eat, you'll not be much use to your daddy when he needs you." He sighed with relief when she sat down and nibbled on the egg filled tortilla.

She ate half of it and finished her coffee.

Several hours later, the surgeon came out. Lucas stood up with Gail, his arms around her shoulders. "Mr. Steele is in recovery. The cancer was more widely spread than we thought. We got as much of it as we could, but couldn't take any more of his lungs." He shook his head. "This type of cancer grows rapidly. He could live several months or a few weeks."

Gail moaned and turned her face to his chest.

"I'm very sorry, folks. We'll keep him as comfortable as we possibly can."

Two days later, they took Sam home. He was weak and pale, but continued to be his crotchety self. In the last few weeks he'd lost considerable weight and his jeans bagged in the seat and hung on his hips. Lucas hated seeing him wasting away and could only imagine what Gail must be feeling.

Gail took a leave of absence from her job and stayed with Sam day and night. Ruth came every day to help clean the house and did some cooking, so Gail only had to heat up most of their meals. Sam's illness wore on Gail. She had trouble sleeping and dark circles formed under her eyes.

By the end of their second week at Sam's, Lucas had seen enough. Gail was killing herself. "Honey, I'm worried about you. I want you to sleep later in the mornings. Let Ruth fix breakfast."

She shook her head. "I can't. I don't want to miss one moment with him."

"I understand, but if you get sick, you'll end up in bed yourself. You won't be any help to him then." Gail finally agreed but couldn't sleep past six o'clock each morning, so they started going to bed earlier in the evening.

After Gail went to sleep, Lucas opened their bedroom door so he'd be able to hear Sam's attempts to get out of bed. He would ease from the bed without waking Gail, and help Sam to the bathroom.

Sharon and Randall came over often and in the fourth week, when Sam got so bad he couldn't be left alone, Randall rotated with Lucas, sitting with him at night.

One night when Lucas sat with him, Sam had difficulty sleeping so they talked. "Gail looks so much like her mama. Do you remember her, Lucas?"

"I have a picture in my mind though I'm not sure if it's real or not. Seems like she always wore gold hoop earrings." Lucas was tempted to reveal part of his dream to Sam. But, it'd serve no purpose and only upset him. And, he had no idea if the woman was June or not.

Sam smiled. "That would be Junie. Wore them regardless of where we were going." He sighed. "Wish I could have made her happy."

"Some women are never happy, no matter how hard you try."

"Yeah, but I didn't try hard enough. When Gail was born, all I could think about was providing for my family." He sighed. "Forgot the importance of enjoying my wife and child." His sunken eyes searched Lucas's face, their pale blue color sending out a spark of strength. "Don't ever make that mistake, Lucas. Remember to have fun."

"I promise I will, Sam."

"I know you love my daughter. You proved it when you waited for her to get her degree, and I want you to know I'm extremely proud to have you as my son-in-law."

Lucas's throat clogged with emotion. "I love you, Sam."

Sam's eyes glittered with tears. "I know that, son, and I love you, too." He coughed and gasped for a minute. "If you and Gail ever have problems, remember things aren't always what they seem on the outside. Don't take them at face value. Love and life can be hard to figure out. Have faith and trust each other. And be able to forgive and forget."

He couldn't speak, but nodded in response. God, he prayed he'd never betray Gail's trust and need her forgiveness.

It had been six weeks since they'd brought Sam home from the hospital. He was skin and bone, nothing like the vital man he'd been the year before.

A couple of times he'd caught Ruth crying during the day. She'd loved Sam for many years. Sam tried to tone down his gruffness around Ruth and Gail, yet it was hard when the pain got bad. Several times Lucas had walked into Sam's room to find Ruth on the bed with Sam, holding him, his face turned to her breasts. He'd quietly eased out and shut the door.

Something woke Lucas. He lay still, waiting to see if Sam needed him, but heard only the hum of the window unit in their bedroom. Then he remembered his father was sitting up with Sam. He heard it again, a gagging noise. He shot out of bed, started for the door, and noticed a sliver of light under the hall bathroom door. Lucas stood in the hall with an ear cocked toward Sam's room waiting for the noise again. When he didn't hear anything, he relaxed thinking it was his father in the bathroom and turned back to the bed. He lay down and reached for Gail to find her space empty. This time the gagging noise turned into retching.

Fear knotted in his belly. Gail had worn herself out and was now sick. He leapt from the bed, strode to the bathroom door, and tapped gently. "Gail, honey, can I come in?"

His answer came in the form of a low moan and more retching. He opened the door and quickly closed it behind him. Gail knelt in front of the toilet and used the seat to support her upper body. Her long dark hair hung down, obscuring her face.

Lucas wet a washcloth and handed it to her.

"Thank you."

He pulled her hair back from her face and tucked it down the back of her gown. "What's wrong? Do you think it was something we had for supper?" He sat on the side of the tub and stroked her back.

"Don't know," she said, and heaved again. Shaking she held the cloth to her face. "What time is it?"

"Almost five o'clock."

She stood on shaky legs and brushed her teeth. "I think I'm going to live now. Wasn't sure there for a while."

He put his arm around her shoulders. "Come on, let's get you back to bed."

"But it's time to get up now."

"We've got thirty minutes. I want to hold you for a while."

They got into bed and Lucas pulled her close. Within five minutes she was sound asleep. Careful not to wake her, he got up and carried his clothes across the hall to the bathroom.

When Ruth came in at six, Lucas had the coffee ready and bacon frying.

"What are you doing up so early?"

"Gail was sick this morning. Got her to go back to sleep for a while. Wish I could make her stay there all morning. This is really tearing her up."

Ruth turned away. "Yeah, I know." She sniffed. "Poor child. To lose her mother when just a baby and now her father. It's not fair."

Lucas grasped Ruth shoulders. "I'm sorry, Ruth. This is awfully hard on you, too. I know you love him."

She nodded and sobbed quietly. When they heard Randall's footsteps on the stairs, she wiped her tears with her apron and started pouring coffee.

"Good morning, son, Ruth. Can I have a cup of that coffee?"

"Coming up," said Ruth.

"Who'd I hear sick in the bathroom this morning?" Randall took a seat at the table.

"Gail, Dad. I don't know what caused it, thought it might be something she ate, but she said she's felt sick the last couple of days." He shook his head. "I think she's worn herself slap dab out."

Ruth started cracking eggs in a bowl. "Could she be pregnant?"

Lucas felt his face heat with embarrassment. He cleared his throat. "No."

"Are you sure, son? Some women's cycles are crazy."

Lucas tried to be civil, but his reply was curt. "There is no way she can be pregnant."

"Could be a stomach virus," said Ruth. "Sometimes they make you miserable before they become full blown."

Steps sounded on the stairs and Lucas left the kitchen to meet Gail. "Dammit, what are you doing out of bed?"

She hugged him. "That little nap made me feel so much better. Anyway, I'm hungry."

Lucas threw up his hands. "Oh well, I tried." He followed her into the kitchen.

Gail kissed Randall's cheek. "Was Daddy awake when you came downstairs?"

Randall pulled her into his arms for a hug. "No, sweetheart, he's still asleep, but I expect the smell of coffee and bacon will wake him soon."

~*~

Gail busied herself getting a tray ready to take upstairs. Her daddy ate a little less each day, but she cherished every morsel she could get down him.

Lucas's arms curled around her waist from behind. He leaned down and kissed the side of her neck. "I'll see you this evening. Please get some rest this afternoon."

She leaned her head back against his warm solid chest and hugged his arms closer. "I'll try."

Gail stepped into her father's room. His eyes were open and he smiled at her. She leaned down and kissed his cheek. "Good morning, Daddy."

"Morning, baby girl."

She handed him a mug of coffee with a large handle, easier for him to grip. His hand trembled as he brought it to his mouth and took a sip. Gail fed him a bite of eggs, and as he chewed, he nodded at her plate. She ate some of her eggs to appease him. This had become a morning ritual when Sam had noticed she'd lost weight and looked drawn and pale. After three bites, he shook his head. "Too tired. You keep eating. Want to talk...you."

A lump formed in Gail's throat, making it hard to swallow the food in her mouth. "Okay."

Sam nodded and closed his eyes a minute. "First,

never forget…how much I…love you." Talking took up precious oxygen he couldn't afford to waste.

"Daddy, please don't talk. Save your strength."

"Need to say…some things before…"

Gail set the food aside and moved her chair closer.

"Ruth and I…close…good woman. Not fair to her…needs you." Gail nodded understanding. "Your mother…only woman I…loved. Didn't…kill her."

"Oh, Daddy, I know you'd never do something like that. They'll find who did it, I promise." She'd see to it.

He nodded. Tears filled his eyes. "You…joy of my…life.

Gail crawled onto the bed as she'd done so many times as a child. Except this time she cradled her father in her arms as he'd snuggled her close when she'd come to him with bad dreams. "I love you, Daddy. You're the best father a girl could ever have." And she cried. Her body shook with great shudders.

He patted her hand as they both cried and murmured broken words of comfort. As her tears subsided, she whispered, "Sleep, Daddy. Rest." She wanted to tell him about being unfaithful to Lucas, ask for his guidance. But, she couldn't burden him with it. He'd be so disappointed in her. Would he think she was just like her mother? No, it was her burden to bear alone. As his breathing eased, she relaxed and dozed.

~*~

Ruth tip-toed into the bedroom and smiled to see father and daughter snuggled together, sleeping, the sound of Sam's oxygen machine the only sound in the room. She reached down to pick up the tray to carry back downstairs, but noticed something wasn't right. Gail's chest gently rose and fell. Sam's didn't.

Fist in her mouth to muffle the sobs, Ruth went downstairs and dialed Lucas's cell phone.

He answered immediately. "Hello."

"Lu...cas, it's...Ruth." Unable to say more, she sobbed into the phone.

"I'll be right there."

~*~

Lucas called his folks and they stopped in the drive behind him and went in to Ruth.

He rushed upstairs to find Gail asleep beside her father. "Oh, baby, I'm so sorry."

His wife looked so peaceful, he didn't want to wake her to face what had occurred, especially not here. Carefully, he lifted her in his arms and carried her to their bedroom. When he laid her on the bed, she smiled at him then curled up on her side and went back to sleep.

She'd never forgive him if he didn't wake her, give her the news. He leaned down and kissed her, tasting her lips until she responded. Finally her lids lifted and she smiled. She reached out for him. He lay down and drew her into his arms. "I'm sorry, sweetheart, your daddy is gone."

Chapter Eleven

"Are you all right, honey?"

Gail had never felt so sick in her life—emotionally and physically. Her father's illness had sapped her, but her guilty conscience had amplified her discomfort. She had a constant case of heartburn and felt so tired it was an effort to keep going. "I'm fine, Lucas." She patted his cheek.

Lucas took her elbow and led her to the gravesite. They'd ridden in her car, having declined the limo service her father had wanted.

People filed to the green tent where Sam's casket waited for a last goodbye. Flowers were heaped around it, filling the air with a multitude of sweet smells. The hot August heat made them almost cloying and Gail had to steel herself to keep from getting sick.

Brother Bailey's words were lost on her. All she could hear was the sound of cars on the highway, the thump of her heart, and then a buzzing in her ears. She swayed and Lucas's arm tightened around her waist. Tilting her head up to his, she smiled and whispered, "I'm fine." Then she fell into a deep, dark pit.

Lucas placed a cool cloth on her forehead. She looked around and tried to get up. They were in her bedroom at the farmhouse.

"Be still, you fainted at the cemetery. Rest for a few minutes."

Lines of worry etched his face. She was becoming a little concerned herself. What was going on with her body? Had she worried herself into developing an ulcer? Or...

"Oh, God."

Lucas leaned over her. "What is it? Are you hurting somewhere?"

She shook her head and closed her eyes so he wouldn't see the stark terror in them. She prayed. *Please, Lord...don't let it happen now.* If she were pregnant with Alex's baby, it would kill Lucas. *Get yourself together, Gail.* She drew in a couple of shaky breaths. "I'm fine now. Please, Lucas, I need to be downstairs with our guests."

He sighed and helped her up. "Okay, but do me a favor, find a place to sit down. You need to see Doc Smith tomorrow."

"Nag, nag, nag." Gail laid her head on his chest and he stroked her hair.

"I love you, honey. It hurts to see you so frail and weak. What would you do if I fainted?"

She squeezed his waist. "Oh, all right, I'll go."

"Good." His hand at her back, he walked her to the door. "I'll go with you."

"No, you will not. You've been away from the stables long enough." She stopped on the stairs. "I'll be fine. You know Doc will call you if you're needed."

He studied her a minute. "We'll see how you feel in the morning."

The house overflowed with Sam's friends. He had no family, but people from several counties knew him and had come to pay their respects. When Alex approached her, Gail almost went to pieces. She'd seen him a couple of times at the office since their trip, but she'd been in a hurry to get things in order for her leave.

Alex took her hand, and she struggled to keep her face calm. "I'm so sorry for your loss, Gail. Sam was well loved in this community. I know he's still considered a suspect in your mother's death, but very few people believe him capable of such a crime."

She pulled her hand from his. "Thank you. That means a lot to me." Tears gathered in her eyes and she gasped for air.

He grabbed her elbow. "Are you all right?"

"I'm fine. Just haven't felt well lately." Gail could have bitten her tongue for mentioning it.

He nodded. "That's understandable. You've been through a rough six weeks." For a minute, he studied her, his face sober. He shoved his hands in his pockets. "About that weekend, Gail, I—"

"Excuse me, I…" Panicked, she turned and hurried away. She bumped into someone and looked up, surprised to see Ben Shaffer. He turned to her, his face a mask of comfort and folded her in his arms. For some reason, she'd felt an immediate connection to this man. His tenderness touched her and she cried for the umpteenth time in the last two days.

Ben patted her back and whispered. "It's going to be okay, honey. Your daddy is at peace." He handed her a pristine white handkerchief. "Now dry those tears. I've got someone I want you to meet." He led her to a slightly plump older woman with silver hair fixed in a short spiky style. Dressed in a three-piece black and white suit with silver accessories, she couldn't be called pretty, but was attractive in her own way.

Ben drew Gail to the woman. "Honey, this young woman is Gail, Ben's daughter and Lucas's wife. Gail, this is my wife, Sarah."

"Your wife?" For the first time in a while, Gail felt joyful. "You got married and didn't invite us?" Gail took Sarah's hands. "I'm so happy to meet you."

"You too, honey, and so sorry about your daddy. Ben talked about what a good time he had visiting with the three of you."

Gail nodded, throat constricting. "He enjoyed Ben, too." She took each of their arms. "Come on. We've got to break the news to Lucas. He'll be thrilled."

Lucas saw them coming and met them half way. He shook hands with Ben and hugged Sarah.

"They got married, Lucas."

He clasped Ben's shoulder. "Well, it's about time."

Ben grinned. "That's exactly what she told me," he said as he pulled Sarah against his hip.

"We need to celebrate one day soon," said Lucas.

Sarah smiled up at Ben. "We're having a big barbecue the second weekend in September."

"That's right and we expect you and Lucas to come," said Ben. "And no motel, you'll bunk with us."

Gail looked at Lucas and he nodded. "We'll be there. Now, you two get something to eat."

When Gail went into the kitchen to get a drink of water, she found Ruth washing dishes. "What are you doing working? I'll not have it, Ruth. You get in the living room and sit down, mingle, do whatever, but you'll not be working in this kitchen today." She pulled Ruth away from the sink, took the apron from around her waist, and pushed her through the kitchen door.

Tom's wife Alice took over at the sink. "Thank

goodness. Poor woman is grieving. She was crazy about your daddy."

"Yeah, she was," said Gail. Filling a glass with water, she returned to the living room.

People were beginning to leave and said their goodbyes and added their condolences. The room was almost empty now. Gail sat down by Ruth and took the older woman's hand.

Ruth sniffed and wiped at her tears. "I'm going to miss him something awful."

Gail's heart twisted. "I know you will. You were with him every day."

"You know your daddy was so proud of you. When your mama left, he was like a man crazed, but when he picked you up or just looked at you, you seemed to comfort him." Ruth patted Gail's hand. "Not many women are as fortunate as you. You had a loving father and now have a loving husband."

Gail nodded and looked around the room until she found Lucas. He stood talking with his folks. Tall and well formed, her husband was a beautiful man. Yes, she was blessed indeed. "Ruth, did Daddy ever ask you to marry him?"

Ruth stayed quiet for a minute. "Yes, he asked me about ten years ago, but I turned him down."

"Why? I thought you loved Daddy."

"Oh, child, I did something awful." She closed her eyes for a minute. When she spoke, she chose her words carefully. "I couldn't marry your father without revealing some things in my past. He said he didn't care about my past, but I did."

Gail could imagine a variety of things a woman wouldn't want to reveal about her past, but none of them seemed to fit her picture of Ruth.

"We'd been sleeping together and oh I loved him so much. Though he loved me, he wasn't in love with me like he was with your mother. When I turned him down again a year later, he said I could continue to work for him, but our relationship was over."

It was hard to imagine her father saying such a thing. He had been a stickler for respectability and would want to provide a good example for his daughter. But why didn't he ever see other women? Who knows, maybe he did. He may have been discreet.

Ruth interrupted her musing. "Are you still reading your mother's diary?"

"What? Her diary? Oh no, Bud still has it. Someone broke into the house and tried to take it. Chief wouldn't let them take it."

"Why on earth would someone want that old diary?"

"Don't have a clue. All it does is talk about Daddy, me, and you." Gail flashed Ruth a grin.

"Me? What did she have to say about me?" Ruth's brows rose in surprise.

"That you interfered when it came to dressing me and that made her so mad." Gail watched Ruth blush.

"Well, I was young, we both were, and thought we knew everything." She grinned. "We had some hot fusses, but always made up."

"That's the impression I got from the diary, as far as I got to read that is." She wondered when Bud would give it back to her or if he would. "Ruth, did you know my mother planned to leave?"

Ruth teared up again and nodded. "She...she planned to come back and get you when she got settled." She covered her mouth with her fist. "That…would have killed…your daddy."

Gail put her arm around the older woman and patted her shoulder. Evidently Ruth had loved her father even back then. Goodness, a love triangle right here where she'd grown up, and she'd never known. "That's in the past, Ruth. Don't dwell on it."

Gail stood and helped Ruth to her feet. "It's been a long day. You go on home and rest."

She watched Ruth collect her purse and head out the door then went into the kitchen. Alice met her at the door. "You're not allowed in unless it's to find something to eat. Sit down here and I'll fix you something." Alice pushed her into a chair, and too tired to argue, Gail let the older woman fuss over her. "Here you go, eat what you can."

Gail ate a bite of the crabmeat macaroni salad. It tasted good, as did the gelatin salad with mandarin oranges. Someone had brought fresh yeast rolls and Alice had heavily buttered one for her. "Mmm, thanks Alice. This is hitting the spot."

"Good, you need to put back on some of the weight you've lost."

Lucas walked through the door and smiled. He kissed the top of her head. "I never thought seeing my wife eat would be a reason for excitement." Alice handed him a filled plate. "Thanks. We sure appreciate all you ladies have done for us."

Alice said, "We were happy to do it, Lucas. Sam was a special man." The other two ladies in the kitchen voiced their agreement. "When you two finish eating, why don't you change clothes and get some fresh air."

"We just might if Gail doesn't want to take a nap."

Gail watched Lucas eat. "I think a walk sounds good. We could go on home and go riding."

Lucas stopped eating. "It'd be nice to go home, but packing would take some time and I want you to rest tonight. Why don't we spend the night and tomorrow morning you can pack. I'll come load our bags at lunch."

The mile walk to the creek was enough exercise to help Gail sleep that night. She'd cried while Lucas held her. Her tears were cleansing this time, not like the ones she'd shed when her father lay in pain and wasting away. He was at peace now. That he lived with Jesus was a given with her. She could see Sam in a robe of white and wondered if he fussed about the material getting in the way. Had he met her mother there? She hoped so.

At six a.m. Gail woke with bile rising in her throat. She hit the floor at a run, barely making it to the toilet before throwing up into the bowl. Her stomach was empty, but the heaving continued. Her physical discomfort didn't compare to the emotional wretchedness going on in her heart and conscience. She carried another man's baby. Sobbing, she continued to gag.

In her misery, she barely heard Lucas come in and wet a washcloth for her face. As before, he pulled her hair back and rubbed her back. "This is—" She retched again and again. "The worst sick I've ever experienced."

"You call Doc Smith first thing this morning," Lucas said. "Better yet, I'm calling him before I leave here."

"Okay, I won't argue." She stood up, washed her

face, and brushed her teeth. "I better start breakfast."

"I can eat at the ranch. Why don't you lie back down for a while? You've been through a lot the last couple of months."

The thought bore consideration, but she had so much to do. It could wait. She needed to feel better. She felt guilty giving in to her need, but she had to get strong for the struggle ahead. Trying not to cry, she gave him a lopsided smile. "You talked me into it."

A few minutes later, Lucas, freshly showered, shaved, and smelling wonderful, leaned over the bed to kiss her good-bye. "Sleep as long as you can, sweetheart. See you at noon."

Gail woke and looked at the clock. She shot straight up in bed. Nine o'clock? It had been years since she'd slept late, but she felt better. She showered, put on shorts and a tee shirt, ate breakfast, and started packing. After a couple of days to rest, she and Ruth would start going through the house, getting it ready to close up. She hadn't decided whether to try to rent it or let it sit vacant. First, she'd need to go through all of Daddy's things and store them in the attic. Thank goodness that decision didn't have to be made right now. There was one more important. What to tell Lucas.

The phone rang. It was Lucas.

"Doc Smith's out for a couple of days and won't be able to see you until Friday. I don't like it. I think you should call your doctor in Austin and go see her."

"Lucas, she's a gynecologist."

"Well, she's still a doctor, right?"

He had a point but... "I'll think about it. Right now I feel fine. Would you believe I slept until nine o'clock?"

He chuckled. "Well, honey, you must have needed the rest. Sometimes you have to listen to what your body is telling you."

"And just what is your body telling you, mister?"

"It misses yours."

"Hmmm, I'm sorry. I've neglected you lately." Truth was she felt so damned guilty she'd been reluctant for him to touch her for fear he'd know she'd been unfaithful. "Maybe tonight I'll pull out the little red teddy you like so much."

"You mean the one that's cut so high on the side I get a good view of your creamy butt?"

"Yes, that'd be the one." His appreciation fueled her passion and desire for him. For the first time in a long while, her body yearned to be joined with his.

He groaned. "Do we have to wait until tonight? I don't know if I'll survive the day. The anticipation might kill me."

She laughed. "You poor man. I think you'll live."

He chuckled. "I better run. See you at noon."

When they drove up in front of their ranch style home, Chief barked and jumped with joy to see them. They scratched his ears and rubbed his neck, but when they went into the house, he followed on their heels.

It felt good to be in her kitchen again. Six weeks of dust had accumulated so she had her work cut out for her. Lucas sliced tomatoes from his mother's garden while she spread salad dressing on slices of bread for sandwiches. When Lucas left, she set about cleaning house.

Friday morning she sat in Doc Smith's office waiting her turn to see him. The last couple of days she hadn't been sick in the mornings, but had a case of the yucks all day long. It wasn't bad enough to put her to bed, but was aggravating.

The door to the examination area opened and Susie called, "Gail, the doctor is ready for you."

Susie took her blood pressure, her temperature, and clucked like a mother hen when she noted Gail's weight loss of seven pounds. She led her into an examination room, and as Gail listed her symptoms, wrote them on her chart. Susie opened a drawer and pulled out a folded gown. "Here, better get undressed and put on this lovely paper gown. I think Doc will want to give you a full examination."

Gail must have looked concerned because Susie patted her hand. "Now don't be looking worried. This is general procedure with this list of symptoms and all Doc's patients have lived so far."

A few minutes later, Doc came into the room. He chatted for a minute to put her at ease and expressed sympathy for the loss of her father.

"Now, let me see, you've lost weight, been vomiting some, tired, and generally feel sick to your stomach."

His bushy eyebrows twitched. "Hmmm. Do you have to pee a lot? Are your breasts tender?"

Gail nodded at both questions.

"I think we better do a pelvic exam."

He flipped a switch and Susie came into the room. When he finished, he helped Gail sit up.

"I'd say, in between seven and eight months, you and Lucas are going to be the proud parents of a little Johnson. Congratulations, Gail."

Gail's heart lodged in her throat. "I'm pregnant?

I'm really pregnant?" Her chin trembled.

Doc's brows drew together. "Aren't you happy?"

She covered her face with her hands. "Oh, my God!" To her mortification, she started blubbering like a baby.

He folded her in his arms. "Now, now, it's just all those hormones doing strange things to your emotions." He patted her back and nodded for Susie to leave the room. "Gail, you can talk to me. What's going through your head? I thought you and Lucas wanted a baby."

"We...we do. But...but I've done something terrible." She drew back and wiped her eyes with the tissue Doc handed her. "I can't talk about it right now."

He studied her for a minute, and then nodded. "Susie will give you a book on prenatal care and I'll give you some prenatal vitamins. You do need to find an OB/GYN as I'm out of the baby delivering business."

All she could do was nod.

"I'm here if you ever need to talk."

On the trip home, a thousand thoughts ran through her mind. A baby. She was pregnant, but the child wasn't Lucas's. What would she tell him tonight?

Chapter Twelve

Gail hadn't been in the house more than ten minutes when Lucas called.

"What did Doc say, hon? Are you all right?"

Voice hoarse from crying, she choked out, "I'm fine, Lucas. I'll tell you all about it when you get home."

He was quiet for a minute. "I'll be there in ten minutes."

When he came through the door, she wanted to fly into his arms, but held back. "I'm not sick."

"Whew, what a relief." He pulled her into his arms and buried his face in her neck. "Why've you been throwing up and so tired then?"

She squeezed his waist. "Come sit down in the living room." Taking his hand, she led him to the sofa. His expression mirrored the turmoil in her chest. "I'm pregnant."

Gail watched the flurry of emotions cross his face. Joy, confusion, doubt, denial and finally anger. His body stiffened. He pulled his hand from hers. The pain etched on his face made Gail gasp.

"Who the hell's the father?"

Her lips trembled, but she finally managed to speak. "I...hope you are."

He looked at her like she'd sprouted an extra head. "You hope?" Disbelief and rage transformed his features. He grabbed her shoulders. "What the hell is that supposed to mean?" He released her and stood. His hands gripped his hair, and he spun on his heel, turning his back to her. "Please, God, tell me this is a bad dream."

"I'm sorry, so sorry, I was drunk and didn't know what I was doing."

He swooped down on her, his hands fisted at his sides. "You bitch. You lying, cheating…"

Gail shrank from him.

Lucas bellowed like a wounded bull and shoved his fist through the wall behind the sofa. When he yanked his fist out, it was bloodied, but it was the expression on his face she wished she'd never seen. It twisted with pain and desolation and the tears pooled in his eyes was evidence she'd destroyed him.

Before she could call out to him, he strode out the door and got in his truck. The tires squealed as he tore away from the house, sending a spray of gravel in his wake.

She rushed to the bathroom, fell to her knees in front of the toilet, and vomited. Her body quaked with the force of the spasms, leaving her weak and shaky, her soul dead.

~*~

It was after midnight when Gail heard Lucas come in. After he'd left that morning, she'd cried for hours and then made herself clean house. When he didn't show up for dinner, she'd left his on the table and gone to bed.

He stumbled around in the dark, and she heard his boots hit the floor. She could feel his eyes on her as he stood beside the bed looking down, and smell the alcohol fumes.

Voice cracking, he moaned softly, "Oh baby, how could you do this to me?"

Her eyes had adjusted to the darkness and she watched him turn and leave, shoulders heaving from sobs.

Pain at his agony ripped through her. She turned and buried her face in the pillow, tried to muffle her pitiful wails coming from her throat. In one moment of weakness, she'd destroyed everything of value to her—Lucas and her marriage. If only she could turn back the clock and not make the trip to California. She wanted to go to him, sooth his pain, but knew nothing could make this better. Several minutes later, she heard light snoring from the living room.

Gail woke early. Eyes closed, she lay still and listened to the sounds around her. Lucas's snoring had subsided to a dull hum, the icemaker dumped cubes, and the trays filled with water. Her head hurt from crying and her eyes protested against the light when she opened them. She forced herself to get up. Lucas's shirt was tossed across the foot of the bed. Out of habit, she picked it up to put in the clothes hamper, but instead brought it to her face. She allowed herself to enjoy his scent. Even with the cigarette smell, it was as familiar as breathing. She stuffed the shirt into the hamper and closed it firmly. Their lives were changed forever. She might as well face the facts.

It didn't take her long to dress and eat a bagel. By the time she heard Lucas stirring, she was ready to leave. Without a word to her husband, she took her purse and left the house.

~*~

Lucas woke to the sound of the carport door opening and closing. He sat up and listened to Gail's car start and drive off. Their words yesterday flashed through his mind, the echo of their intensity keeping time with the pounding pulse in his head. Pain sliced through his heart. His wife had been with another man. Was it just to have a baby or did she care for this man?

Nauseated from his night of beer, he staggered to the bathroom and threw up. Under the showerhead spray, he leaned into the wall and let the hot water run over his aching body. If only it could ease the pain in his heart. When the water cooled, he washed and rinsed. In the kitchen, no coffee had been made, and the dinner he'd not come home to eat last night still sat on the table. Gail had been pissed he hadn't come home. Well that was too bad.

Minutes later, he got in his truck and drove to the stables. He'd stop by the bunkhouse and eat. It took all his willpower to keep from turning onto the road leading to Sam's place. What good would it do to see her? It wouldn't change the facts, just make matters worse.

Lucas worked late on purpose. He didn't want to see Gail, to think about the child growing inside her—a child not his. But it was time to face her and make a clean break. His sorrow had escalated into anger, a cold feeling, almost of hate.

When he could see into the carport, his stomach dropped with dread. Gail's car was missing. His emotions were mixed. If she'd already left, it was probably for the best. Chief met him as he got out of the truck. "Hey boy, where's Gail? Where is she, huh?"

Chief gave him several yips and followed him into

the house. All the lights were out, and last night's dinner still littered the table. His stomach dropped at the finality of the evidence—she'd moved out. Maybe he should be grateful because it prevented another confrontation. He sat down and stared around the empty kitchen. Chief whined and Lucas rubbed his head.

Chief's ears perked up. Lucas caught his breath at the sound of Gail's car pulling into the carport. He jumped up and rushed into the bedroom. By the time Gail entered the house, he was in the shower. No way he'd let her know he'd been moping about. He held his breath, wondering if she'd come in like she usually did and say hello, but she didn't.

Dressed, he entered the kitchen to find her at the stove. Neither spoke. He gathered the dishes off the table and scraped and loaded the dishwasher. She'd put on coffee and started Spanish omelets. He sliced tomatoes and made toast.

Gail sat plates on the table and they sat down. "I'm sorry I'm late. I laid down for a minute and slept two hours."

Lucas cleared his throat. "It doesn't matter."

She nodded and they ate in silence. The quiet grew thick with tension, hurt, and unsaid words. His throat constricted so tightly it hurt. He glanced up to see Gail trying to swallow her food. She took a sip of coffee and the look of panic on her face worsened.

"Can I get you a glass of water?"

"Please." He sat it before her. "Thank you." She finally managed to swallow and took another drink from the glass. Tears glittered in her eyes.

Lucas watched her try another small bite and force it down. He finished his omelet and opened the freezer.

"How about a dish of ice cream? Maybe that will go down easier."

She couldn't speak, but nodded. He fixed them each a bowl and tried to relax as he watched her eat. They cleaned the kitchen together as they had many times in their marriage. But the camaraderie was gone. Lucas mourned its loss. He couldn't swallow his hurt and pride and pretend the child was his. When the baby kicked inside her, could he take joy in its movements and the changes taking place in Gail's body? He wanted to, God how he wanted to, but he couldn't. He'd always wonder if the baby's real father would be waiting for a chance to announce to the world the child was his. Let folks know Lucas Johnson couldn't father a child.

No dammit, their marriage was over. He'd never trust Gail again. "We need to talk."

Gail squared her shoulders and sat down at the table. He sat across from her, not the place beside her where he usually sat.

"I know who the baby's father is. Alex is out of town right now, but when he gets back, I intend to kick his ass for taking advantage of you."

She tried to speak, but he held up his hand. Voice hoarse, he growled out, "I don't want to hear any of it, Gail, so shut up and listen to me."

Her chin jutted as she tried to hold her emotions in check.

"Tell me, did you sleep with Alex just to get pregnant?"

The color drained from her face. She stood, her body shaking in anger. Before he could react, she was screaming and pounding him on the chest with her fists, almost toppling his chair. "How could...you? You stupid…damned shit… I—"

Bolting out of the teetering chair, he grabbed her wrists and shook. "Stop it." She jerked away from him, her body racked with sobs. His gut twisted. "I want you out of this house tomorrow. I'll get some of the men to come help you move." He fought the pain in his throat. "As to whether or not I'll give the baby my name, I haven't decided. But, I'll take care of you financially."

She faced him, eyes dead of emotion. "That won't be necessary. I can take care of us both. And as far as your name goes, neither the baby nor I need it."

Pain sliced through him like a knife. "That's right, I suppose you'll both be Guthries." He slapped the table. "Fine by me."

"You're a fool, Lucas. A damn fool." Her words were calm and clipped. "I may have been unfaithful, but it's possible this child is yours, and you're denying it before you even know for sure."

He stuck his face inches from hers. "You're forgetting one thing, sugar. I'm unable to father a child."

"That's right, sweetheart," she spat. "A low sperm count means you're sterile, and we know you sure as hell don't believe in miracles."

Her chin gripped tightly in his hand, he made her look at him. "You were my miracle, Gail. And see how our marriage turned out?"

"If it's any consolation to you, I've never been sorrier about anything in my entire life. I hate myself more than you'll ever be able to."

She yanked away from him, turned, and was gone from the room. He stood in the kitchen, listening as she removed items from their bedroom and bath. He steeled himself against the longing in his heart, tried to tune out the sounds. He heard Gail turn on the shower and later the guest bedroom door close. The slam was like a death sentence.

He let Chief out for a minute, locked up, and walked into the bedroom. Before he closed the door, he called the dog, but Chief ignored him. Lucas stepped into the hall and found Chief curled up in front of the guest bedroom door. Hurt at his dog's defection, he turned and closed the door.

~*~

Gail curled into a ball and closed her eyes against the pain piercing her heart. She understood Lucas's pain. All these years she'd loved him, had been true to him, and in one weak moment, she'd destroyed it all. The thought made her stomach roil. She shivered in disgust. Oh God, the hate on his face would live with her forever. Deep sobs wracked her body. She covered her mouth to stifle them, not wanting Lucas to know how much she hurt.

The door opened, and Chief padded into the room. He placed his cold nose against her chest and whined. Wrapping her arms around his neck, she cried harder. Lucas stood in the doorway, barely visible in the moonlight. He quietly backed out of the room and closed the door.

~*~

He leaned out the window and watched as a car pulled into the clearing and turned out its lights. For a short moment, they lit up the shiny new car hidden in the trees. A woman opened the door and as the interior light expelled the darkness, he could see the woman's face. It was Junie, Gail's mama. The door slammed with a bang, and she rushed into the arms of the man hidden in the shadows of the big trees. Lucas turned to his mother and started to speak. "Mama, that—"

"Shh, son. Be quiet now."

Sharon Johnson started the car and left the clearing, using the moonlight to guide her out. When they were on paved road, she turned on the headlights. His mother and daddy had argued after supper. She'd put him in the car to go for a drive, to cool off she said, and parked on the cliff edge of the creek. They listened to the hum of cicadas and other night creatures while gazing down at the dark water below.

Lucas woke to the sound of the door to the carport opening and closing. He jumped from the bed, pulled on jeans, and ran into the hall just as Gail came back in the house. When she saw him, she stopped for a second and then walked past him into the guest room. She snapped a suitcase closed and lifted it from the bed.

"You don't need to be carrying that." He took it from her and followed her out to her car.

"Thank you. I'll come get the rest of my things when you're not here, so you won't have to see me."

Hands in his back pockets, he smirked. "That's good because the sight of you turns my stomach. You're just like your mother, a slut. It wouldn't surprise me if Alex wasn't the first man you've spread your legs for."

Her hand cracked across his cheek. He welcomed the sting. Chin high and trembling slightly, she stared at him a long time. His words were brutal, he'd meant them to be, but her reaction wasn't what he expected. He wanted tears, raging, begging. All he got was her calm perusal. It ended with, "Goodbye, Lucas."

Without another word, she got in her car and drove away. Lucas sat at the kitchen table for a long time, haunted by the message in her eyes. Her goodbye was final, not an 'I hope we can work it out'. Good, it's what he wanted. He rose from the table, finished dressing, and left for the stables.

He located Tom. "Get Jim to drive over to Sam's place and help Gail with whatever she needs done." Lucas kept his back to Tom. One look at his face, and his good friend would know something was wrong.

"Sure. Jim will jump at the chance. He's been trying to catch Ruth's eye for years."

"Thanks, Tom."

"Sure thing."

Lucas's cell phone rang. He checked caller ID. It was his father. "Hi, Dad."

"Come up to the house. I want to talk to you."

Lucas found Randall at the kitchen table, drinking coffee. As usual his silver hair was neat, and he wore jeans and a starched western shirt. For a man approaching sixty, Randall Johnson was a picture of health and fitness. Lucas poured himself a cup and sat down. His father watched him, but Lucas couldn't meet his eyes. He took a swig of coffee and looked around. "Where's Mom?"

"She's over at Sam's place, or I guess I should say Gail's place."

Lucas clenched his jaws to keep his rage from rolling out in a torrent.

"What the hell's going on with you two, son?"

Lucas didn't flinch and met his father's eyes. "We're splitting up."

Randall snorted. "Well, hell's bells, since she's

moving out, I figured as much."

Lucas rubbed the back of his neck. "She cheated on me, Dad. While on the business trip in California, she slept with another man."

~*~

Sharon Johnson stared in horror at her daughter-in-law across the kitchen table. At Gail's news, Ruth wailed and covered her mouth with her fist.

"Let me get this straight. You slept with Alex Guthrie and the child you're pregnant with, the one my son has longed for, might not be his." She slapped the table in fury and felt exultant when Gail jumped and Ruth screeched. "Did I miss anything?"

Tears streaming down her face, Gail met her glare. "No...I think that about covers it."

"You little bitch, you're just like your cheating mother."

Gail stood, shoving back her chair. Her face pinched with pain, she said, "You leave my mother out of this. Think what you want of me, I deserve it, but she's not here to defend herself."

Sharon vibrated with anger as she got up from the table. It took all her restraint to not slap the young woman. "You won't get one red cent from Lucas, not one damn thing from that house except what you brought to it."

"I want nothing from him. Now I want you out of my house."

"Gladly. If I never see you again, it'll be too soon. My son gave you everything a woman could ever want, and you...you put a knife in his back." Sharon could no longer restrain her sobs. "How...could you do it?"

"I'm sorry, so sorry. I was sick and worried about

Daddy, drank too much, and I didn't know what I'd done until the next morning."

"Drunk?" She grabbed her car keys off the counter. "Let me tell you something, missy. If this child is my grandchild, we'll fight you for custody. No drunken slut is going to raise a Johnson."

Gail's mouth opened and closed, but no sound came out. Whirling, she yanked open a drawer, removed a rolling pin, brandishing it in the air. Sharon gaped in fear and stepped back against the wall. She watched in shock as Gail pounded dishes on the table, shoving them to the floor. Then breathing hard, she stepped back from the wreckage and looked Sharon straight in the eye. "Don't threaten me. This baby is mine."

Why, the girl's crazy. Even more reason to get custody. "We'll see—"

"That's enough, Sharon." Ruth grabbed her arm and steered her out of the kitchen. "Your own reputation isn't as pristine as you'd like everyone to think, so you better watch yourself."

~*~

Lucas hadn't slept much last night, and dealing with his folks wasn't what he wanted to be doing this morning. His father's face was ashen as he sputtered and struggled for words, "Oh, son, I'm sorry. Was it that womanizer Alex Guthrie?"

"She didn't say, but I know it was. He's been attracted to her ever since she went to work there." *And I was fool enough to continue to let her go off on these trips.* She'd seemed immune to the man, so he'd felt he needn't worry.

"So, is she in love with the man?"

Lucas choked on the words. "Don't know, don't care. She's pretty torn up over what she's done, ashamed. But it's what she deserves." He wanted to kill Alex for taking advantage of her. Lucas's voice broke. "She's pregnant, Dad."

He watched the play of emotions on his father's face—joy, confusion, and then suspicion. Randall's hands fisted. "She thinks this baby is Alex's?"

His face heated and he coughed to cover his embarrassment and humiliation. "Um, I found out last month it's unlikely I'll ever father a child." He dropped his head into his hands and massaged his aching temples.

"Aw, hell, son." He pounded the table, rattling their cups. "How could Gail do this to you? I can't wait to tell her what I think of her. All these years..." He shook his head sadly.

They both turned as his mother came in the house. She set her purse on the kitchen counter and turned to her son.

"Hi, Mom."

She hugged him from behind, and her cheek against his, murmured, "Lucas. I'm sorry, son." Her familiar scent made his heart ache more. He covered her arms with his and fought the tears that threatened to fall.

"So, I guess you'll be filing for divorce then."

"Yes." The sooner he was free of her, the better. Yet the decision didn't offer comfort. For the thousandth time, he asked himself how this could have happened to them.

Hand on Lucas's shoulder, she said, "And when you file, I want you to ask for a DNA test. If the child is yours, you fight for custody."

If the baby was his... If Gail carried his baby, he'd damn well get joint custody and share his child's life.

He stood to leave, and someone knocked on the back door. His mother answered it. "Hello, Bud. What are you doing out this way?"

Bud held his hat in his hand and nodded toward Randall and Lucas. "Morning, Sharon. Can I come in?"

"Sure." She stepped back so he could enter. "Have you got time to sit down for a cup of coffee?"

"That'd be dandy if it's already made."

"Have a seat," Randall said.

He took the chair Lucas had vacated. Sharon sat a cup front of him. "Thanks, Sharon. Randall, I hate to bother you folks this morning, but I need to talk to you and Sharon." He fixed Lucas with a stare. "Alone."

Chapter Thirteen

"What's this all about, Bud?"

He took a slurp of his hot coffee, sat the cup back on the table and watched the Johnsons for reactions. "It's about the murders of June Steele and Lamar Jacobs."

Sharon visibly paled. Randall took her hand. "We'll be glad to tell you everything we know."

Taking a pen and small tablet from his shirt pocket, he flipped it open. "Good. Let's start with…did either of you know Lamar?"

Randall spoke up. "Yes, Sharon did. I met him just the one time."

Bud watched as the man comforted his wife. She looked ready to crumble. Randall moved his chair closer to hers and put his arm around her shoulders. "It'll be okay, honey. It's time to get this off your chest."

She bit her lip and nodded.

"Sharon, were you having an affair with Lamar?"

Her chin shot up. "No, absolutely not. We were friends, that's all."

"Did your husband know about this friendship?"

Shaking her head, she glanced at Randall. "No."

"In June's diary, near her last entry, she writes that you, Randall, caught your wife with Lamar and threatened to kill him if he came near her again." He watched Randall closely. "Is that true?"

Randall's large fist struck the table and Sharon jumped. "It damn sure is. The man was trying to make time with my wife by pretending to be her friend." He combed his hair with his fingers. "Sharon and I were having some problems at the time, and she confided in him. I saw exactly what was going on, followed them one day to a restaurant outside of Austin."

"Sharon, did you really believe Lamar was seeing you only as a friend, that he didn't hope your relationship would go farther?"

She flushed and ducked her head. "No, I knew what he hoped for. I acted stupid, but saw it as a way to get back at Randall."

Randall's jaw flexed. Hmm, evidently the man didn't know that little bit of information. Sharon must have pleaded innocence as to where the meetings would lead.

Bud cleared his throat. "How many days before June Steele disappeared was this?"

Sharon glanced at Randall. "Two, three days?"

"Yeah, I'd say three."

"Did you know June was seeing Lamar and planned to leave with him?"

She nodded. "Once I saw her meet him at the creek. I suspected she planned to leave, but didn't realize it would be so soon."

"There is an entry in the diary that says you and June had an argument about Lamar. Is this true?"

"Yes, she thought I was romantically involved with him. But I wasn't."

"Why didn't you tell Sam Steele about Lamar Jacobs, especially after June disappeared?"

"I was embarrassed and ashamed. I didn't want anyone to know."

"Did it ever occur to either of you that knowing might have let Sam Steele have some closure all these years?"

Sharon burst into tears, and pressed her face into Randall's chest. Hands hugging her shoulders, he tucked her closer. From their behavior, the couple obviously had a good relationship now. Of course, their manner today could be misleading.

"We discussed it, Bud, but decided it wouldn't help anything." Right now Randall didn't look so sure.

"You didn't think they might have been able to track them using Lamar's license plate number?"

"We never figured June would stay gone long. Thought she'd be back any day, begging Sam to give her another chance." Randall sighed. "As time crept on, it just seemed easier to try not to remember." Bud didn't respond. He'd let them stew for a minute and see what kind of response he got. "I know, it was damned selfish of us and we've regretted it for years."

"One other thing, June's diary says you women knew about the deep hole in the creek. Is that true?"

Sharon grabbed a napkin and dried the tears on her face. "Yes, we found it one day while fishing from the bank. The water was low that summer. We noticed a large dark spot where we couldn't see bottom. June went in and explored to see how big around it was."

"Was that the summer June disappeared?"

She thought for a minute. "No, I think it was the one before she left."

"How come you never told your husbands or anyone else about the hole?"

"Just never seemed to be a good reason, I guess."

Bud finished off his coffee and reviewed his notes. "I'll need you both to come down to the station this afternoon and give a formal statement. I need to know where you were on the days in question and the names of people who can verify your whereabouts." He stood and took his hat from the rack by the back door. "Thank you for your help, and for the coffee, ma'am."

~*~

Gail fixed herself a cup of hot tea and sat at the kitchen table. Sharon's threats and harsh words had left her trembling and on edge. No one would take her baby from her. No one.

Ruth was dusting the living room when someone knocked at the door. With a screech, she jerked and covered her heart with her hand. She was beside herself about something, had been acting funny all morning. Gail couldn't imagine her being that jumpy about her moving home.

Gail opened the door. Jim, one of Lucas's hands, stood on the porch, hat in his hand. "Morning, Miss Gail, Tom sent me over to help out with some heavy work you need doing." He caught sight of Ruth and his smile grew broader. "Howdy, Ruth."

Ruth's response of, "Hello, Jim," lacked enthusiasm and the older man's smile shrunk.

True to his word, Lucas had sent help. She doubted it was out of consideration. He just wanted her out of the house as soon as possible. Well, the feeling was mutual. "Thank you, Jim. If you'll meet me at the house at three this afternoon, I'll have some boxes ready for you."

He doffed his hat and nodded. "I'll see you, then."

Gail turned to Ruth. "What is wrong with you today? Are you sick?"

Ruth shrugged. "I don't know. Guess it's your father's death and now this." She waved at Gail's suitcases sitting by the stairs. "I'm just on edge. Pay me no mind."

She hugged the older woman. "If you don't feel up to working, let me know. Most of this stuff can wait until another time."

"No, I want to help you get settled." She sniffed. "I don't know what to think with all this news on top of your daddy's death." She shook her head. "If Sam were alive, I shudder to think what he'd have to say to you."

Gail didn't doubt Ruth's words, and having to tell her father she'd been unfaithful horrified her. Her hand moved to her stomach. But, he'd have loved this child. "Please, Ruth, don't mention our problems to anyone. It's no one's business but ours."

"I won't say a word." Ruth snorted. "People are so gossipy around here, it'll be interesting to sit back and see what kind of stories they come up with."

Gail picked up the two suitcases and started for the stairs.

Ruth rushed to take them. "You'll not be doing any toting. Your father would rise from his grave and come after me if I let you do something to hurt yourself and his grandchild." As if shocked by her words, the older woman paled and put her hand on her bosom. She muttered something under her breath.

She followed Ruth up the stairs and went into her room. Clothes lay across her bed, so she gathered coat hangers and started hanging them up. It felt so strange to be back here without Lucas. How would she manage without him in her life? A deep sense of despair washed over her. How could she have slept with Alex Guthrie? God, was she a slut, or did the alcohol cause her to lose all her good sense? This should be such a time of joy, yet here she sat, pregnant, and didn't know the identity of her child's father. She wanted to curl up on the bed and weep, but instead went to work.

A terrifying scream echoed down the attic stairs. Gail rushed from her room and collided with Ruth in the hall. Face white with fear, she trembled from head to toe.

"What is it? Did you see a mouse?"

Ruth covered her heart with her hand and gasped for air. "Ghost, oh God, it's his ghost. She told him." Her eyes rolled up and she fell into a dead faint.

~*~

Early Monday morning, Bud stopped by the house. He removed his hat. "Morning Gail, I didn't expect to see you here."

"Hi, Sheriff, what can I do for you?"

"Need to speak with Ruth if she's here."

Gail stepped back. "Come on in and have a cup of coffee. Ruth will be downstairs in just a minute."

"Coffee sounds good." He followed her into the kitchen and hung his hat on the rung of a chair. "Sure sorry about your daddy. He was a fine man."

"Thank you. I sure miss him. Seems like he's everywhere I look around here."

Bud nodded. "'Spect it'll be that way for a long time." He cleared his throat. "Want you to know I never believed for a minute Sam committed those murders, but he's still on the list of suspects."

Gail bristled and started to speak. Bud held up a

hand. "I know what you're going to say, but until we can prove otherwise, that's the way things stand. I want to be open and upfront about the situation."

She didn't like it, but could appreciate his honesty and nodded her understanding.

"I don't know what you need to talk to Ruth about, but she's been mighty edgy lately. She fainted yesterday, so tread lightly. Said she'd seen Daddy's ghost."

Before he could respond, Ruth swept through the swinging kitchen door, stopped and nodded when she saw Bud. "Sheriff."

"Ruth, I need to talk with you. Can you sit down for a minute?"

"What's this all about?" she asked.

Bud glanced at Gail. "Would you excuse us?"

Gail nodded and went upstairs. What would Bud want with Ruth? She was one of the most law-abiding citizens around. Gail hoped he wouldn't say anything to upset her. Her episode with "the ghost" had left her shaken. Gail didn't want to see a repeat performance. She'd been afraid the older woman had suffered a heart attack.

A short while later Gail heard Bud leaving and went down to check on Ruth. She sat at the kitchen table, staring into space. "Are you all right?"

Ruth's eyes looked haunted, but she nodded. "I'm fine. He and the assistant DA have been reading June's diary. There was an entry in it about the three of us swimming down at Possum Creek and finding that deep hole."

"You knew about it?" Gail sat down across from her. Ruth dropped her eyes and nodded. "Why didn't you tell Bud that back when the car was found?"

She shrugged. "Wouldn't have made any difference. We just happened to find it one summer when the creek was low."

"You said the three of us. You, Mama, and who?"

"Why Sharon Johnson, of course. We swam together lots in those days and took you kids with us."

"How come I never knew about the excursions?"

"Don't know. Expect it was never important. Guess it is now as Bud's already talked to Sharon."

Gail didn't know what to think. She wished she could have the diary back to finish reading it.

"Sometime after that, June and Sharon had a falling out about something. June was mad as all get out."

"You don't know why?"

"Nope, but sometimes I wonder if Sharon wasn't seeing someone on the sly." Ruth had always been nosey and inclined to gossip. Surely she had an inkling.

Gail was puzzled. Randall and Sharon were devoted to each other. She couldn't imagine either being interested in someone else. Like she never dreamed she'd get involved with someone else herself. One just never knows.

"I heard June and Sharon arguing one time and June said, 'Stay away from him, Sharon, I mean it.' Of course I knew your Mama was seeing someone, but didn't know who. I'm thinking they were both seeing the same man."

Gail's stomach churned. This was a picture she didn't want embellished on her mind. Not Sharon. It was bad enough her mother had been involved with another man.

She didn't want to hear anymore. "I think I better

check to make sure I have something to wear into Austin tomorrow."

Ruth went home at six p.m. and Gail felt lost in the big house. She sat in her father's favorite chair. The smell of stale cigarette smoke reached her nostrils and her stomach turned over. She moved to the sofa. The chair would have to be shampooed one day soon.

It was eight o'clock when she went up to bed. Loneliness choked her. She hugged the spare pillow and gave in to the tears she'd kept bottled inside all day.

~*~

Gail's appointment with Dr. Lane went well. She was pronounced to be in good health, but they drew blood to make sure. "Since you're RH negative and Lucas is positive, we'll also be doing a Coombs test periodically to check for RH sensitization. Are you familiar with the issues associated with RH disease?"

"Yes. I've done some reading since trying to get pregnant."

"Good." The doctor closed her chart and stood. "You get dressed. I'll see you in my office in a few minutes."

Dr. Lane strolled into her office and rather than sitting behind her desk, took the chair beside Gail. "Now, I can see something is bothering you. What is it?"

Gail told her everything and Dr. Lane kept handing her tissues. Finally, she quieted.

"Is there any chance this man could have drugged you?"

"You mean like the date rape drug?" The thought had never entered her mind. "No, I don't think so. He's a womanizer, but not a criminal. I have only myself to blame for drinking too much."

"We've all made mistakes. Give Lucas a chance, maybe he'll see that and forgive you."

Yeah, right. Like Lucas is going to listen to anything I have to say.

"Now, there is a new test that allows you to know definitely who the father is. I'm not talking about the amniocentesis or chorionic villus sampling. It's a non-invasive test and won't hurt the baby or you. The baby's DNA can be collected from your blood and compared to your husband's. There are a variety of ways his DNA can be collected."

"I'll mention it to Lucas."

"Do you think the other man would submit to testing?"

Gail cringed at the thought of asking. "I don't know."

"It's not absolutely necessary. If you want to be discreet, you can bring in a couple of his hairs with the root attached, a piece of chewing gum, a water bottle. Anything that would have a sample of his DNA. Of course, it could only be used for your personal information."

She giggled at the thought of yanking out some of Alex's perfectly styled hair. It was the first time she'd laughed in a while and felt good. "I'll think about it."

The doctor must have known what she was thinking as she grinned. "Let me know. We have your blood samples. Didn't you say your husband had seen Dr. Jamison? He can leave a blood sample there. Our offices work together all the time."

Dr. Lane stood and walked Gail to the door. "Try not to worry. It won't change the facts. Concentrate on your precious baby and let Lucas work through whether or not he can forgive you."

The next morning, Gail woke to find Chief sitting on the back porch. He acted excited to see her and danced around to show his enthusiasm.

"Hey, boy, what are you doing here?" She wondered if Lucas knew where he was and called him.

He answered on the second ring, his voice brusque and detached. "Yes."

The sound sent her heart into her throat. "I just wanted to let you know Chief is here in case you've been looking for him."

"I dropped him off this morning. He misses you and I'm tired of his moping around. I sat his dish and food on the porch."

He would miss the animal. She felt guilty but... "Thank you. It'll be nice having some company."

"I've got to go."

"Wait. I saw Dr. Lane yesterday. She said the baby's DNA cells can be collected from my blood. If you want, Dr. Jamison can take a sample of yours and they'll test them."

Lucas remained quiet for a long time. She could hear him breathing. When he spoke, his voice broke. "You're damn right I want." He hung up.

She'd not gone three feet when the phone rang. It was Bud. "Gail, we've matched the fingerprints on your book. They belong to Ruth."

Gail couldn't have been more shocked if he'd said they were Sharon's fingerprints. She dropped into a chair. "But why would she come into the house on the sly?"

"Said she wanted to read what your mother said

about her."

"I'd have loaned it to her if she'd asked."

His voice gruff, he asked. "Do you want to press charges?"

Press charges against Ruth? The woman who'd cared for her and her father all these years. "No." But she'd hurt Chief. Most of the blood in the drive was from her wound, but she'd hit him several times on the head. "I don't know what to do."

"I think you should. We don't have any proof, but Ruth could have easily committed the murders. She had access to the gun and also knew your mother's plans."

Gail was speechless. Ruth a murderer, that was ludicrous...she just couldn't see Ruth shooting two people in the head. "She didn't have a motive to kill them."

"Not one that we know of yet. Are you sure you won't change your mind and press charges?"

"I can't. I'm sorry for all the trouble, Bud."

He sighed. "All right, guess that's that."

"When can I have the diary back?"

"Don't know. You'll need to talk to the assistant DA, Robert Pruitt, as he's reading it now. Keeps looking for clues to the murder. If Ruth is still working for you, be careful."

"That's ridiculous. She would never hurt me and you know it. Ruth practically raised me, Bud."

"You mind what I say, young woman. People aren't always what they seem."

She sighed. "Okay, I will. And I'll talk to Robert to see if he has any idea when I'll be able to get the diary back." Ruth capable of murder? Gail couldn't see it. But wasn't that why criminals were hard to catch? No one believed them capable of the crimes they'd committed. Their victims especially. The thought made her shiver. She'd better get her mind on something else.

Gail drove into town and stopped by the DA's office. Robert was busy, but his secretary said he'd be free in a few minutes. She sat down and flipped through a copy of *National Geographic.* She'd just gotten into a story about sunken treasure in the Gulf of Mexico when Robert came out to greet her.

"Hello, Gail, this is a surprise. Come on in."

His office was plain yet neat. She sat in a hard wood chair facing his desk.

"You here about the diary?"

"Yes, I'm hoping you're finished and I can take it home. I never did get all the way through it."

He leaned back in his chair and folded his arms across his waist. "I need to keep it awhile longer, but I've been over it again and again and not found anything that might lead us to the murderer. I've made two photocopies, one as a backup and one for you. You find anything of interest to this case, let me know." He pulled a stack of papers from the bottom desk drawer and handed it to her.

"Thank you, I will."

He cleared his throat. "This is none of my business, but there's a rumor going around that you and Lucas have separated."

"Yes, it's true. I'd appreciate it if you'd keep it to yourself."

He nodded. "You bet. I'm sorry. Hope you'll be able to patch things up."

"I don't think that's possible." She thanked him for the diary and left to buy groceries. When she got home,

Ruth was in the kitchen, cleaning. Chief watched her every move. Ruth seemed grateful to see her.

"Oh, I'm glad you're home. I know this dog has good reason to distrust me, but I can't work with him staring at me."

"Come on, Chief. Go outside." He stood in the door looking back at Ruth. "I'll be fine, boy. Go on."

She turned back to Ruth, who stood wringing her hands. "I'm...sorry for what I did. I don't know what got into me...but I wanted to see that diary so bad." She swiped at the tears on her cheeks. "I'd hoped to read it...and...put it back before you missed it."

"Why didn't you just ask?"

She ducked her head. "I didn't want you to know I was concerned about the spats your mother and I had. Didn't know what she might have said about me."

Her reason didn't make sense to Gail, but who could figure out how other people thought? "I can almost forgive you for coming into our home uninvited, but I'll never forgive you for hitting Chief. Don't do anything like that again, Ruth."

"Oh, God, I didn't mean to hurt him. Honest. I won't, I promise. And thank you for not pressing charges." Bud must have informed her of Gail's decision.

That evening, Chief followed Gail upstairs and curled up on the rag rug by her bed. She slipped between the covers with the diary pages and started where she'd left off before.

Today I met the nicest man at the drug store. We chatted for a minute about job opportunities. He said a person could make good money in Canada. His name is Lamar Jacobs.

Chapter Fourteen

It was Saturday morning. Lucas had worked himself into a stupor all week, hoping he'd be so tired when he got home he'd be able to fall asleep. But it didn't work. Over and over, the facts raced through his mind. He was sterile, Gail had sex with Alex, and he couldn't forgive her for betraying him. He hated her, he missed her, and he ached for her. He wanted to drive himself into her body and erase the memory of another man from both their minds.

The following week he had an appointment with Dr. Jamison to give blood for the paternity test. By now everyone on the ranch and in town knew he and Gail had split up, and though curious, no one asked questions. He was tired of eating his own cooking and by himself. Tonight he'd go out for a steak, stop at Bubba's for a few beers, and then maybe he'd fall asleep when he fell into bed.

He walked Butterscotch to the pasture gate and removed her tether rope. She loped off, kicking up her heels to join her mother. On his way to the bunkhouse for lunch, he saw Bud's cruiser coming up the road. Lucas changed directions and walked toward the sheriff's car. Bud rolled down the window. Lucas put both hands on the door, leaned down, and asked, "What's up, Bud?"

"Need to talk to you a minute. Got time?"

"Sure, come on to the bunkhouse and we'll grab a plate and find a quiet place to eat outside."

Bud grinned and heaved his large frame from his cruiser. "Best invitation I've had all day. Wonder what Shorty's cooking up today."

"Well, it is Wednesday so I'd say we're having the usual, meatloaf." Shorty had a schedule and stuck to it faithfully. If he varied, someone usually complained.

They grabbed a plate, plastic silverware, and tea and sat on the tailgate of Lucas's pickup. For a minute they were quiet. Just past a field of grass, Lucas could see his house. A month ago he'd stared in that direction and been anxious to get home to Gail. Now he didn't even have Chief waiting for him.

Bud sat his plate aside and wiped his mouth on his napkin. "You know I fingerprinted your folks and Ruth."

Lucas nodded and tensed for what Bud might say next.

"Ruth's fingerprints were on the diary. She said she'd wanted to read what June had written about her, but was too embarrassed to ask Gail if she could see it."

Blood roared in his ears. The nerve of the woman. Cozy up and then pull a stunt like that. He would tell the woman what he thought the next time he saw her. "Sounds like a damned weak excuse to me." Lucas remembered how carefully Chief watched Ruth when she was at the house.

"Don't fly with me either, but Gail didn't want to press charges. Wondered if you were of the same mind. You can press them yourself, you know."

Had Gail lost all her good sense? Lucas scratched his chin. He needed a shave. Lately he'd found himself being slovenly in a way he'd never been before. "Yes, do it. I'll come down this afternoon to sign a complaint."

Bud nodded. "Okay, glad to hear it." They tossed their disposable utensils in a trashcan outside the door of the bunkhouse. "Thank you for the lunch."

"You're welcome. Thanks for coming out, Bud."

Bud waved and walked toward his car, then stopped and turned back. "Thought you'd want to know, Robert Pruitt released a copy of the diary to Gail yesterday. He's gone through it with a fine tooth comb, but hasn't been able to discover any leads on who might have committed the murders." He got in his car. "Call me if you hear anything."

"Will do."

Bud made a U-turn around Lucas and stopped again. He rolled down the passenger window.

"By the way, Gail knows Sam hasn't been cleared as a suspect. It's only fair you know both your parents are suspects, too. We're checking on their alibis right now."

"You're wasting your time. Neither one of my folks is a murderer."

"I hope you're right."

~*~

Gail returned to work the following week. Morning sickness continued to plague her, but she'd learned when it hit, not to fight it. Just get it over with. Alex hadn't returned from vacation and she was grateful not to have to face him yet.

Lucas's vindictiveness in filing charges against Ruth still appalled her. The woman had been taken downtown, booked, and appeared before a judge. She'd been given a sentence of 100 hours of community service. He was probably right to do it, as Ruth had committed a crime. She tended to be too softhearted and one day the tendency would turn around and bite her.

On Saturday, she drove into town and picked up cleaning supplies, paint, and wallpaper for the baby's room. She'd decided on a duck theme in blues and yellows. Her heart constricted at the checkout counter when she thought how much Lucas would have enjoyed planning and decorating their baby's room. But, it appeared this baby was hers, not theirs.

At one o'clock, she met Sandra at the On the Square Cafe to eat. The lunch rush over, they took a booth in the back corner with plenty of privacy. Though she'd prefer to have a burger and fries, she'd settle on Mary's vegetable plate.

Sandra stood and hugged her and then looked Gail over with a critical eye. "What has Lucas done? I'll kick his ass for you, sister, just give the word."

Gail laughed. "You're a sweetheart, but that's not necessary."

"It's true, then? You've left him?"

Gail took a deep breath. "Yes, it's true. More like he threw me out."

Her friend gaped in shock. "What on earth for?"

Gail debated whether or not to tell her she was pregnant. This should be such a joyful time. She needed someone to be happy for her. Gail lowered her voice. "I'm pregnant, but Lucas doesn't believe he's the father."

A variety of emotions flickered across Sandra's face. The last was bewilderment. "But why?"

As Gail told her about Lucas's visit to a specialist, her lips started trembling and she bit the bottom one to still them. "And...and I slept with Alex when we were in California on that business trip."

For once Sandra was speechless. Then, brows furrowed, lips pinched, she sputtered, "My God! What were you thinking?"

Gail flinched at Sandra's evident disappointment. "I wasn't. I got drunk and don't remember a whole lot."

"Could you be mistaken? I mean, maybe—"

Gail shook her head. "What I do remember is leaving the bar and Alex having to hold me up. I started crying about Daddy. The next thing I remember is him comforting me, then we're kissing...and then my dress was around my waist..." Sandra reached out and grabbed her hand. "When I woke up, I was naked."

Sandra's disdain turned to pity. "Oh, honey, so the baby could be Alex's."

She nodded.

"Have you talked to him?"

"No, he's been out of town on vacation. He should be back this weekend. I saw Dr. Lane this week and she took some blood samples. Lucas is seeing the doctor for blood work to be used for paternity testing." She so wanted Lucas to be the father. Regardless, he'd never forgive her. Their life together was over. If Alex proved to be the father, she would accept the fact and allow him time with the baby if he wanted it. And she'd get by.

"I know what you're thinking, Gail," Sandra said. "You've made a bad mistake. And Lucas may never forgive you, but don't let your hurt keep you from being happy about this baby."

Gail nodded. "Let's order and talk about something else. I'm thinking about getting my hair cut."

Sandra arched a brow. "What'd you have in mind?"

"Something easy to take care of, like chin length and smooth. A cut that would only require blow-drying yet with enough length to pull back if I wanted to."

"With a little feathering around the face, it would be perfect for you."

Lucas loved her long hair, but she didn't need to worry about pleasing him anymore. She'd wear her hair to suit herself. And with the baby coming, she didn't want to spend a lot of time on it.

"I think I'm going to take the plunge after lunch. You want to go with me and keep me from backing out?"

"I'd love to." Sandra grinned. "I wouldn't miss this for the world. You've not had a haircut for as long as I've known you."

Sandra was right. Oh, she'd had her hair trimmed, but never cut off. Just the thought made her queasy, but when they got to Betty's Beauty Barn and Josie, Betty's daughter, started fussing over her, she relaxed. When she left the beauty shop, she felt ten pounds lighter.

~*~

Saturday evening, after a shower and shave, Lucas drove to the steak house situated just outside of town. He ordered a twelve-ounce sirloin with the trimmings and ate the whole thing. It filled the hole in his belly, but not the empty space in his heart. Eating alone wasn't any more fun here than it was at home. At least the food tasted better. He wanted a beer.

Bubba's, as usual on a Saturday night, was

crowded so he opted for a stool at the bar. After his third beer, he noticed Robert, Jason and their wives at a corner table. He pushed his way through the dancers to reach them.

Both Jason and Robert stood to greet him. Robert pulled up a chair for him, and he sat down and turned to the ladies. "Hello, Patty, Cheryl, you both look lovely tonight."

"Well, thank you, Lucas," Cheryl said. "Sorry I can't say the same about you. You're not looking your best. How are you?"

The waitress approached the table and Lucas ordered another beer, then turned to the women. "As well as can be expected."

Patty took his hand. "Do you want to talk about it?"

Lucas shook his head, his throat thick with misery. "Nope, nothing to talk about. It's over."

Jason spoke up. "Any time you need to talk, you know where to find us."

"Thanks, I appreciate it."

Lucas smelled her cloying perfume before he heard her voice. How he'd ever thought the woman was attractive remained a mystery to him now. Yes, she had a great body and enjoyed sex, but she didn't stir him emotionally. No one could but Gail. To hell with emotions, right now he needed a distraction.

"Lucas, honey, I didn't expect to see you here. Where's the little wife?"

Lucas turned. "Hello, Tabitha. As you can see, Gail's not with me."

She pursed her lips. "Oh dear, that's right, you're separated. I'm so sorry."

"It's nice of you to be concerned."

"But that's what old friends are for, sugar." She took the arm he'd slung over the chair back and tugged. "Come on, dance this number with me."

Lucas lifted her hand from his arm and raised it to his lips for a quick kiss. "Not right now, Tabitha. Maybe later."

As she stalked off, Cheryl said, "That woman is pure poison. Please don't get involved with her again. What you ever saw in her I'll never know."

Lucas almost laughed at the expression on his friends' faces.

Robert hugged her and laughed. "It's a man thing, honey."

She snorted. "I would make a comment about the location of men's brains, but I can see it would go over your heads."

Lucas hooted with laughter and the rest joined in. The experience was refreshing and one he'd not enjoyed in a while. Suddenly his pain resurfaced and called him to task. Before he could tamp it down, he looked up and caught Alex Guthrie watching him from the bar. He pushed back his chair. "Good to see you, guys. I've got business to tend to."

Alex met him near the door, and as if prearranged, they walked outside together. Neither one stopped until they were at the back of the building. It sat in front of about thirty acres of undeveloped land.

Lucas took in his adversary's appearance. Today he wasn't wearing his suit or a polo shirt and khakis. He was dressed in jeans and boots.

"I hear you wanted to see me. From the look on your face, you don't have to tell me what about." The sorry bastard had the audacity to grin.

"You got my wife drunk and took advantage of her in a weakened state."

"Ho, ho, so that's what she told you?"

Lucas threw a punch and caught Alex in the mouth. Blood spurted and he wiped it away with his sleeve. "You're a sorry sack of shit, Alex. You're going to pay for what you did to her." He hit him again. This time Alex moved and the blow glanced off the side of his head. He quickly recovered and landed two quick blows to Lucas's stomach.

They were equally matched in size and weight. They circled each other like two rogue bears, then started throwing punches. A crowd formed, but Lucas was oblivious as he pounded away at his enemy. Robert and Jason tried to break them apart.

Lucas yelled, "Get the hell away from me."

Finally three police cars came screaming to a halt, barely missing the spectators. Bud and a deputy grabbed Lucas, while two local police officers latched on to Alex. As they were forced into two different vehicles, hands cuffed behind them, Alex jeered. "Oh, and just for the record, she yelled 'Alex' when she came."

Lucas could take no more. He roared like a wounded bull and jerked free. Bent over, he charged head first and knocked an officer on his butt to reach Alex. He felt a blow to the back of his head and his knees buckled.

~*~

Monday morning, when Gail walked into the office, Sue and one of the waitresses from On the Square Cafe had their heads together, whispering.

182

"Good morning, Sue, Veronica."

They started and jerked apart. Both women spoke, but Gail noticed the flush that rose on Sue's face and the smirk on Veronica's.

Gail cringed inwardly, but pretended nothing was a miss. She knocked on Ron's office door and stuck her head in. "Have you got a minute?"

He looked up and smiled, then motioned to a chair. "Sure, have a seat." When settled in her chair, he asked, "What's on your mind?"

His expression kind, she suspected he knew exactly what she wanted to say. And what the two women were discussing outside in the lobby.

"I want you and Alex to know I'm pregnant and will need a six weeks leave of absence in approximately six months."

"That's wonderful, Gail. Congratulations."

"Thank you." She looked down at her hands. "I'm sure you've heard Lucas and I are separated."

"Yes, I'd heard, but hoped it wasn't true. Is it possible you'll reconcile?"

Her voice trembled. "No, I don't think so." She stood up and he hurried around his desk to see her out.

Ron placed his hand on her shoulder and gave her an awkward pat. "Gail, we think a lot of you here. If we can help in any way, let us know."

She nodded. On the way back to her office, she saw Alex enter his, closing the door behind him. Taking a deep breath, she decided she might as well get this over with. She knocked and heard his, "come in."

His back was to her as he watched someone on the courthouse lawn. "Alex."

He whirled to face her and smiled. If you could call

the expression on his battered face a smile. "Not too pretty, huh?"

"My goodness, what on earth happened?"

"Lucas and I had a meeting of the minds Saturday. Had you not heard about our visit to the hospital and then the jail?"

Gail's legs weakened, her vision blurred. He rushed around the desk to get her a chair. "Would you like a glass of water? I'm sorry, I thought you'd heard."

She could only look at him. Her lips trembled and she covered her mouth with her hand. Alex handed her the glass of water and propped his hip on the end of the desk. She took several sips. "Lucas looks about the same as I do. He's okay."

She nodded.

"How'd he find out about California? When it took so long for him to extract revenge, I figured you hadn't told him."

"I'm pregnant, Alex." She waited for him to say something, but he looked at her like he didn't understand what she was saying. "The baby could be yours. Lucas is sure it is. He threw me out. Not that I blame him."

His jaw dropped. "I'm going to be a father?" His expression of shock turned smug. "Well, well. How about that?"

"We're having paternity testing."

He nodded and moved to look out the window again, his back to her. "Ah, I see. So, if Lucas is the father, he'll take you back."

She dropped her head and studied the hem of her skirt. "No, I doubt he'll ever forgive me."

"You know I've always been attracted to you, Gail.

If I thought for a minute you loved me, I'd offer to marry you and raise the child regardless of who the father is."

His offer surprised her, but with his back to her, she couldn't see his eyes. Was he being honest? It didn't matter. She couldn't ever marry him.

"I'm sorry. I'll always love Lucas and am willing to raise the child on my own." He turned and fixed her with a stare. "Oh, if you're the father, of course you'll have access to your child. I didn't mean to imply otherwise."

"That's more than fair."

She stood to leave, glad the confrontation was over.

He held up a hand. "Please, stay a minute more. I need to come clean with you."

What was he talking about? She sank down into the chair.

He tried to smile and winced. "Nothing happened between us that night. Your baby can't be mine."

"Wha…"

"You and I did not have sex."

"But the next morning…"

He held up his hands. "I know. You're wondering what happened to your clothes. I undressed you so you'd be unsure." He didn't look the least remorseful. "It was an evil thing to do, but I wanted you so bad. Then, when I touched you, you cried out for Lucas and then passed out cold. I was sexually frustrated and royally pissed."

"But—"

"Yes, you were crying about your father, you kissed me and I took advantage. It never got any further than me unzipping your dress and baring your breasts." He coughed. "Uh, I did see your charms when I undressed you, but I did it quickly and didn't take advantage of your unconsciousness."

She jerked up from the chair. "You asshole. You're despicable." Dizzy, she fell back into the chair, crying. "How could you let me suffer all these weeks?"

"I'm truly sorry. I tried to tell you at your father's wake, but you panicked and rushed off." He shrugged. "Then I went out of town. I should have told you the next morning, but you were so frosty, and played the wounded party so well, I just…"

Ron burst through the door shutting it behind him. "What the hell is going on in here? I could hear you in my office with the door closed."

Gail kept quiet. Let Alex explain his way out of this. He said, "Gail and I were clarifying an issue."

Ron snorted and fixed Alex with a stare of disgust. "So, the rumors are true. You and Gail shacked up while we were in California."

Gail blushed to the roots of her hair.

"No, that's not exactly what…"

She didn't want to hear another word from Alex's mouth. He might not be truthful with Ron, but right now she didn't care. She tuned him out and took several deep breaths to calm herself, and then left the two men together.

Sue caught her the minute she neared the door to her office. "Gail, there's a man waiting in there to see you."

He stood as she entered. "Mrs. Johnson?"

"Yes, what can I do for you, Mr…

"Samuelson, ma'am, Michael Samuelson." He

handed her a fat sealed envelope. "Please sign here."

She signed her name to a form. He quickly took it, nodded and left. The return address read Cheryl Pruitt, Attorney at Law. Her heart stopped. She grabbed the desk to steady herself. Lucas had filed for divorce before he knew if she carried his child. Now it was final. There would be no forgiveness, no reconciliation. Lucas was right. Miracles didn't exist.

Chapter Fifteen

So, it was over. Her five-year marriage was dead. Well, she wouldn't delay the issue. She grabbed her purse, stuffed the envelope inside, and left her office.

"Sue, I'm leaving for an hour or so. If anyone needs me, I'll be at Jeff Taylor's office." Before she could answer, Gail strode out the door. That should give Sue more fodder for gossip.

Jeff had been her daddy's lawyer. Now he would be hers. His secretary Lorene talked on the phone when she walked in. She said, "Gotta go. Bye," and hung up. "Hi, Gail, what can I do for you this morning?" Gail had no doubt the woman knew exactly why she was there, but was too much of a professional to let on.

"Is Jeff in?"

She rose from her desk. "Sure, honey, let me see if he's got time to talk to you." Hips bouncing underneath the stretched polyester pants, she strode into her boss's office without knocking. She'd worked for Jeff as long as Gail could remember, so who was boss was debatable.

Lorene came back out with Jeff on her heels. "Gail, come on in." He turned back to his secretary as she slid into the office chair. "Hold all my calls."

"Will do."

Jeff took her arm and led her to a chair. "I'm so sorry about your daddy."

Gail sat in the overstuffed leather club chair. "Thank you. It's been hard. I miss him."

"I'm sure you do. And especially now, hmmm?" His expression was sympathetic. He'd probably heard all manner of stories from people going through divorce. Would hers shock him at all?

"Yeah, especially now." She removed the envelope from her purse and laid it on his desk. "So, you've already heard?"

He scratched his chin. "After the fight at Bubba's Saturday night, I doubt there's a person in the county that doesn't know. Shame folks around here thrive on gossip so." He picked up the envelope, opened it and studied the pages. Then he took off his glasses and looked at her.

"Have you read this?"

"Yes."

"Did you understand it, have any questions about anything?"

No, it was all plain as mud. She shook her head.

"Do you want to contest the divorce, change any of the stipulations?"

"No."

"Of course you know the divorce won't be final until after the baby is born, paternity is confirmed, and final arrangements for child support and visitation are settled."

"I understand. But, I want to get it over with, off my mind so I can move on."

He watched her for a minute, then cleared his throat. "I think you should ask for a settlement of some kind. Lucas can afford it and you may need a nest egg to fall back on."

Maybe she should, but she didn't want anything from him. If the baby was his, he wanted him or her to bear his name. He wanted full visitation rights and would pay child support. Of the wedding gifts they'd received, she could have what she wanted, any furniture they'd bought, and her car. "I don't want a thing from him, Jeff. He's running cattle on daddy's land and I'll ask for a lease fee. If you would, please draw up a lease agreement for 600 acres. Charge whatever the going price is right now."

"Gail, are you sure you two won't reconcile? Have you thought about counseling or a trial separation?"

In her mind there wasn't a chance, and evidently not in Lucas's either. "No. He's made up his mind." Should she tell Jeff the truth? Lucas had filed for the divorce on irreconcilable differences. He could've used the charge of adultery. At least she had that to be grateful for. "There is something I want to tell you, but I don't want Lucas to know. I found out this morning Alex and I did not have sex. I was drunk, and he made it look like we had, but I'd passed out."

"My God, that bastard. I may add a few more bruises to his face." He frowned. "And why aren't you telling your husband this right now instead of me?"

"Because the trust is already broken. Lucas filed for this divorce even before he knew whether or not he was the child's father. Frankly, I don't want to be married to him anymore." Picking up a pen off his desk, she reached for the papers and started signing them. "Do you think you can have these delivered to Lucas today?"

He nodded. "Gail, think of your child. Don't sign this without giving it more thought."

"I know what I'm doing, Jeff. For the first time in several months, I have peace of mind. This is what Lucas wants." She removed her wedding band and diamond engagement ring and placed them on his ink blotter. "Be sure these are included in the envelope with the signed papers."

Jeff shook his head and sighed. "It'll be done as you ask. I'll send someone over to your office so you can sign the lease agreement and have it delivered at the same time."

~*~

When Gail returned to work, Alex's office was empty. Ron, still red-faced, looked ready to blow at any minute. For the first time, it occurred to her that her job might not be as secure as she'd thought. If Ron and Alex fired her, she might have to move to find a job to support herself and the baby. She had Sue bring her something back for lunch and worked to make up for the time she'd been out. Because of the time she'd been off with her daddy, work was backed up and she'd be working long hours for a month to catch up.

Around two o'clock, Ron came into her office. Thank goodness his coloring had returned to normal. The fact didn't ease her mind much though. He sat down across from her desk. "We need to talk."

"I'm sorry, Ron. If you want my resignation, I'll give it to you today."

He held up a hand. "Wait. Let me say something first." She waited while he struggled with something in his mind. "I'm embarrassed and ashamed of the scandal this incident has generated and the tarnish it's put on our company image."

Gail felt her hopes of staying drop. He was right.

Not that it would affect their out-of-town business, but it might run off some of their local customers.

"I can't believe you'd act so shamelessly. However, I realize you were in a vulnerable state-of-mind at the time with your father's terminal illness. The fact Alex plied you with alcohol and took advantage is despicable." He glared at her. "You're a grown woman and should know when you've had too much to drink."

She sank a little lower in her seat. "I don't think it's possible for you and Alex to work here together. One of you has to go."

"I understand. I'll clean out my desk this afternoon."

"Fortunately for you, that won't be necessary. Alex wants to sell his share of the company and move to Austin. It'll be tight, but I think I can afford it. We'll have to hold off on buying the new equipment you and Alex picked out, but..." He shrugged. "We've made it this long without it."

Tears filled her eyes. "You mean I can stay?"

"Isn't that what I've been saying for the past five minutes?" He looked surprised that it wasn't clear to her. "Yes, you can stay. I know your behavior in California was out of character for you. Unfortunately, I've suspected Alex's activities at conventions weren't what I'd consider..." He seemed to be at a loss for words. "Anyway, I'm glad he's leaving. If, in the future, you feel you'd like to buy his partnership, let me know and we'll discuss it."

"Thank you, Ron. I won't disappoint you again."

~*~

Gail hadn't been home ten minutes when a car drove up. Tired and worn out emotionally, she wasn't ready to face another soul. Pounding sounded on the door. "Open up Gail, it's me, Sandra. I know you're in there, girlfriend. Let me in."

Knowing Sandra wouldn't leave without talking to her, Gail pulled on a robe and went downstairs. One look at her friend's face and she knew the news was out. She fell into Sandra's arms and sobbed.

"Oh, honey, I'm so sorry." Sandra patted her back in sympathy. "Come on, let's sit down on the sofa. Tell me all about it."

Gail told her everything, her talk with Alex, with her lawyer, and then with Ron.

"And you signed those papers after what Alex told you? What were you thinking, girl? You love Lucas and telling him what you'd learned would've changed everything."

"I was so damn mad and hurt," she choked out. "He filed for divorce before he knew if he was this child's father or not."

Sandra shook her head. "He's hurt, too, Gail. You might have done the same thing. I know you still love him. If you don't tell him and set things right, you may not get another chance."

Gail didn't like the sound of those words, but Lucas wasn't the only one who'd been hurt. His hasty decision cut her to the quick. No, she'd done the right thing. "I can't right now."

Sandra shook her head. "You're fooling yourself, Gail. That pride of yours won't keep you warm on cold nights and make you laugh and smile. Don't leave this as it is and regret it for the rest of your life."

~*~

Lucas rubbed down Grayboy and turned him into

his stall with a bag of oats. They'd had a long afternoon checking on the cattle he'd turned onto Gail's land. His bruised ribs had complained all day. He could've let one of the hands do it, but figured the pain was good. It would keep his mind off other matters.

Just as he walked out of the barn, he saw Michael Samuelson drive up. Maybe Cheryl had something else for him to sign. He wondered if Gail had been served papers yet, and for the tenth time that day wondered if he'd done the right thing. His appointment with Dr. Jamison wasn't until tomorrow. He could've waited until he knew if he was the baby's father. But he'd been so damn mad, hurt, destroyed that he'd bothered Cheryl on Sunday to get the papers drawn up. He'd been filled with satisfaction Sunday night, but this morning doubt had plagued him.

"Hey, Lucas." Michael waited for him at his vehicle, a beat up Ford Bronco.

"Hello, Mike, got something for me from Cheryl?"

The other man's smile faded. "No, uh, this is from Jeff Taylor." He handed him the thick envelope with a form for his signature on the top. His stomach dropped to his toes, and for a minute he felt lightheaded. Michael handed him a pen. "Need to sign right here." He pointed to a line.

Lucas scrawled his signature and returned the pen. "Thanks."

"Yeah." Lucas turned on his heel and headed for his truck. He got in and sat holding the envelope with both hands. His heart pounded in his chest and a deep feeling of finality came over him. He let anger set in and camouflage the hurt. Didn't take her long to counter his offer. Bet she wanted money, but she sure as hell wasn't going to get it. With his pocketknife, he slit the seal and looked inside. Along with the folded papers was a small manila packet about the size of something to hold a key. He dropped it in his shirt pocket.

He unfolded the papers and started to read. The first page was a lease agreement for her land. Though surprised she'd thought about leasing so quickly, the price and terms were fair. He set it aside and turned to the divorce papers. With each word, his heart grew colder. She didn't make one counter offer, didn't ask for anything, and had petitioned to have her maiden name restored. Just like that, they'd set in motion the dissolution of their marriage. No squabbling, bickering over property, no heat—all calm, restrained, and cold.

A deep sense of grief washed over Lucas. He dropped his head back against the seat and closed his eyes. Gail, his wife, had slept with another man and torn his life asunder. How could she have done it? They'd had everything. Except a child. They could have adopted children. Hell, he might've even considered a sperm bank. But no, she gets drunk, screws another man, and turns his life to shit.

Tears dropped from beneath his lashes and ran down his cheeks. He sat up and brushed them away with his hands. In the still warm weather, the residue evaporated quickly. Remembering the packet, he removed it from his pocket. He dumped the contents into his palm. Gail's wedding and engagement rings lay there, winking at him in the fading light. He closed his fist over them and surrendered to his despair. Sobs shook his body, their sound filling the cab of his truck. He turned on the radio and upped the volume in hopes of hiding the resonance of his anguish.

~*~

Tuesday Lucas drove into Austin to see Dr. Jamison. He sat in the plush office chair while the doctor looked over his file. "There's a note in here from Dr. Lane. She has your wife's blood sample and is requesting one from you for paternity testing."

"My soon-to-be ex-wife is pregnant. I have doubts the child is mine. Not only do I have an extremely low sperm count, but my wife has been unfaithful."

"Oh dear, I hate to hear that."

"What, that my wife is pregnant or that I doubt I'm the father?"

"Why both, of course." Dr. Jamison looked back at his notes. "If you hadn't rushed out of here so fast back in August I would have explained to you that science is not always exact."

"What's that supposed to mean? You told me it would be a miracle if I ever fathered a child."

"Yes, that's what I said, but if you'd have let me finish, I'd have told you I've seen those miracles happen time after time." He took off his glasses and slipped them in his lab coat pocket. "Not as many as I'd like, but…"

Lucas felt like he was choking. Was it possible he could be the father? "Did those couples have paternity tests?"

The doctor shrugged. "Some did, some didn't."

"And?" asked Lucas.

"In most cases, the husband was the father, in others, they were not." He leaned back in his chair and steepled his hands. "Let me tell you something, son. Some of those men who discovered they weren't the father didn't really care anymore. The child their wife carried became their child."

"How could a man forgive his wife for getting pregnant by someone else?"

"Some of the men saw it as a gift of love on their wife's part. She loved him so much she was willing to turn to another man to give him a child. In those cases, the couple couldn't afford sperm bank prices." He shrugged. "And others felt it the ultimate betrayal and the couple divorced. But I have to say, among the couples where the men doubted and the child was his, the divorce rate was higher. His doubt destroyed her love for him."

For a moment Lucas doubted his decision to file for the divorce so quickly. But, no, she'd been unfaithful. He'd never be able to trust her again.

Dr. Jamison stood up. "Since you're here, let's go ahead and get both samples—one for a sperm count and one for DNA." Lucas followed him to an examination room. Thank goodness he wasn't going to have to strip this time. "For the paternity test, we can swab your mouth and use the buccal cells to match DNA." He took a long cotton swab and raked it around in his mouth and returned it to the vial it had come in. With a marker, he labeled it.

"How accurate is this test?" It seemed too simple to him to be any good.

"It's between 95-99% accurate. Do you know if the other man will be donating a sample for paternity testing?"

Lucas felt the muscles across his shoulders and neck tense and knot. He didn't give a rat's ass whether Alex Guthrie gave a sample or not. His anger was no reason to be uncivil, so he choked down his irritation. "I don't know."

Opening a door, he pulled out one of the containers for the sperm collection. He labeled it and handed it to Lucas. "You know the routine. Room number two is vacant."

His distaste must have shown because the doctor patted him on the back and smiled sympathetically. "I'll call you personally as soon as I get the sperm count back. The paternity test takes several weeks, so be patient."

~*~

Lucas patted Butterscotch's rump as he put her in the stall with her mother. He reached up and stroked the mare's neck. "She's doing well, mama. You can be proud of her progress."

His cell phone rang, startling both the mother and colt. Butterscotch skittered to her mother's flank and the mare turned, barring her baby from view. Lucas stepped out and closed the door before answering. "Hello..."

"Mr. Johnson, please hold for Dr. Jamison."

His heart thundered to the beat of the music as he waited on hold for the doctor to pick up.

"Lucas, this is Dr. Jamison. Are you where you can talk a minute?"

"Yes, sir, no one's here, but me and the horses."

"Okay, here it is. Your sperm count is up to almost double what it was before. Now, it's still not like it should be, but better." He cleared his throat. "I'm assuming you've not been having intercourse lately."

Lucas's face heated and he was glad the doctor couldn't see him. Why it should matter considering their conversation, he didn't know. "No, sir, Gail and I are separated."

"That could account for the rise. Been thinking about the fact that you ride a horse often. In some cases, a lot of time in the saddle has been known to affect a man's ability to produce sperm."

Good grief, he couldn't give up riding, could he? "You really think that could make a difference?"

"You never know. Just like some men who wear jockey shorts have to switch to boxers. Jockeys hold the testicles too close to the body, producing more heat— too much for the production of sperm. You wear jockeys?"

He cleared his throat. "Yes, sir."

"Change to boxers, then. Now, I know as a rancher you can't give up horseback riding, but easing back on it will help in sperm production. I'll call you when I get the paternity results."

"I...thank you for calling me personally, Dr. Jamison."

"You're welcome."

Chapter Sixteen

Sam's place, no, Gail's place now, looked different in the winter moonlight. Through the trees, bare of leaves, light glowed through the downstairs windows. In the summer, the cottonwoods around the house almost obscured it from view. Now their limbs looked like skeleton bones curling around the structure. A short distance away, live oaks grew so thick it was impossible to see through them. Deer loved the area.

Lucas sat on Grayboy and watched shadows pass by the windows. He hadn't intended to ride this far, or intrude on Gail's privacy, but was now glad he had. The house was too isolated and anyone could slip up unseen. Of course Chief would alert her, but she needed some outdoor lighting. He'd send Jim over to put up a motion detector light at each corner of the house. The one in the back would illuminate the garage if she had to drive in at night. It was the least he could do for Sam's daughter.

"Let's go home, boy."

The ride had comforted him. As he undressed, he lifted Gail's rings from the glass dresser tray on top of her vanity. The platinum engagement ring held a three-quarter karat princess cut diamond solitaire. It was smaller than what he'd wanted to buy, but Gail insisted anything bigger would look gaudy. She'd been right. The ring looked beautiful on her hand and suited her.

The wedding band was smooth and slightly wider. He tried to slip it on his little finger but it wouldn't reach his knuckle. Sighing, he placed them back on the tray, showered, and crawled into bed.

Arms folded under his head, he stared at the ceiling and remembered the night he'd come home from Austin. The day Ruth had come into their home and invaded their privacy. He and Gail have made love several times during the night. Was it possible he'd made her pregnant? The possibility sent a surge of joy through his body to be quickly replaced with pain and sadness. Their marriage was over, but if the child was his, he'd be the best father he could and treasure every moment they had together.

The news Alex had left town came as a big surprise. He'd thought Alex and Gail... Hell, he didn't know what he'd expected, but it wasn't his rival leaving town. Gail continued to surprise him. He never dreamed she'd sign those divorce papers so quickly. If he'd hoped she'd beg and plead for another chance, he'd been sorely disappointed. And if she had, would he have given it?

~*~

Jim worked to attach something to the eave of her house when she drove in the drive. She hit the garage door opener and pulled into the double garage her daddy had built when she was in high school. Chief greeted her as she slid out of the Lexus.

"Hey, boy, what's Jim doing here, hun?"

Chief barked and trotted over to the ladder. Jim called down. "Hey, Gail. Putting up some motion detector lights for security."

"Whose idea was that?" As if she didn't know.

Why couldn't he let her be? He didn't want her, so she wished he would leave her the hell alone.

"Lucas's I suppose. He sent me." He climbed down from the ladder. "I'm sure sorry to hear about you two splittin' up. Just don't seem right."

"Thank you, Jim. I appreciate you helping me, but please tell Lucas to let me take care of myself. I don't need him tending to my business."

The older man appeared shocked. "He's just trying to be helpful."

Gail choked back an angry epitaph. "Maybe, but I don't need or want his help."

She went into the house and called the hardware store to see how much the lights cost. To the price, she added twenty percent to cover Jim's labor. Then she called Lucas. He didn't answer, probably on purpose. At the beep, she recorded her message.

"Keep your good deeds to yourself. I don't need or want your help with anything. I'm sending a check to cover the lights and Jim's labor." She hung up.

~*~

Lucas received the call on a Friday morning in the middle of November. He'd driven to town to pick up supplies and had just parked his truck when his cell phone rang. When he saw Dr. Jamison's name and number, his heart jumped into his throat. He croaked out, "Hello."

"Lucas, this is Doctor Jamison. I've got those results. Where are you?"

"I'm parked in front of the hardware store."

"Good. Don't want you running off the road. The results show you're definitely the baby's father. Congratulations, Lucas."

Lucas couldn't speak. Tears welled in his eyes and he fought for control. He tried again, but only managed a croak.

"I understand, son. No need to say anything. Call if I can help you in any way. "Oh, do you want to know the child's sex?"

He managed to croak out, "Yes."

Dr. Jamison laughed. "It's a girl." The line went dead.

He punched the off button and dropped his phone in the passenger seat. A girl, they were having a sweet baby with dark hair and blue eyes like Gail. God, he was so happy he wanted to jump out of the truck and shout to the heavens. He and Gail were having a child. A grin stretched his face, but his joy dimmed as an ache formed in the pit of his stomach. They were no longer a couple and would never be one again. Gail had been unfaithful and though she'd been drunk, and not fully to blame, he couldn't get past it. He would miss so much of his child's life—her birth, watching her nurse at Gail's breast, and slipping in at night to smooth the covers and watch her sleep. He prayed their child would be healthy. He sighed. What a turn his life had taken. Starting the truck, he backed out and was halfway home when he remembered he'd forgotten to pick up his supplies at the hardware store.

~*~

Gail had just gotten home when her phone rang. She kicked off her shoes and reached for the wall phone in the kitchen. "Hello."

"Gail? Dr. Lane here."

Her heart jumped into her throat. She sat down at the table. "Hello, Doctor, are you calling about the paternity tests?"

"Yes. Lucas is definitely your baby's father."

"I know. I learned from Alex that we weren't intimate."

"Do you want to know the baby's sex?"

Did she? "Yes."

"It's a baby girl. For her sake, I hope things work out for you and Lucas."

Tears pooled in her eyes and rolled down her cheeks. She batted them away with her hand. "Lucas filed for divorce. I'm not contesting." Her voice broke. "I...I didn't tell him about Alex's confession."

Silence loomed for a minute.

"Are you sure you're doing the right thing?"

"No, but it's done."

"I'm very sorry. You take care of yourself and I'll see you soon." She disconnected.

Gail dropped her head onto her arms and cried. Chief whined and nuzzled her leg. She bent to hug him.

"I'm okay, boy. We're having a baby girl, Chief. What do you think about that?"

Chief yipped and she managed a shaky laugh.

Oh, Lucas, what happened to us? I destroyed our happiness before we had a chance to experience a family.

She jumped out of her skin when the phone rang again. Who could be calling now? She looked at the caller ID. It was Lucas and she didn't want to talk to him. On the 5th ring the answering machine picked up.

"Gail?" She stuffed a fist in her mouth at the sound of his voice. Had he heard about the baby already? He cleared his throat. "Dr. Jamison called with the news." His voice broke. "I'm so happy about the baby...our daughter." She let the tears run freely, grateful she was alone. "I...I wish things were different." After a moment of silence, he hung up. Gail gasped for air, trying to prevent the sobs, but failed.

~*~

Saturday morning, Gail sipped her tea at the kitchen table while she read the last entry in her mother's diary.

Today I'm leaving. It hurts to leave my baby girl, but I can't take her until I have a job. I'll be returning for her as soon as possible. If Sam suspects something, he's not let on. He's a good man and my going will break his heart, but staying and pretending is wrong.

Ruth knows my plans but has promised to tell no one. Lamar has offered me a ride to Canada. Thank goodness Randall stepped in and Sharon is out of the picture. I can't say I'm in love with Lamar, but he's interesting and is offering me a chance for a more exciting life.

I took one last peek at my sleeping daughter and kissed her sweet face. Mommy will be back, sweetie.

Gail wiped a tear from her cheek. How could a mother leave her child? She placed her hand on the one growing inside her. The little toot had played around all night. She thought she'd never get to sleep.

She heard a car pull up. Chief stood and yipped a greeting at the back door. Oh dear, it must be Lucas. *What's he doing here?* She opened the door and Chief ran to greet him as he strode toward the house. In his sheepskin jacket, jeans, and hat, he looked the typical rancher. She watched his loose-jointed gait as he approached and swallowed her self-pity at losing him.

Sweeping his hat off, he ran a hand through his

thick hair. "Good morning. I'm sorry for not calling. Can we talk a minute?"

"About what? Seems everything has been said."

Jaw tense, he bit out the words. "It would help if we could keep this civil."

Gail stepped back so he could come in. She didn't invite him to sit down or offer him coffee.

He picked up the copy of June's diary and flipped through the pages. "Learn anything?"

"Is that what you're here about?"

"You're not going to make this easy, are you?" When she didn't answer, he leaned against the kitchen counter. "Do you ever wonder how your mother's suitcase got back in this house, in the attic?"

Of course she wondered, all the time. Angry, she sputtered, "Yes, but you'll never make me believe Daddy did it."

He frowned. "I'd never try to make you believe that. I don't think he did it either, but somebody sure as hell did."

She took a calming breath and nodded.

Lucas folded his arms across his chest. "Why didn't you press charges against Ruth?"

"She just wanted to see the diary, Lucas. It's not like she tried to take money or something valuable."

"She broke into our home, Gail. She took your father's key and invaded our privacy and hurt Chief. You should've pressed charges."

"Lucas, she's a member of the family. Would you have pressed charges if your mother or father came into our home uninvited?"

Gail knew she'd hit a nerve when his nostrils flared. "That's not the same thing and you know it."

"Yes, that's right—they're not *that* kind of people."

"Dammit, Gail, that's not what I meant and you know it."

She walked away, but he caught her at the door. His hands were gentle on her shoulders. "Have you ever thought it might have been Ruth who killed your mother and that man?"

"Yes, I have, but I don't believe Ruth capable of murder, especially not of murdering my mother, a woman she loved."

"Think about it some more. How did that suitcase get in the attic? She knew where your father kept his guns and she wanted to read the diary bad enough to break into our home."

Gail's chest felt like it would explode. What he said made sense but...

The front door opened and Ruth called out. "Yoo-hoo, it's me, Gail."

Lucas squeezed her shoulders. "Just think about it, please."

She nodded and pushed through the kitchen door. Lucas followed.

At the sight of him, Ruth blushed scarlet and stammered. "Lucas, I... It's good to see you."

"I wish I could say the same."

Gail's jaw dropped and she screeched, "Lucas!"

"What? I'm not as forgiving as you, Gail." He looked at Ruth. "If I'd had my way, Ruth, you'd have gone to jail rather than put in hours of public service. Understand this, your little story about the diary didn't fool me one bit."

Ruth's chin quivered. "I'm sorry, so sorry, I don't

know what got into me, but I did want to read—"

Lucas held up his hand. "Save it for someone else, Ruth. And don't ever lay a hand on another one of my animals." He turned to Gail. "Remember what I said."

He pushed through the swinging door. A second later she heard the closing of the back door and the slap of the screen door.

"He hates me now," Ruth cried. She burst into tears.

Gail put her arm around the sobbing woman. "Don't worry, he'll get over it in time." She wished she knew that for a fact because she'd rarely seen Lucas so angry. "Why don't you work on Daddy's room today? Put all the clothes in his closet in boxes and we'll take them into town to the church."

Ruth nodded, hung her coat in the closet, and started upstairs.

Gail found Ruth in her father's room hidden in the long closet that traveled the length of one wall and opened into the next bedroom. As a child Gail had loved to play in the dark area. It was her secret tunnel.

"Ruth?"

A squeal came from inside and Ruth's head emerged from among the clothes. "You scared the dickens out of me."

Gail chuckled as she fingered some of the hanging garments. "Sorry. I didn't realize Daddy had so many clothes."

"Honey, I don't think he ever threw anything away. Even some of your mama's old clothes are stuck back in here."

"Really? I'd like to see those. Bet they're pretty funky looking."

Ruth snorted. "Maybe, but hang on to them long enough and they'll be in style again."

Gail stepped back and looked at the boxes Ruth had already filled. She picked up a shirt and breathed in the scent of starch and fresh air. An old suit coat still held onto the smell of stale cigarette smoke. She dropped them back into the box.

"I think I'll lie down for a while."

In her room, she stretched out on the bed, pulled a throw over her, and nestled her head into the pillow. She'd sleep for just a few minutes.

~*~

Ruth went downstairs and ate a quick bite. Going through Sam's things depressed her. And his room was creepy. She could feel his presence in the room looking over her shoulder. Once she'd jerked around thinking someone had touched her. She shivered. After stacking her plate in the sink, she went back upstairs.

The boxes she'd filled and labeled were closed and ready to be carted away. A few of Sam's things still remained in the closet and drawers, but Gail would want to decide about those. The room had grown chilly and she looked around to see if a window was open. All were closed tight. She peeked outside to see if the temperature had dropped. From the intensity of the sun, it looked to have warmed up. She shrugged and started to turn away from the window when she felt a cold draft of air hit her neck. Jerking around, she probed the corners of the room, her eyes straining to see whatever had spooked her. Nothing.

Hugging herself, she tried to warm up and started for the door. It was time to get out of here. As she passed the old wardrobe with its murky mirror, she caught her reflection. She reached up to brush a curl from her forehead when another reflection joined hers. Sam stared at her, his eyes filled with hate. Frozen, unable to move, she gaped in horror as his white image turned into two hands. They closed around her neck, cutting off her air. A low hiss echoed around her.

Did you think I wouldn't find out?

Frantic, Ruth clutched her throat, trying to break the hold as she hung in the air and was shaken like a rag doll. Kicking, trying to scream, she struggled with the unseen force. Suddenly the grip relaxed, she fell to the floor, and drew in a deep breath. Smoke hit her lungs and they instantly rebelled. Keening in fear, gasping and coughing, she finally managed to choke out a scream.

~*~

Gail woke to a woman's screams. She jumped up from the bed and ran into the hall. Ruth flew from her father's room, stumbling, half crawling on the floor wailing, "Nooo, nooo." Gail thrust out her arms to prevent colliding.

She grasped the older woman's shoulders. "What is it? What's wrong?"

Ruth clutched her around the legs and buried her face against her knees. "Gh-ost...your daddy's ghost."

The woman shook so bad her shudders vibrated up Gail's body. She bent and rubbed Ruth's back. "You don't believe in ghosts. Something just spooked you in there."

Ruth lifted her head and shook it violently. "No...it was him. I saw him in that old mirror. He tried to choke me to death."

Gail wanted to laugh, but fear crept in and stole the

inclination. The woman had gone over the edge or was about to. She pulled Ruth up off the floor. "Come on now, you know how wavy that old mirror is. I don't doubt you saw something reflected there, but it wasn't Daddy."

She pulled away and moved down the hall. "Come on, let's go back in there and look around."

"No, no, I'm scared," Ruth keened. She grabbed onto Gail's arm, dug in her heels, and wouldn't let go.

Gail pried Ruth's fingers from her arm. "Let go, Ruth. Either come with me or wait here." Sobbing, Ruth wrapped her arms around her waist, shook her head, and backed up. She spun on her heel and ran downstairs. Gail heard the door open and bang closed.

Cold air struck her as she entered. She rubbed her arms to warm them. Boxes sat around the room. Everything looked normal. She shrugged and started to turn away when she caught a whiff of cigarette smoke. Her gaze flew to the mirror and the reflection of a smoke ring. As she stared in shock, it left the mirror, grew larger, and then dissipated. She opened her mouth to scream, yet a sense of calm washed over her. The tenseness left her body. She smiled and choked out a laugh. She wanted to say, "Hello, Daddy," but she didn't believe in ghosts. Her imagination was running wild, and Ruth needed a vacation or a doctor. Darned if she might not need one, too.

Chapter Seventeen

The first Friday in December, just before closing, Gail looked up to see Lucas standing in the doorway of her office. As always, his handsome visage made her heart flutter. He wore starched jeans with a suede leather coat over a white shirt. She slowly released her breath to calm herself. Lines had appeared around his mouth and eyes that hadn't been there when she'd last seen him. "What are you doing here?"

He twirled his hat in his hand. "I wanted to see if you'd go to dinner with me tonight. So we could talk."

"What about? Can't we discuss it here?"

"I'd rather not."

She wanted to be fair. "All right." He helped her into her coat and they left the building with a dozen pairs of eyes watching them go.

At the curb, he said, "I can bring you back for your car or you can follow me."

"Where are we going?"

"How about the steak house?"

"Fine, I'll follow you then." It was on her way home and she didn't see any need for them to make the trip back to town for her car.

Lucas waited for her when she pulled into the big parking lot. When he closed her car door, after helping her out, he took both of her arms and studied her face. A sad expression crossed his face. He reached up to run his fingers through her hair.

Gail froze, her heart in her throat at the familiarity of his tender touch.

"You've cut your hair." He smiled with what she assumed was regret. "I noticed it awhile back when at your house, but was too mad about Ruth to mention it. It suits you, but I'll miss your long tresses."

The wind caught a strand and blew it across her face. She brushed it back. "It'll be easier to take care of when the baby arrives."

Lucas nodded, and as if suddenly remembering the cool temperature, took her arm and they walked toward the restaurant. They were escorted to a booth at the back and sat facing each other.

They studied the menus for a minute. When the waitress returned, Gail ordered salmon and steamed vegetables. Lucas ordered his usual, steak.

Lucas cleared his throat. "How are you feeling? Any more morning sickness?"

"I feel good, haven't been sick in several weeks."

He nodded. "You look good. Pregnancy agrees with you. For a while there, you had me worried. I thought you had some dread disease."

"Yeah, well I felt like it, too." She shuddered. "Morning sickness is terrible. Much worse than a stomach virus."

"I'm glad you're over that part." He played with his silverware. "I hope you don't mind, but I called and talked to Dr. Lane today. She said you and the baby are doing well."

Gail didn't know what to say. She couldn't decide whether to be angry or touched. Touched won out.

Voice thick, Lucas said, "I'm glad."

She smiled faintly and nodded, the moment awkward. Gail felt sorry for the man across from her, the man she'd given her heart to. Pain etched his brow and she had to bite her lip to keep from crying. All the years she'd known him, he'd seemed so sure of himself, so brave and strong. His vulnerability felt like a dagger to her heart. She knew he wanted this baby and it hurt that he didn't want her, too. Again she wondered if she was wrong not to tell him the truth.

The waitress approached and slid plates in front of them. During the meal they kept the conversation neutral and for a short time, Gail forgot they were separated.

"That was delicious. You really should try something besides beef."

"That'd be a betrayal of my profession." He pushed his plate back. "Actually, your salmon did look good. Maybe next time I'll try it."

"I'll believe it when I see it."

"Would you like dessert?"

"Goodness, no. I couldn't eat another bite. You go ahead though."

Lucas ordered apple pie and coffee. Gail had a cup of hot tea. She sipped it and watched Lucas eat his pie. When he'd eaten the last bite, she asked, "What did you want to talk to me about?"

His relaxed body stiffened and he studied his empty plate for a minute before lifting his eyes to hers. "Have you talked to Alex, told him he's not the baby's father?"

"No, Alex and I don't keep in touch."

His jaw dropped. It would be hard for Lucas to understand a man not being interested in his child. And she wasn't being truthful, since the man knew he couldn't be. "He never thought he was the father."

"What. Why not?"

She reached for her handbag and coat. "I think I better go. Chief needs feeding." *And I don't want to answer any more of your questions.*

He took money from his wallet and tossed it on the table.

Gail stood and slipped into her coat. Lucas took her arm and walked her to her car.

She retrieved her keys. "Thank you for dinner."

"Gail, we didn't get to finish talking. Can I come over for a minute?" He smiled. "I'd like to see Chief, too. I miss him."

How could she deny him time with his dog? "All right. Just for a short while."

~*~

Gail parked in the garage Sam had built ten or so years ago. When Chief saw his truck, he started barking and leaping into the air. He pulled in behind Gail and got out and greeted his dog. They played for a minute and then he walked in the back door with Gail.

"I'll put on a pot of coffee."

Lucas took the carafe from her and moved to the sink. "You go ahead and change clothes, I'll make it."

"All right."

A few minutes later she came back downstairs in leggings and a warm knit shirt. He tried not to stare at her shapely legs and the small mound protruding under the shirt. He'd about give his arm to be able to splay his hand across it and feel the life growing there.

Gail filled him a cup and quickly made a cup of hot tea in the microwave. They took their drinks into the living room. She curled up on the sofa and he took her daddy's recliner.

He looked around the room. She'd done a little decorating, purchased a new rug and curtains. It looked homey and comfortable as always. In the corner, at the foot of the stairs, were a gallon of paint and several rolls of wallpaper. From where he sat, it looked like the paper had ducks on it. She'd purchased decorations for the baby's room. His heart dropped to his stomach. He wished they could share the project. After all, it was his child too. For several weeks, he'd been struggling with the idea of forgiving her and taking her back. Her unfaithfulness hadn't been planned, stupid on her part, but she hadn't set out to hurt him. He didn't want to still love her, but he did. He turned to see her watching him.

His throat tightened, making it hard to talk. "You shouldn't be painting. It might hurt the baby."

"I talked to Dr. Lane. She said in a well ventilated area, the fumes wouldn't hurt her."

The image of a dark haired toddler formed in his mind. The picture was so adorable he felt even more miserable. He cleared his throat. "I could help you paint. You don't need to be standing on a ladder. Let me help you."

Taking a sip of her tea, she stared off into space. Lucas saw the tears in her eyes and his confusion grew. She'd hurt him and damned if she didn't act like he was the one at fault.

"Never mind, forget I asked."

"What else did you want to talk about, Lucas?"

"I would like to go with you to Austin for your next check-up." There, he'd said it. He had a right to know how she and the baby were doing.

"Okay, I'll let you know what day and time the week before."

Her ease in agreeing surprised Lucas. Maybe she thought his involvement would help him forgive her. If she'd hoped for reconciliation, why had she signed the divorce papers so quickly? And returned her rings. It hurt to think they'd meant so little to her.

"Why did you sign the divorce papers so fast, without fighting for anything?" If she'd wanted to hurt him further, she'd succeeded. "Did you even read them?"

"Yes, I read them and they're fair. Why should I fight you for something I don't need just to be vindictive? I have everything I need right here. As far as the wedding gifts go, I don't want anything to remind me of what we had together. Yes, I was at fault, but you made it clear forgiveness wasn't in your vocabulary." She gasped out a sob. "And you didn't even have the decency to wait to see if you were this child's father before you filed."

"How dare you condemn me after what you did?"

"I didn't hurt you on purpose. Can you truthfully say you didn't file with such speed to hurt me, get back at me?"

He didn't answer.

She sneered. "I didn't think so. That's why I immediately went to Jeff. He wanted me to contest, to ask for a settlement, but I wanted you to have what you sought—a divorce from the woman who'd betrayed you." She dropped her feet to the floor and slammed her cup on the coffee table. "And now that you have it, why can't you leave me alone? Stop sending Jim over here to do odd jobs. I can damn well take care of myself and I don't want you worrying about me, thinking about me. Just leave me the hell alone."

She shot up, reached over, and yanked the coffee cup from his hand. "It'll be bad enough you'll be here visiting the baby after she's born and going with me to the doctor on occasion. I'd like you to leave."

Lucas was stunned beyond belief. The gall of the woman trying to make him into the bad guy. He stood up. "This divorce isn't my fault and no matter how you twist things around, you're the one who screwed around with another man."

Her face colored. For a minute he thought she'd slap him. Hell if he knew why. She wasn't the injured party. He'd welcome the sting on his jaw to ease the ache in his heart.

"That's right. I'm a slut. I've known one other man besides you." Her face twisted in torment. "Of course you can't say you've only been with one other woman besides me. If we can stay below ten, it would be a miracle, wouldn't it?" Tears ran down her face as she spat out, "And you know what's such a shame?" The laughter that ripped from her mouth wasn't the pretty sound he'd always loved. "I don't remember a thing about my night of sin. I can't even say if he's better in the sack than you are."

~*~

Gail hated herself for not telling Lucas the truth. But he acted so damned high and mighty. If he'd just waited a while longer to file for divorce, at least until he knew he was the baby's father, she would have. Evidently he'd been furious when he and Alex had fought. He'd probably been embarrassed everyone in town had known what'd happened or supposedly had anyway.

She dried her tears and brewed another cup of tea. Her Christmas lights twinkled, reminding her of how lonely she'd be this year without her father and Lucas. Sharon, anger having cooled slightly, had invited her to dinner with them, but she'd probably not go. Being around Lucas caused too much pain.

She really didn't blame Sharon for her harsh words the day she'd learned about Gail's infidelity. In her shoes, Gail would have felt the same way. The threat about taking her child was something else entirely. They were words thrown in anger and she didn't really believe the Johnsons would fight for custody. A child needed her grandparents. She'd forgive Sharon for her daughter's sake.

If she told Lucas the truth now, if he wanted her back, she feared it would be more for the baby's sake than because he loved her. Plus, knowing Alex had seen her naked might be as bad for Lucas as the sex act itself. Who knew how a man's mind worked?

The only way they could reconcile is if Lucas forgave her for being stupid and could love her as much as he had before. She couldn't accept anything less. It would be better to raise the baby apart than live together in a marriage lacking in total love and trust.

~*~

The drive from Gail's to Bubba's went by in a blur. Her last remark had sent him stomping out of the house. He'd wanted to slap her and the thought horrified him. What did the women he'd been with before they'd gotten together have to do with anything? Not a damn thing. Gail was grasping at straws to make herself feel better, trying to excuse her behavior and make him feel bad.

He grabbed a stool at the crowded bar and ordered two beers. The first he threw back and emptied in three gulps. The second he savored as he watched the reflection of the dancers in the mirror. As usual on Friday nights, Bubba's was packed. Christmas would be in a couple of weeks so colored lights and greenery hung in swags from the posts separating the dance floor from the tables.

Tabitha passed by, partnered with one of Jason's ranch hands. She grinned and wiggled her fingers in his direction. Dressed seductively as usual in tight black jeans and a leopard skin knit top, her outfit left little to imagine as to what she wore underneath. The woman dressed like a slut, but Lucas knew she was selective when it came to her bed partners. Why she wanted to give the impression of a loose woman, he didn't know. Maybe insecurity on her part.

In the mirror, Lucas watched Tabitha approach. He swiveled on the stool and waited, watching the fluid movement of her breasts and hips. She stopped in front of him. "How about this dance, cowboy?"

Why the hell not? He grinned. "My pleasure, darlin'."

The song was a slow number and Tabitha pressed against him in eager invitation. He savored the feel of her soft breasts pressed against him. His body responded and he pulled her closer. When the music stopped, he draped his arm across her shoulders and led her to a vacant table. "You with somebody tonight?"

"Nope, came with a bunch of girlfriends." She scooted her chair close to his and laid her hand on his leg. "They won't miss me."

Lucas signaled the waitress. "What are you drinking?"

"Same as always, sugar."

He ordered four beers and a plate of hot wings.

"So, you and the wife haven't worked things out?"

"Are you really interested or just making conversation?"

"Why of course I'm interested."

When she'd first moved to town, he'd been a freshman in college. They'd spent a lot of time together, a good part of it in bed. Then she'd moved and he'd started seeing someone else.

"No, I've filed for divorce."

She smiled seductively. "So, the rumors are true. She cheated with Alex Guthrie and you kicked her out."

He turned, put his arm over the back of her chair, and fixed her with a steady glare. "I don't want to talk about my marriage. If you plan to hang around me tonight, drop it."

"Okay, sugar, whatever you say."

She pulled his head down. His face mere inches from hers, he battled with his conscience. Then remembered Gail's words. His lips met Tabitha's in a searing kiss. He'd meant to banish his wife's image from his mind, but the kiss only emphasized the shallowness of this encounter. Hurting, he was deep in the dumps. Hopefully a few beers would ease his grief.

Their hot wings arrived. Lucas enjoyed the heat of the pepper and the soothing cold beer as it eased the fire in his mouth. As soon as they'd emptied the plate, Tabitha pulled him back onto the dance floor. He enjoyed the loud music and exercise. And for a short while, he forgot his life was in shambles.

"Let's go. I'll give you a ride home."

"Sure, baby. Let me visit the ladies room first. I'll meet you by the door."

When he stopped in front of her house, he killed the engine and walked around to help her out. It was dark around her place, no lights on inside or out. The neighbor's dog started barking, but quit when his owner gave a sharp command.

"How do you keep from breaking a leg without any light?"

She giggled. "Stand here a minute and your eyes will adjust."

The air felt cool and she shivered. He rubbed his hands up and down her arms, easing the goose bumps away. She moaned and leaned toward him. Their mouths met and the kiss was primitive and hot. She broke away and pulled him up the steps onto her porch. As she struggled to get the key in the lock, his hands covered her breasts, his arousal pressed against her buttocks. The door opened and they fell into the room. He kicked the door shut and followed Tabitha into her bedroom.

Chapter Eighteen

As usual, Lucas woke as the sun crept over the horizon and lightened the sky. As the haze of sleep lifted, awareness he wasn't alone sunk in. Warmth radiated from the woman nestled against his side. Joy leapt in his heart and he turned to snuggle Gail closer, only to freeze at the sight of blond hair draped over his arm. Tabitha still slept, her face looking younger than her years without the heavy makeup. *Oh, God. What have I done?* Anger had overridden his good sense. He shouldn't be here. He was still married and by noon word that he'd shacked up with Tabitha would be bandied about town. Plus, it wasn't fair to Tabitha. He didn't care about her and their night together might give her false hope. His behavior would be viewed by Gail as the final insult. Remorse settled in his belly. He'd let his wounded pride dictate his actions. Not a fact to be proud of. Disgusted with himself, he shut his eyes to try to blot out the picture of his stupidity.

Tabitha mumbled something in her sleep and rolled onto her side. He quickly eased his arm from under her head, got up, and gathered his clothes. In the living room, he dressed and searched the kitchen for something to write on. Beside the refrigerator, he found a pad and pencil. He wrote a note for Tabitha and walked back into the bedroom to leave it on the bedside table.

As he let himself out the front door, the neighbor's dog started barking again. The curtains lifted and then dropped as he rounded his truck to get in. The dog continued to bark. His truck roared to life and he drove out of the small housing area, feeling worse than he had when he'd left Gail's the night before. His only comfort was he'd had enough sense to ask Tabitha if she had condoms and she had.

~*~

Ruth arrived early Saturday morning. Gail was anxious to get started on painting the baby's room, but needed the furniture moved. She called Jim. An hour later, he and Jamie, a kid who worked for Lucas, were on the back porch.

"Morning, Miss Gail, Ruth." Jim tipped his hat. The boy nodded shyly.

"Come on in." She moved so they could enter the big kitchen. The odor of Ruth's baking filled the air and Jamie looked with interest toward the oven. "Now that I have you here, I wonder if after you moved the furniture you'd be interested in doing some painting for me. I'll pay you whatever you think is fair."

"We've got all day as far as I know." He turned to Jamie. "You game, son?"

"Yes, sir."

Gail led them from the kitchen to the stairs. "Come on up."

Jim stood just inside the room and surveyed the three-piece set. "Where you plan to put all this stuff?"

The bedroom suite was an old cheap set purchased in the 1940's. Veneered wood had been popular and many of the styles were rounded. The handles appeared to be Bakelite. Some people were trying to replicate the look, but not her.

"I'll have to put it in the garage for now. Know anyone who'd want a vintage set like this?"

"Might be that antique store downtown would sell it for you. Lord knows, she's got a lot of junk like this old thing. Has big prices on it, too."

His suggestion wasn't a bad idea. Then she wouldn't have to worry about finding someone to take it. "Would you mind taking it in for me?"

"Not at all." Jim started taking drawers out of the chest. He nodded toward the bed. "What about the mattress and springs?"

"Guess they'll have to go in the garage."

It didn't take the two men long to load the furniture and leave for town. When they returned, Jim handed Gail a check for $400.00. She was stunned the three pieces had brought that much. "Thanks, Jim. With this I may have you two do all the work in the baby's room."

"Be glad to. We'll see how much we can get done today."

Ruth sat a plate of cinnamon buns on the table. "First have some coffee and a sweet roll."

"Ruth, darlin', I thought you'd never ask."

Gail tried not to giggle at the indignant expression on the woman's face. She smacked him with an oven mitt. "I am not your darlin' and I'll thank you to remember that."

Jim snorted. "Could be, if you'd loosen up a little." He sat down and helped himself to a roll. "Mmm, mmm. Delicious." Reaching over, he pulled out a seat for Jamie. "Have a seat, boy. Don't ever say no to good eats like this."

Jamie ducked his head and sat down at the table.

After three rolls each, Jim and Jamie were ready to talk business.

Gail had a pad and pencil and started making a diagram. "I want the paper on the bottom half and paint on the upper half. Then I'm going to buy two inch molding to put around the room where they join."

"You want the molding, baseboards, and door frames painted?" Jim asked.

"I think white would look good. What do you think?"

"What color crib do you plan on getting? I'd go with the same color wood. Kinda tie everything together."

Gail bit her lip as she thought. There was so much baby furniture to choose from and she'd not had a chance to look other than in the catalogue. "I think I'd like to keep the furniture a medium oak. It would go with the house better."

She stood and pulled the JC Penney catalogue out of a drawer. The page was marked with a paper clip. When she sat it on the table, it fell open to the crib she'd almost settled on. "This is what I think I want." It was a Jenny Lind style with a matching chest and dressing table. The old rocker from the sewing room would be perfect with it.

Ruth leaned in to look. "Oh, I like that, it has an old-fashioned look." She poured them all another cup of coffee. "Why not just clean up the baseboards and frames and stain the molding to match?"

"That's a great idea. Sounds perfect." She turned to Jim and Jamie. "You two up to it?"

"You bet."

"Yes, ma'am." Jamie's head bobbed up and down.

"Then, let's get to work. The supplies are at the foot of the stairs." They left the kitchen and she started to follow.

Ruth hovered near the sink, drawing dishwater.

"Leave that, Ruth. Don't you want to help us with the painting?"

She kept her eyes on the rising water. "No, y'all go ahead. I think I'll clean up down here and wax the kitchen floor."

Gail looked down at the shiny floor. It'd been waxed less than a month ago, and with just the two of them traipsing in and out, it didn't need it again. Something wasn't right, and Gail was afraid it had to do with Ruth's fear of her daddy's room. Or, she should say, his supposed ghost. She hadn't been back up there since her last scare.

"Ruth, Daddy's ghost is not upstairs in his bedroom. If he wanted to haunt us, he'd have the full run of the place."

Ruth's shoulders tensed. "If it's okay with you, I'd like to finish up down here and go home. I don't feel so well."

"Ruth—"

The older woman spun around. Face pale and pinched, her eyes looked wildly around the room. Gail took a step toward her, but Ruth put out her hands to ward her off.

"No, I gotta go. Sorry." She tore off her apron, grabbed her purse off the counter, and while stuffing her arms in her coat, backed out the door. "I'm sorry."

"Ruth, please, I'm worried about you." Gail reached out for her arm.

She jerked free and hissed. "Don't touch me."

Afraid she'd cause the woman to fall down the porch steps, Gail moved back. "You need to see Doc. You're taking Daddy's death too hard. I know you loved him, but…"

Before she could finish, Ruth turned and was down the steps, running in the direction of her car. At the door of her Ford, she looked back at Gail, and then got in and drove away.

Gail didn't know what to think or who to call, but she feared Ruth was having a nervous breakdown. Since her daddy's death, Ruth had lost weight and jumped if a feather dropped. She'd never been a nervous person, or at least didn't seem so to Gail. But she'd been wrapped up in her own life, so probably wouldn't have noticed.

Trying to decide what to do, she walked upstairs. Maybe Ruth needed time away from here. There were too many memories in this house for her to cope with right now.

Jim had cracked two windows to provide a cross breeze and cut the paint fumes. Both men were taping around the woodwork so she opened a can of paint and poured some into the roller pan. Rolling on the paint relaxed her and she loved watching the color transform the room. With the three of them working, it didn't take long to finish the job. They stood back and admired their work.

"Looks real good," Jim said. "Nice and cheerful for a baby."

It was a good color, not too bright, but not pale either. "Yeah, it does. I love it."

"You want us to start the wallpaper today?"

"No, let's wait until tomorrow. Do you mind

working Sunday afternoon?"

They both agreed to be there at one o´clock. When she'd seen them to the door and locked up, she returned to the nursery. She couldn't resist putting up a couple of sheets of paper. Little yellow ducks floated along in blue water. An occasional bullfrog perched on a lily pad surrounded by reeds added additional color and rhythm to the design. She was pleased with her choices.

Gail tried to call and check on Ruth, but she kept getting her answering machine. Sunday morning she tried again. No luck. Hopefully she'd see her at church. Sharon and Randall were waiting for her on the church steps.

Sharon said, "I know I said some hateful things to you, and I'm not taking them all back, but you are the mother of our son's child. Will you sit with us this morning, Gail?"

"Okay. I'd like that." As they walked in, they drew a lot of attention and she couldn't help but notice a buzz of something in the air. Instead of sitting by his wife, Randall sat on Gail's other side. She was wedged in between the two older people. Odd, they'd never seemed this clingy before.

Randall put his arm around her and whispered. "I can't tell you how excited we are about a granddaughter."

"I'm pleased too, though I'd have been just as happy about a boy."

He chuckled. "Yeah, us, too."

As they left the church, Gail received several sympathetic glances. Childhood friends stopped to chat and offer congratulations on the baby and sympathy about the divorce. She didn't understand why they were being so solicitous today. Their attention made her uncomfortable. Noticing her agitation, Randall and Sharon whisked her off to the parking lot. Sharon took her arm. "Why don't you come over for lunch today? We'd love to visit with you."

"I'd like to, but Jim and Jamie are meeting me at one o'clock to paper the nursery."

"The nursery. Did you hear that, Randall? She's started the nursery. Can we come see it?"

"Of course. It should be finished by next weekend."

"Have you picked out furniture?" Sharon's eyes sparkled with pleasure.

"Yes, it's a medium oak spindle type crib. I just love it and it'll look great in the room. Though I have to admit, it was hard to make up my mind."

Randall cleared his throat. "Let us buy the set for our grandchild? It'd mean a great deal to us." Gail looked up at Lucas's father and saw the sincerity in his eyes. His resemblance to Lucas made her throat tighten.

"I'd like that, too. Thank you."

Sharon hugged her. "Thank you." There were tears in her eyes and Gail struggled to keep hers at bay. "Tell Jim to bring us the particulars on the set and we'll get it to you next week."

Randall kissed her forehead. "Take care of yourself. We're here if you need us."

~*~

It wasn't until Gail was in the car on her way home that she remembered Ruth hadn't been in church. She swung by her house, but her car wasn't in the drive. Ruth's sister didn't live in Stony Creek any longer and as far as Gail knew, Ruth had no other living relatives.

She'd call the sister tomorrow if she hadn't heard from Ruth by then.

Jim and Jamie were waiting for her on the back steps. Chief kept them company and got his ears scratched for his efforts. He left them when she got out and greeted her excitedly.

"Hey, boy, are you taking care of our company?"

He woofed and ran back to the men.

"Have you guys eaten?"

"Yes, ma'am, ate at the bunkhouse."

Jim opened the screen door and held it while she used her key. Chief followed them in the house and went to his water bowl. "You guys go ahead and get started then. I'm going to change and eat something real quick."

"Take your time. We can handle this. Can't say I'd want to hang paper for a living, but do know my way around it."

She hung her coat in the entry closet as they trudged upstairs. Jim hollered down, "Hey, this piece you put up looks good. Little bugger's gonna love these ducks."

"Thanks. I hope so."

In her bedroom she changed into stretch pants, a loose top, and tennis shoes. She stuck her head in the nursery door and it appeared the two men knew what they were doing. Jamie painted the adhesive to the wall while Jim measured, cut, and placed it on the wall. Jamie came along behind and smoothed it with a wide, short bristled brush, and then wiped the surface clean with a damp sponge.

"You guys are doing such a good job, I don't think you need me."

Jamie grinned. "You can supervise, ma'am." The boy acted more at ease today.

"I'm good at that."

Downstairs, she heated leftover beef and barley soup and fixed a sandwich. It was a filling lunch and the hot soup warmed her. She sat her dishes in the sink and went upstairs. Hopefully, climbing these stairs ten times a day would help her keep the weight off. In the nursery, she sat in the rocker she'd dragged from the sewing room the night before and watched.

Jim asked. "Ruth coming over today? Didn't expect her to leave so soon yesterday."

"I didn't either." She didn't know how much to tell him. "She wasn't feeling well and I'm worried. I tried several times last night to call her and again this morning. She wasn't in church, and when I drove by her house, her car wasn't in the drive." With her toes, she sat the rocker in motion. "I'm hoping she went to see her sister."

"Probably did. If you don't hear from her soon, let me know, will you?"

She nodded. "Oh, I just remembered. Randall and Sharon want to buy the baby's furniture. I'm going downstairs and tear that page out of the catalogue so they'll know what I want."

"That's all those two can talk about these days. They're mighty pleased."

"I'll be right back."

She'd moved the catalogue so it took her a minute to find it. The page tore out easily and she folded it so it'd fit in Jim's pocket.

As she climbed the stairs, she heard Jamie say, "I don't understand Lucas."

"Not your place to understand him, son. People can be hard to figure and trying will get you nowhere. He's your boss and a good man."

"But she's so nice and pretty. I can't believe he'd shack up with someone like Tabitha. What could he have been thinking?"

"As you well know, men don't always think with their brains."

"Well, I don't like it. Half the town knows he spent the night at her place Friday night. When she hears about it…"

Gail's legs gave out from under her and she sat down on the stair step. Her heart pounded in her chest. Jealousy and hurt choked her. It took all her willpower to keep from crying out. Biting her fist to keep quiet, she eased back down the stairs. Taking an old coat from the closet, she left through the back door and started walking, Chief on her heels. That's why Sharon and Randall had surrounded her this morning. They were standing beside her to prevent more gossip.

When she was far enough away not to be heard, she released the tears. Sobs wracked her body as she cried out her grief. She dropped to her knees, the dampness of the cold dirt seeped through her leggings as she wailed. "Oh Lucas, what have I done?

Chapter Nineteen

Monday morning, Gail called Lucas. The sound of his, "hello" twisted the knot inside her tighter.

"Lucas, you wanted to know about my next appointment with Dr. Lane. It's next Monday at eleven o'clock."

"I'll meet you there."

For just a moment, disappointment nagged her, but she thrust it aside. They had no business going together. Too much had been said already. "Do you know where her office is located?"

"I'll find it. See you there." Before she could respond, he disconnected.

Gail closed her eyes and dropped her head back against the desk chair cushion. Lucas had slept with Tabitha, and Gail knew she was partly to blame. If she'd controlled her anger and hurt, and told him the truth, maybe things could have been different. Had he been with her again? She forced herself to relax and not think about the mess that had become her life.

When she couldn't reach Ruth, she called her sister in Houston. Judy hadn't heard from her, but promised to call if she did. Unable to let it go, Gail called and talked to Bud. He came by her office later in the afternoon. "Did you find out anything?"

"Neighbor said she saw her leave Saturday afternoon with two suitcases. She gave me Ruth's extra key. Couldn't find anything unusual in the house." He tilted his hat forward and scratched the back of his head. "Maybe she needed to get out of town for a few days."

She nodded. "Maybe, but it's just not like her."

"If we don't hear from her within a few weeks, we'll put out an alert to watch for her car."

A couple of weeks seemed like forever. Ruth was a grown woman. She had suitcases so she hadn't been forced from her home. They had no choice but to wait. "Thanks, Bud. I appreciate you checking for me."

"No problem. If I hear anything, I'll let you know."

Gail came home one afternoon to find a note that JuneBug was in a stall in the barn. She dressed in sweats, stepped into tennis shoes, and grabbed a coat on her way out the door. Chief followed on her heels.

The mare heard her enter and whinnied a greeting. "Hey, girl. I've missed you." Junebug nudged her in the chest. Gail dropped her head to the horse's forelock and rubbed her neck affectionately. Her saddle lay across the neighboring stall, the bridle on a nail on a post. Within a few minutes, she had Junebug saddled and led her out of the stall.

She hadn't gained much weight, but lifting herself into the saddle took more effort than it had in the past. Being on the mare's back once again felt wonderful. She wouldn't let her run, just take a leisurely pace. Out of habit, she turned her toward the gorge. Junebug knew the way and took off in a slow gallop. The wind cooled Gail's face and her heart thumped with exhilaration at being on horseback again. She laughed out loud for the first time in weeks.

The grass approaching the gorge was dry, yet the

few live oaks and salt cedars remained green. No wildflowers were in bloom, but to Gail the land was still beautiful, familiar. It was like an old friend, one that would always be there for her. She stopped at the basin's rim. Junebug wanted to go further, but Gail reined her in. Too many memories lived below. Ones too close to her heart.

Junebug's ears flicked up and she nickered a greeting. A horse across the wide expanse answered in response. Her breath caught in her throat at the sight of Lucas atop Grayboy on the far side of the chasm. He didn't move, just stared. She returned his gaze, grateful the distance was too great for him to see the longing in her eyes. Gail couldn't look away. Her hands gripped the reins and she fought to keep from kicking Junebug into motion down the slope. Before she could force her eyes from him, Lucas turned his horse and rode slowly away.

She hadn't been in the house five minutes when the phone rang. Before she could say hello, Lucas's voice echoed across the line. "What the hell were you doing riding? If I'd known you didn't have sense enough to take care of yourself and our baby, I'd never have brought Junebug over."

For a minute she couldn't speak. His anger palpable, she could hear his rapid breathing. "I was careful and won't be riding anymore until after she's born. I have no intention of hurting myself or this baby."

She hung up, furious he'd question her judgment. Maybe riding was a little reckless, but she'd been careful.

~*~

Lucas ordered a beer and found a table. He'd no sooner sat down when Jason joined him. "Hey, Jason, where's Patty?"

Jason waved to the waitress and said, "She's at home with the kids." He placed his drink order and turned back.

"Since when did you start hanging out at Bubba's without your wife?" The idea didn't sit well with Lucas.

"Believe it or not, she sent me to talk some sense into you, old friend." The look Jason sent him conveyed his disapproval. For some reason, his condemnation hurt.

Lucas took a healthy slug of his beer. "Well, you're wasting your time."

Jason sat and didn't say anything, just stared at him. His scrutiny got on Lucas's nerves. "All right, spit it out and then leave me alone."

"I never thought the day would arrive when I could be ashamed by your behavior. Screwing around with someone like Tabitha when—"

"Shut up, I don't want to hear it."

"That's too damn bad. You're going to listen to me if I have to take you outside and beat the shit out of you."

"Try it and see what you get for your trouble." Lucas was itching for a fight. He needed to let off some frustration, but it wasn't his good friend he wanted to hurt. Another round with Alex Guthrie would do a lot to salve his irritability.

"You're a fool, Lucas. Your wife made a mistake and she's paying for it. But, it's shameful the way you've taken up with Tabitha before the divorce is final. You're going to be a father. Be a man that child can be proud of."

Lucas closed his hand around the bottle of beer. He wanted to squeeze until it broke. "Are you through?"

"No. You better make up your mind if you can forgive Gail or not."

"That's easy for you to say. Your wife didn't screw another man."

"Yes, you're right. But, if the rumors are correct, Gail was depressed, worried about her father, and Alex got her drunk. It's not like she set out to cheat on you. And she didn't lie to you either. Her honesty deserves some consideration."

Sometimes Lucas wished she had lied.

"If you'd make a mistake, don't you think you'd be worthy of a second chance?"

"No, I wouldn't. Anyway, I'd never do that to her."

"Right, you're perfect, aren't you? All these years I thought you had one of the strongest loves I'd ever seen. Hell, Lucas, maybe you love yourself more than you're capable of loving anyone else. You put Gail on a pedestal and forgot she was human."

Lucas hit the table with his fist. "Dammit, man, she betrayed me."

"Yes, she did, but she's asked your forgiveness, hasn't she?" His gaze didn't waver. "Make up your mind, Lucas. She didn't cheat to hurt you. She got drunk and made a terrible mistake. Quit flaunting Tabitha, at least until after the divorce. If you can't forgive her, I can think of several men who'll be glad to step in and help raise your child." He shrugged. "But, maybe that's okay with you."

Jason stood up and nodded toward the door. "Your date is here so I'll give you some privacy."

~*~

Friday night Randall called. "The baby's furniture is here. Can Lucas and I come over tomorrow and set it up?"

Jim and Jamie arrived first. The molding to divide the painted area from the papered had been cut and stained, so all they had to do was level it and nail it to the wall. Jim had brought a nail gun and a long extension cord. Before they started, she heard knocking on the front door.

"That must be Randall and Lucas." She couldn't help but notice the look that passed between Jim and the boy. As if to clarify things, she added, "They've brought the baby furniture."

They filed down the stairs. Randall met her. Hands on her shoulders, he said, "You can't come up until we finish."

She laughed. "Okay, I'll put on a pot of coffee." With four men in the room there wouldn't be room for her anyway. Lucas came in carrying one end of a large box. She tried to smile. His gaze flicked to her for a mere second and then returned to his burden.

She put on a pot of coffee and brewed a pot of tea for herself. One of the ladies at work had been teaching her to knit during lunch break, so she brought out her practice sample and worked on it. From upstairs she heard the noise of men's laughter blended with the thumping of the electric nail gun. Thirty minutes later they came down the stairs and went back to Lucas's truck. Back and forth they went.

Finally, she heard Randall call. "You can come up now."

Gail didn't know what to think as she maneuvered

the stairs. The men stood back as she entered the room and then moved so she could see behind them. The crib she'd seen in the catalogue stood elegantly against the far wall. It was filled with a large stuffed duck and had an animal mobile suspended from the headboard. Each adjacent wall held a chest and the changing table.

Tears filled her eyes and she croaked, "Oh my goodness. It's so beautiful." She hugged Randall. "Thank you."

He patted her back. "You're welcome, sweetheart. Lucas and I were happy to do this for you and the child."

She sniffed and smiled up at him.

Lucas. He stood by the crib, running his hands over the smooth spindles. His shoulders were rigid. She turned back to Randall for help to discover he and the others had left.

"Lucas?" He turned and she saw the sheen of tears in his eyes. "Thank you. It's beautiful." He nodded and turned back to the crib.

Silence loomed between them. Finally, hands stuffed in his pockets, he faced her. "You've done a good job on the room. I like it. Have you decided on a name for her yet?"

"I've been thinking of Samantha after Daddy."

"Your daddy was a good man. He'd be as proud as the prize bull at the fair."

Brushing tears off her cheeks, she laughed. "Yeah, he would, wouldn't he?"

The smile died on his face. "Her name will be Johnson, won't it?"

Her heart thudded in her chest. "Of course."

He waved toward the door. "We better get

downstairs."

Randall walked around the table, pouring coffee when they entered the kitchen.

Gail took a cake from the refrigerator. "Anyone care for a slice?"

"Hmmm, looks delicious," said Jim. "Is it one of Ruth's?"

"No, afraid not. I baked this one last night." She served them each a slice and then sat down beside Randall.

Jim sipped his coffee. "Where's Ruth been hiding these days? Don't see her much anymore. She's not sick, is she?"

Gail studied her cup for a minute. "I haven't seen or heard from her in a week. Bud checked on her for me and her neighbor said she'd left with two suitcases last Saturday afternoon."

Randall and Lucas exchanged looks that reeked of censure. She wanted to deny their silent accusations, but decided to keep her mouth shut. "I'm worried sick about her."

Lucas cleared his throat, his expression different from the one he'd worn a second before. "She probably just needed time away from this town and memories."

"I think she's taking Daddy's death pretty hard, so maybe you're right. Plus, it was so soon after finding out about Mama. It's just been a bit much."

A strained silence followed. Gail struggled to ease the tension. She stood. "Who wants more coffee?"

Jim pushed his chair back. "Not for me and Jamie. We need to get back and take care of some things Tom has lined up for us." Jamie washed down his second piece of cake with the last of his coffee. "Enjoyed the cake."

She hugged the older man. "Thank you so much, Jim." Jamie blushed when she caught him in a hug. "You too, Jamie. You were a big help."

Randall stood. "We better get going, too."

Lucas started for the stairs. "I left something in the baby's room. I'll meet you at the truck, Dad."

~*~

Taking two steps at a time, Lucas rushed up the stairs and slowed as he entered the nursery. Closing the door, he stood for a moment taking in every inch of the room. His heart clenched with regret that he didn't live here, wouldn't be at Samantha's beck and call every night. He sat down in the rocker and set it in motion. Gail would sit here to nurse her, soothe her tummy aches, and experience her first smiles, coos, and gurgles. He'd be on the outside looking in. Jason's words from last night echoed in his head. Could he forgive, forget, and move forward?

~*~

Lucas waited when Gail pulled in the parking lot of the medical complex. He helped her from the car and held her arm as she navigated the steps into the building. She wanted to turn to him and plead with him for another chance. Of course that wasn't possible. She'd kept something from him and now he—

"Are you all right?" he asked as they stood in the elevator.

She tried to smile. "Fine. Just thinking."

The door opened and they walked down the long hall to a corner office. Inside, Gail signed in at the desk while Lucas waited and then they sat down. Fifteen minutes later they were shown into an examination room. The nurse took her vital signs and handed her a plastic cup. "There are packets in the bathroom. Be sure we get a clean sample."

Lucas was reading a pamphlet on prenatal care when she got back. No sooner had she sat down on the examination table than Dr. Lane knocked and breezed through the door.

"Hello, Gail." She shook hands with Lucas. "Good to see you here with your wife." If he had any objection to the term wife, he didn't show it. She sat on the stool and reviewed the nurse's notes. "How're you feeling? Still having any nausea?"

"No, I feel fine."

"Hmm, I see you haven't gained any weight since your last visit. Are you trying to avoid gaining?"

Lucas shot her an accusing glare. "No, I'm eating properly and regularly. I'm not always hungry and have to force myself to eat sometimes." Her chin trembled slightly and she struggled to still it.

"How are you sleeping?" Dr. Lane's eyes were assessing as she waited for her response.

"Not too good some nights. Others, fine."

"Is your job stressful?"

"No, tiring some days, but starting in February, I'll work half days and the last month will work from home."

"That's good. Lie back, I think I'll do an ultrasound today and see how your little girl is progressing."

Gail lay down while Dr. Lane extended the table to hold her legs. The doctor placed a sheet over her lap to provide some privacy. Gail tugged her slacks down to her hips and folded her blouse up.

~*~

Lucas couldn't take his eyes off Gail's abdomen. It was slightly rounded and a few white lines stood out against her pale skin. He wanted to reach out and cover it with his hand, see what it felt like with his child inside.

"Okay, you know the routine. Be prepared for the cold."

Gail shivered when the gel hit her tummy. Dr. Lane spread it over her belly with a microphone-like device. Lucas moved so he could see the monitor better. He'd read about ultrasounds, but never seen one.

She checked the vital organs and the placenta. When the baby's profile became fully visible on the screen, Lucas couldn't hold in the gasp that escaped from his chest. "Oh my God, look at her. She's perfect."

"Yes, she is," said Dr. Lane. "Though she's on schedule, I'd still like to see you put on some weight before your next appointment, Gail." She handed Gail some paper towels to clean off the gel. "And, I want you to work on getting more sleep. I don't like to prescribe medicine if I can keep from it, but you need rest."

"What about horseback riding?" Lucas asked. "Should she stop?"

Gail tossed him a frigid glare. Dammit, he had to know. He didn't think Gail would be reckless, but he wanted the issue clarified.

"I think it'd be best not to ride from now on."

Dr. Lane handed Lucas a slip of paper. He looked down to see a picture of their baby. If she'd handed him a check for a million dollars, he couldn't have been more surprised or thrilled. "Thanks, Doctor." He tucked it into his chest pocket. On the drive home, he couldn't resist patting the pocket to make sure it was still there. Jason's words haunted him again. The thought of Gail marrying another man made him deathly ill. His daughter calling someone else daddy was too horrible to contemplate.

Chapter Twenty

Gail had declined Sharon's invitation to spend Christmas Day with them. The strain between her and Lucas would be too much to handle. She'd taken gifts over to them, even one for Lucas. The memory of what she'd bought him made her smile. She hadn't intended to buy something as nice, but once she saw it, she knew it was perfect. She'd been strolling through one of Austin's art galleries when she spotted a painting of a horse and rider that resembled Lucas and Grayboy. The stallion galloped at full speed with its lean rider, hand on his hat to keep it on, bent over the horse's neck. She hadn't been able to look away.

Sharon and Randall had come by the previous evening with a gift and to see the nursery. Sharon "oohed" and "aahed" over the way the room had pulled together. She still hadn't heard from Ruth. No one had.

She'd put up a small tree. Its clear lights twinkled, casting their glow around the room as did the white angel on top. The mantel held sprigs of greenery, candles and her Nativity set. It was almost six o'clock and already dark. She lit the candles and added a couple of logs to the fire. The only light she had on in the room was the one between the new recliner she'd bought and the sofa. Christmas carols drifted through the house thanks to her new CD player. It had been her Christmas gift to herself. Curled up on the sofa with a cup of hot-spiced tea, she worked on the baby afghan she was knitting. She'd finally gotten the hang of the needlework and was pleased with how the blanket was coming along.

Car lights flashed through the front windows and the spotlights turned on. Chief sat by the door, body wriggling in joy. Her heart skipped a beat. She'd been afraid Lucas would come by, but more scared he wouldn't. They'd not talked since the day she'd seen the doctor.

His knock propelled her toward the door. Lucas stood on the porch, carrying a square, wrapped package and two foil-covered plates, one stacked on top of the other. His grin faltered, as if not heartfelt. "Ho, ho, ho, Merry Christmas."

Gail smiled nervously and stepped back so he could enter. "Merry Christmas to you, too." As he passed, his spicy aftershave teased her nostrils and sent an arrow of desire and longing through her. It was so intense she thought she'd cry out.

"Mom sent you some dinner, actually enough for both of us. We don't want to disappoint Dr. Lane the next time you get on those scales."

Gail took the foil-covered plates from him and he put the present under the tree. She went ahead of him though the swinging door into the kitchen.

"Hmmm, looks delicious." Turkey, cornbread dressing, mashed potatoes, green beans, and cranberry sauce. "Sit down, I'll get us something to drink."

"Water for me."

She fixed two glasses of water and placed them, silverware, and napkins on the table. Lucas pulled a foil package from his pocket. Chief sat at his feet, tail wagging. "You knew I wouldn't forget your turkey dinner, didn't you, boy?" He opened the foil and sat it on the floor for the dog. Chief devoured it in less than a minute, and then tucked his head under Lucas's arm. Lucas patted his side. "You're welcome, fella."

"Your mom is a wonderful cook."

"Yeah, she is." Face sober, he looked down at his plate. "We missed you today. Christmas just wasn't the same without you."

Gail nodded. "I missed being there, but didn't think I could handle it. Too many memories." She shot him a shaky smile. This had been the loneliest day of her life.

Voice hoarse, he studied his plate. "Yeah, for me, too." He finished eating and shoved his plate back. She pushed hers back, too. "Can't you eat more than that?"

Hand over her belly, she shook her head. "I'm stuffed. I'd eaten a little something before you got here."

Suddenly the baby kicked and she jumped.

"What's wrong?"

"Samantha kicked me." She splayed both hands over her tummy and laughed. "I think she's going to be a soccer player."

Raw hunger lined Lucas's face. He leaned forward, his eyes on the mound in her lap. She moved to stand in front of him. "Here, feel." His large hands covered her and they waited. Surprisingly, she kicked again. Lucas jumped and then chuckled.

Gail stood between his knees. His hands lingered on her, hoping for more movement. He was so close. She studied the shape of his head and the dent in his hair from wearing a hat. The urge to smooth it was strong. It'd be so easy to step closer and put her arms around his neck, hold him close.

His forehead touched the spot where his hands had been and rested there a moment. Her hand cupped the nape of his neck. Neither spoke. Pulling back, he said, "I've got to go." Standing, he looked at her one last time and strode toward the living room.

She followed him. "Lucas, don't go."

He'd pulled on his coat. The guilt of keeping Alex's revelation ate at her. It was wrong to keep it from Lucas.

When she touched his arm, he wouldn't look at her. "I've got to. Thank you for the painting of me and Grayboy." Voice gruff, he added, "I'll cherish it...always."

"Please, I need to tell you something." *Please stay,* her heart begged.

Eyes narrowed, he studied her with suspicion, but waited.

"It'll be easier if you'll sit down." When he was settled in the recliner, she sat on the sofa, hands clasped on her knees.

"Alex and I didn't have sex that night."

Nostrils flaring, he shook he head. "If this is some kind of a joke, it's not funny."

She shook her head. "It's no joke. I was as surprised as you are. Evidently I passed out. Angry, Alex stripped me so I'd think the worst the next morning." Head in her hands, she added, "And I did."

His face resembled stone. She couldn't tell if he believed her or not, but at least she'd told him.

When he spoke, his jaw clenched and the words came out in a bark. "And just when did he share this bit of news with you?"

Her eyes met his. "Fifteen minutes before I got your divorce papers."

He opened and closed his mouth, but no words came out. Finally he choked out, "Then why the hell did you sign them?"

"I was angry and hurt. How do you think I felt getting divorce papers so fast, before you knew if this baby was yours or not?" She swiped at the tears on her face.

"Not as bad as I felt when Alex said you screamed his name when you climaxed."

Hands fisted at her mouth, her body shook with sobs. "Oh my God, I'm so sorry, Lucas."

Standing up, he spat out, "Yeah, well, I'm sorry, too. Sorry as hell you didn't have the courage to tell me the day we argued." He jerked on his jacket. "Even sorrier that in my anger and hurt, I turned to another woman. All the hurt and anger could have been erased with a few words from you."

"You think knowing the truth would have fixed everything?" She snapped her fingers. "You'd forgive me just like that, Lucas?" His face confirmed her fears. "No, I didn't think so."

He strode to the door and opened it. Looking back he said, "It would have been a start." And then he was gone.

Gail sat on the sofa, staring at the fire until it died down and she grew cold.

As she bent to unplug the tree lights, she noticed the gaily wrapped package Lucas had brought. She couldn't imagine what he'd buy for her now, surely not jewelry and lingerie as he had when they were together. The box was too large anyway. It was about twelve inches square, and when she lifted it to her lap, found it heavy. Untying the green silk ribbon, she sat it aside and tore off the paper. She lifted the lid, removed Styrofoam packing, and gasped. It was a beautiful Lladro figure of a woman with long, dark hair bending over a cradle. A smile of anticipation on her face, the figure lovingly touched the cradle, while her other hand lay protectively over her protruding abdomen. The scene played out on a pastel, round rag rug and a dog sat at the woman's feet. The dog looked a lot like Chief.

Gail choked out a tearful laugh. "Look, Chief, here we both are waiting for Samantha." She held the figurine out and the dog sniffed it. The woman did look amazingly like her before she'd cut her hair. How had Lucas found the beautiful piece? It was so personal and well thought out, it touched her deeply.

She closed the doors on the fireplace, carried the gift up to the nursery and sat it on the side table beside the rocking chair. When the baby started exploring, she'd have to move it, but for now, the spot was perfect.

The next morning, she wrote Lucas a thank you note for the gift. He wouldn't welcome a phone call from her. After a long cry the night before, she'd fallen asleep and slept soundly—a change from her prior habit of waking multiple times to stare at the shadows cast by the moonlight on the wall. Clearing her conscience with Lucas had helped. Though she mourned for the love she and Lucas had shared, it was evident the breach between them was irreparable. She'd have to live with the fact and face Lucas with courage and self-conviction when he visited Samantha. She wouldn't moan and groan in an effort to make his life miserable.

In the nursery, she turned the rocker so she could

see outside and wiped tears from her cheeks as she looked at the ugly storage shed below. Something needed to be done about that eyesore. The baby would be looking out the window a lot, and she wanted her to see beautiful colors and breathe in delightful scents. She'd read babies learned through their senses so she'd see that her child's were sufficiently stimulated.

A new roof and painting the door would improve the shed's looks. Blooming shrubs on each side would be pretty. A pink Rose of Sharon on one side and maybe a native hibiscus with red flame-colored flowers on the other. Next time she went to Austin, she'd pick up the plants and put them in the ground in late February.

She got up and went down the hall to the spare room. It was stacked full of junk she needed to go through and get rid of. Her grandmother's old sewing machine was still usable, so she'd keep it, but she wanted to make room for her computer. She'd start with the boxes. They were filled with patterns from the 1940's and 1950's. Surely someone needed old patterns, but who?

~*~

Almost three months had passed and still no word from Ruth. Even Bud was concerned now and had authorities across the country keeping an eye out for her vehicle. Lucas met Gail at her doctor's office each month for her check-up. His concern for her and the baby's health was genuine. They were civil, but the air crackled with the tension between them. Gail caught bits of gossip. Lucas often frequented Bubba's with Tabitha and left with her. It hurt, but she was powerless to do anything about it.

One Saturday, late in February, Gail worked in her office until noon, ate some lunch, and then took a nap. Warm sunlight streaming through the window woke her. She stretched, enjoying the feel of the rays warming her flesh. Chief lay on the rug by the bed. He stood and shook his frame from his head to his tail.

"Hey, boy, let's get outside and enjoy the sunshine."

It was in the high 60's so she put a sweater on over her sweats and they took off down toward the stables. Junebug heard them coming and whinnied a welcome. Gail missed riding, but wouldn't dare take a chance on getting thrown. Not that the mare would intentionally toss her, but she could stumble or step in a hole.

"Have you missed our outings, girl?" She patted the mare's neck and fed her a couple of sugar cubes. "Won't be too long now. You've had a colt or two, so you know how it is, don't ya? Gotta' take it easy when we're pregnant." Junebug tossed her head and nickered.

"I'll see if Jim can't get one of his grandsons to come over and ride you more often." Jim stopped by every day to make sure the horse had feed and water. They'd built the barn to allow the horses to leave their stall and run in the paddock if the weather wasn't too cold.

Gail and Chief walked back to the house. She stopped at the storage shed, and with the heel of her sneaker, drew a circle where she wanted her shrubs planted. It was still warm and several hours until the sun went down. She went in the shed to find a shovel. The ground around the building was soft and didn't require a lot of effort to move the dirt. She had a hole about fifteen inches deep when Chief became interested in her project. He got in the hole and started tossing dirt back with both front feet, whining as he did so.

"What's the matter with you, boy?" Tired, she leaned on the shovel and watched the dog with amusement. Until he uncovered scraps of cloth. "What on earth?"

She knelt in the dirt and worked to unearth the cloth. It was a man's shirt, one of her father's old ones from the looks of it, covered with dark brown stains. Could it be blood? Laying it aside, she continued to dig. A handle appeared and she tugged on it to reveal the top half of a handbag. Stunned, she sat back on her butt. The purse wasn't hers, wasn't like any she'd ever carried. It resembled those she'd seen in vintage shops from the '70s or '80s.

Fear and dread washed over her. *No, not my daddy. Please God, not my daddy.* Shaking from exertion and nerves, she ordered Chief to guard and went inside and called Bud. To her surprise, Lucas arrived first with the sheriff pulling in behind him. She didn't need this, to see him right now when she felt so vulnerable. Why had Bud called him?

She sat on the back steps. Lucas said something to Bud, and then walked over to her. "Are you all right?"

Shaking, she nodded. He sat down beside her. "I know it looks bad, but don't jump to conclusions."

"Daddy did it. He...killed Mama." Her chin trembled and she couldn't make it stop. "But he swore he didn't do it. Daddy never lied to me," she wailed.

Lucas pulled her up off the step. "Come inside, let's get your hands washed and fix you a cup of hot tea. That'll help calm you."

Gail was cold. She grabbed the afghan off the back

of the sofa and curled up in it. Her teeth chattered.

Lucas handed her a cup of tea. "Do I need to call Dr. Lane?"

She shook her head. "I don't think so. Let me get this tea down and see."

Lucas watched her until she'd emptied the cup. "Do you want another?"

"No, thank you."

He walked to the back door and called for Chief. The dog trotted into the living room, jumped up on the sofa, and lay down next to her. He was warm. She stroked his back and cried. He whined and nudged her affectionately. She wrapped both arms around his neck, and buried her face in his fur.

The back door opened and closed, telling her Lucas had gone out. She thought back to the stains on the blue chambray shirt. They weren't splatter stains, but big blotches of color like it had been used for cleanup. For a minute she felt better, but then remembered the purse. For the life of her, she couldn't think of anyone other than her mother it could have belonged to. Her grandmother had died in the 1950s so it couldn't have been hers.

Additional police cars drove up. Gail heard voices of men from the back. She felt better, so got up and went into the kitchen to make coffee. Bright lights flooded the area and cameras flashed. From the kitchen window, she watched as they meticulously lifted items from the ground and put them in either paper or plastic bags. It was getting dark out and colder by the minute. When the coffee was ready, she stuck her head out the door.

"Bud, when you're ready, I've made coffee for

anyone who wants a cup."

Lucas came in. "They'll be in shortly. Sit down, I'll pour for them. You should be in there on the sofa."

"I'm fine. Have they found anything else?"

He kept his back to her and his shoulders stiffened. "Yeah, they did. Bud will tell you when he comes inside."

"Oh Lord, this is such a mess. I still don't believe Daddy did it, do you?" He turned and she searched his face.

His forehead was furrowed with worry, his lips tight with tension. "No, I don't think he did."

Bud tapped on the door and walked inside with two deputies behind him. He held a large Ziploc bag in his hand with the purse inside and three brown paper bags. "Let's have a cup of coffee and then we'll talk."

In a hurry, all four men poured the brew down their throats and set their cups on the counter. Bud turned to one of his deputies. "Pete, I want you to take the evidence to the forensics lab in Austin."

Pete nodded and picked up the bags. The other deputies followed him out the door. Gail wanted to protest, but knew every speck of evidence needed to be closely examined and not compromised by people handling things. Couldn't Bud at least tell her if the purse was her mother's or not?

Bud cleared his throat. "I know you're dying to know what's in the handbag, but sending it to Austin is the best way. They'll have some information for us tomorrow and I'll be sure and let you know something."

Gail wanted to cry. Bud must have seen her misery. Voice gruff, he said, "Now, young woman, don't go condemning your daddy just because we found this out back. It probably is your mother's, but we found some other evidence out there."

She looked at him through her tears. "What?"

"Found a woman's blood-splattered dress and shoes."

Chapter Twenty One

"We don't know who owned the dress, but I think we all have a good idea. Until we hear on the evidence, let's not speculate. We'll hear something from the forensics lab. I'll call as soon as I know something."

Lucas walked out with the sheriff. Within a few minutes he was back inside, looking in the refrigerator and pantry. He laid out chicken breasts, frozen broccoli, and rice. "You go lay down with your feet up. I'll have something ready to eat in about thirty minutes."

Too numb to argue, Gail did as he said. Chief followed on her heels and lay down at her feet. She snuggled into the afghan and closed her eyes. How had her life become such a nightmare? Was it possible Ruth had murdered her mother and Lamar Jacobs? The woman who'd been a fixture around this house for as long as Gail could remember? It was too hard to comprehend.

"It's ready." Lucas stuck his head around the kitchen door. "You want to eat at the table or on TV trays?"

"Let's eat in here." She tossed back the afghan. "I'll get the trays."

"Stay put, I know where they are."

Gail let Lucas wait on her. It felt good, but Lucas had always been sensitive to how she felt and went out of his way to ease her. Considering their circumstances, it felt odd. He was looking out for their baby.

"Thank you. This looks and smells wonderful."

"Make me proud and eat every bite."

She looked at her plate. It was fuller than she'd have filled it. "I'll try, but remember my stomach doesn't have as much room as it normally does. I don't want to get heartburn."

He nodded. "Okay, eat what you can. Just don't pick at it."

Lucas cleaned up the kitchen and brought her a cup of tea, coffee for himself. "I think it best if I spend the night."

She looked up from her cup. He stared into the brew in his mug. "Thank you, that's very thoughtful, but not necessary. I'll be fine by myself. Chief's here."

"Can Chief dial a phone if you go into premature labor or something?" He held up his hand. "Just forget it, I'm staying. Don't worry, I don't intend to try to jump your bones."

Gail blushed. "I never thought you would. After all, it's not like you're starved for sex. You have Tabitha to see to your sexual needs."

He spat the hateful words at her. "And we all know whose fault that is, don't we?"

~*~

Lucas watched Gail's blush turn pale. Her chin trembled and he wanted to kick himself for the insensitive words, but dammit, it was true. She steadied it and raised it a notch.

"Yes, we do. Mine. I take full responsibility and will bear the guilt for the rest of my life. If it's any consolation to you, the news of your night together almost killed me."

Her pain hit him in the gut. He no longer knew which ache was his and which hers. Their hurting ran together to form one big knot in his chest. "Gail, I—"

She shook her head. "No, don't say anything, let me finish." He waited while she struggled for control. "I bear the blame for the first time you were with Tabitha, but not the following times." She looked up at him, her face twisted. "So, I assume since you've continued to see her, there is no hope for the two of us. After the divorce, I won't interfere in your life or try to cause problems. When Samantha is old enough, we'll work out a visitation schedule so you can have her for weekends."

He cleared his throat. "You've done a lot of thinking."

"Yes, I have. I was careless, and in a weak moment when worried about Daddy, I drank too much, and in my intoxicated state, I turned to Alex for comfort. Not sexual comfort, but a shoulder to cry on, and then I kissed him and it turned sexual. In my stupid state-of-mind, I'd made him into you. He said I called his name?" She shook her head. "He lied. I remember calling out for you and that's the last thing I recall."

Lucas wanted to weep. He dropped his head into his hands. God, what a mess. "I don't know what to say, I—"

"There's nothing more to say, Lucas. I want you to be happy. I love you and probably always will. But, I screwed up. It's time I accepted that and moved on, as you seem to have." She stood, folded the afghan, and laid it over the back of the sofa. With a sad smile, she said. "You can sleep in Daddy's room tonight. I hope his ghost doesn't keep you awake."

He sat there and listened to her footsteps as she climbed the stairs. Chief trotted toward him and laid his head on his leg. In a daze, he patted the dog's back. "Go on upstairs with Gail, boy."

For the first hour, Sam's pillow was too fluffy. The second, his mattress was too soft. No matter how he turned he couldn't get comfortable. In truth, it wasn't his body needing comfort, but his heart and mind. He'd replayed the last eight months in his head, starting with Gail's fertility tests. They'd had so much, yet wanted more. Would things have been different if they'd been content to live life and take what it offered without getting in a hurry?

He must have finally dozed, but the room had grown colder and he reached down to the foot of the bed to pull the extra quilt over him. His nose twitched as he caught the scent of tobacco. The drop in temperature had probably brought out the smell of cigarette smoke that clung to Sam's clothes. He snuggled deeper under the cover and closed his eyes.

A whisper of something touched his face. His eyes flew open as a smoke ring erupted from an invisible source aimed at his face. It was followed by another and another. Lucas lay still and watched the perfectly formed circles reach him and disintegrate. Maybe he was still asleep. He sat up in the bed and the display continued. A shiver ran up his spine. Sam was the only person he knew who could blow smoke rings like what he saw.

"Sam, is that you?"

His answer came in the form of a smoke ring that hovered in the air and pulsed. *Guess that's a yes.* "Guess you're pretty pissed about my and Gail's problems." The smoke grew so thick Lucas coughed. "Yeah, don't blame you. Wish I could say I'd fix it, but don't know if it's possible." He waited for another response. One didn't come.

Lucas woke coughing. Smoke, he was choking on smoke. The whole thing had been a dream and the house was on fire. He lunged out of bed and raced down the hall to Gail's room, and then realized there was no smoke. Just outside her door, he stopped to think. Chief would've sensed the fire and alerted them. He must have been dreaming. Unable to return to bed without checking on Gail, he quietly opened the door and peeked in. Chief lifted his head, and his tail thumped the floor. A sigh of relief rushed from Lucas's chest. All appeared well in there.

He closed the door and returned to Sam's room. Stale cigarette smoke met him as he entered. Back in bed, he pondered what had happened. Had it been a dream? Seconds before he dozed off again, a small smoke ring danced before his face, and then disappeared.

~*~

Two weeks later, on Monday morning, Bud called and asked her to stop by. He waved her into his office as soon as she arrived. "Have the evidence report back. Thought you'd want to know what we've got." Bud pulled a chair up closer to his desk and she sat down. "I'm sorry to tell you, the purse is your mother's, but I suspect you had a good idea it was." His frown conveyed sympathy.

"I guessed it was, but wasn't sure." She was glad the question had been answered.

Bud slipped on latex gloves. "I feel you should get

to see your mother's things."

Gail's throat tightened. "I appreciate it."

He sat the clear zip-lock bag in the center of his desk and removed the handbag. It was the size of a hardback book, made of red patent leather, and closed with a gold-tone clasp at the top.

Bud's hands were thick so he had difficulty maneuvering inside the small space. Finally his hand emerged with a small red billfold. Gail thought she'd seen one like it called a French purse. It had a change pocket and a snap opening where a driver's license and credit cards were stored. She started to shake and fisted her hands for stability. Bud opened it and folded it back to look at the driver's license. Face somber, he turned it toward Gail. "Says June Steele, issue date November of 1980." He sat it aside. "Now, let's see what else we can find in this purse."

He pulled out a compact, a tube of blood red lipstick, and a handkerchief. Stuck between its folds lay a small sheet of paper. Bud carefully unfolded it and read it out loud.

June, I'll meet you at Possum Creek with your suitcase. You know where. I'll drop Gail off at Judy's on the way.

He turned it over. "There's no signature."

Gail stood up, moved behind Bud's desk, and looked over his shoulder. "Let me see. The handwriting looks familiar." Her legs felt like rubber. She groped for the chair. "Oh God, I can't believe she could do it— murder my mother. They were friends. Mama said so in her diary."

Bud's face was grim. "I need you to tell me. Who do you believe this handwriting belongs to? We've collected samples from her house, compared them, so have a pretty good idea, but I want to hear her name."

"Let me see the note again. I want to be sure."

He turned the note toward her. She looked into Bud's eyes and nodded. "It's Ruth's handwriting."

~*~

A handwriting expert verified that Ruth wrote the note. Bud put out an APB for her arrest. The town buzzed. News bulletins aired on national television requesting information on Ruth in connection with the murders of June Steele and Lamar Jacobs. Gail tried to stay busy so she didn't have to think about the woman who'd half raised her and the evil she'd done. She was tired of being the object of speculation and gossip. Hopefully it would soon all be over.

On Tuesday night at nine o'clock, the story was Greta's topic of discussion on the Fox News Channel. Pictures of Ruth were splattered across the screen. Wednesday morning, the police in Laredo, Texas were given a tip and Ruth was apprehended sleeping in her car while parked between two travel trailers in the parking lot at Walmart. A Federal Marshall escorted her back to Stony Creek on Friday.

Bud called her at work the following Monday. "Ruth is asking to talk to you. I'll tell her you said no if you don't want to see her." She didn't want to face the woman, but needed answers.

"When's a good time, Bud?"

"Any time that's convenient for you. Just let us know when you're coming."

The jail was a busy place. Through the glass surrounding his office, Bud saw her when she entered. He walked the man in his office out and came to meet her.

He took her arm and led her to a room with a table and two chairs. "Are you sure you're up to this?"

She was calm this morning and ready to get the confrontation over with. "I think so. I'd like to put it behind me."

"Okay, if you're sure. A deputy will always be in the room with you."

"Is that necessary?" She didn't think for a minute Ruth would try to hurt her.

"Just procedure. The assistant DA would like to see you before you leave." He left the room, and Pete replaced him.

"Howdy, ma'am. Sure sorry to see you here in these circumstances."

Not knowing what to say, she nodded.

Bud returned with Ruth in handcuffs. He helped her into a chair. "You've got ten minutes."

Gail couldn't stand to see the cuffs on the woman who'd taken care of her since babyhood. She choked out. "Bud, please, can you take off the cuffs?"

He frowned, but removed them, then left the room.

Ruth looked awful. Her hair was a mess and mascara streaks lined her face. The orange pantsuit she had on was a size too big and hung on her frame. Hand trembling, she raised it to try to smooth her hair. "I know I look a mess. Bud hasn't gotten my things from the house yet."

"You look fine, Ruth."

The older woman's eyes finally met Gail's. Her lips trembled. "Nothing I say will bring your mama back, but I want you to know I've suffered every day of my life for it." Tears rolled down the mascara trails on her cheeks. Gail handed her a Kleenex and Ruth wiped the moisture away. She wadded the blackened tissue into a ball and squeezed it with her fist.

"I lied about a lot of things to cover up what I'd done." She covered her mouth with her hand and tried to stem the sobs. "I would have left years ago, but felt I owed it to you to stay. But...but I...tried not to...to let you get too close to me." Her body shook. "That was my penance. To never have you love me like a mother."

Gail gaped. She'd thought of Ruth as a surrogate mother, or had she? That wasn't important right now. "But why, Ruth, why did you do it?"

"I loved your daddy long before your mother came along, but he never knew it. He never looked at me once until I came to work for them and then it was only as help for June."

She hit the table with her fist, and Gail jumped.

Ruth stood, shoving her chair back, and screamed, "She planned to take you away! I couldn't let her do that." Her tears suddenly dried and her voice rose to a snarl of hate. "It would have killed your daddy, and me!" She pounded her chest. "You should have been my child. Mine!"

Gail stared in horror as the crazed woman fell to the floor wailing, pulling at her hair.

Gail didn't realize she was trembling, about to sink to the floor, until she felt Pete's arm around her burgeoning waist, helping her to the door where Bud met her. In his office, he seated her in a comfortable chair. One of the women appeared with a glass of water.

"Here, drink this," said Bud. "It may help. You're not going to faint on us, are you? Should I call Doc?"

She sipped the water, then shook her head. "No, no, I'm fine, just give me a minute."

She leaned her head against the chair back and closed her eyes. *Please Lord, let me wake up in a minute. Let this all be a nightmare.* Tears stung her eyes and she drew in deep gulps of air. *Get a grip, Gail. This is not good for the baby. Buck up, deal with it.*

Gail sat up in her chair. Bud visibly heaved a sigh of relief. "I'm better now. Where's Robert?"

"He's right outside if you're up to talking to him. It can wait if you want."

"No, let's get it over with."

Robert didn't keep her too long. Mouth drawn in a tight line, he pulled a chair up close to her side. He clasped her hand. "I'm sorry to bother you more, Gail, but wanted you to hear this from me before word is out. The state will be asking for the death penalty."

"Death?" This news was the final straw. "I…" The room spun and she fell down, down into a deep black hole.

She heard voices from far off. "Gail, come on, honey, wake up." Someone was patting her cheek.

"Doc's on his way, Bud. Lucas, too."

The floor felt cold and hard but someone had rolled a coat up to put under her neck and several coats covered her body. Lucas came through the door like a roaring bull.

"Get back, get out of my way, Gail, oh baby." Before she could say a word, he'd scooped her up in his arms and sat in the chair with her cradled like a child. "Give me those coats." He tucked them around her. "I want another one for her feet."

Someone ran to find another one and it was

wrapped around her rubber-soled shoes.

"Dammit, why wasn't I told she planned to see Ruth?"

Pete stuttered, "Well, hell, Lucas, since you're getting a divorce, we didn't know as you'd want to be called. We're not mind readers, you know."

She struggled to overcome the weakness she felt. "There was no need. I'm fine, Lucas. Just had a little shock."

He snorted. "Shock, my ass—"

Pete hollered from the hallway. "Here's Doc."

Gail relaxed as the matter-of-fact doctor waltzed into the room and cast his eyes around the room. "What the hell do you think this is, a freak show?" He shooed them away. "Get out of here and do something—like work."

Everyone left but Bud, Robert, and Lucas.

Doc pulled a chair up and looked at her eyes, checked her pulse, and checked her blood pressure. He put his instruments back in his bag and took her hand. "Now, young woman, what happened here?"

Gail explained how weak she'd felt and how she'd blacked out. "I feel fine now."

"Hmmm, well, your blood pressure is up. I want you to come by the office and let me check it again. I'll call that doctor of yours in Austin. Then we'll see what needs to be done."

"Really, Doc, I feel fine. I just want to go home."

Lucas spoke up. "You'll go home as soon as Doc says you can." He stood and lowered her into the chair. "You sit right here and don't move until I get back." He turned to Doc. "I'll warm up the truck and bring her right over."

Lucas returned with a blanket. He wrapped her in it and picked her up again.

"This is ridiculous. I'm not a baby, you know. I can walk and drive my own car."

He kept walking. "No, you're not a baby, but it's my baby you're carrying around in there, and while I'm able, you'll not do anything to jeopardize her."

She sputtered. "You think I'd do something to hurt this baby?"

"I didn't say that and you know it."

"I don't know any such thing. I'll have you know I've taken care of this baby when you didn't even believe it was yours and I sure as hell can now, too." She struggled in his arms. "Put me down."

"Stop it. You're drawing a crowd."

She froze and looked around. People had stopped on the sidewalk and stood as if waiting for the next scene. Lucas's face appeared cast in stone. She clamped her mouth shut.

Just as Lucas set her on the seat, Pete came running out of the sheriff's office, carrying Gail's purse and coat. Lucas took them and threw them in her lap. He was mad and she didn't care. To suggest she wouldn't take care of this baby was uncalled for.

In one of Doc's examining rooms, Gail lay on the table, covered with the blanket. She was grateful for its warmth though she'd never let on to Lucas. He sat in one of the chairs, looking like a thundercloud.

Doc came in bringing a wisp of cool air with him. "Well, I talked to Doctor Lane and she said your blood pressure's been good to date, Gail. Let's check it again and see if it's down."

He strapped on the cuff and checked it. "It's almost

back to what Dr. Lane said was your normal. She suggested I do an ultrasound to be on the safe side."

Gail started to object and say everything felt fine, but noticed the look of concern and anticipation on Lucas's face.

"Let's get you out of this mummy cloth. Suppose this was Lucas's method of wrapping."

She giggled and watched Lucas blush.

After the ultrasound, Doc announced everything appeared to be normal. "But, as a precaution, your orders are to go home and stay in bed today. Get up only to go to the bathroom and eat. No climbing stairs. Come in and have your blood pressure checked again in the morning. If it's good, you can go back to normal activities." He tapped her on the nose. "Are we clear?"

"Yes, Doc, clear as a bell."

He grinned and left the room.

Lucas said, "Guess that means I'll be spending the night again."

"That's not necessary. I can get someone to come over and fix my meals."

"I will take care of you, Gail. You're carrying my child and I aim to be there when you need me." Chin thrust forward, his expression brooked no argument.

Gail's heart raced at his look of determination. He cared for the baby, but perhaps he still cared for her, too. Maybe if she tweaked his temper enough, he'd admit it. She wanted him back, but only if he truly loved her and didn't just want the baby. "All right, if staying away from Bubba's isn't too painful for you. After all, Tabitha might hook up with another man if you're not there. I wouldn't want you to get sexually frustrated."

Chapter Twenty Two

They were quiet on the ride into town. Their night together had been strained. He'd wanted to throttle her, but fed and waited on her so she wouldn't have to get up. She didn't relax her guard around him and kept an emotional distance. Her remark about Bubba's and Tabitha had burned his butt. He didn't give a rat's ass who the woman left with. She'd been someone to ease his loneliness, someone to dance with, talk to, and have sex with. But for Gail to mention his behavior so matter-of-factly, like she didn't care, didn't sit right with him. Ah, hell, he needed to end the relationship with Tabitha, if you could call their brief encounters a relationship.

Gail had given up on them, on their life together as a family, and given him the freedom to do what he wanted and still have access to their child. Dammit, how dare she give up so easily? She should be fighting for what they'd had.

He glanced at her as she rode along in his pickup. Her color was good and she looked pretty in her pink maternity top. Who'd know that yesterday she'd faced her mother's murderer, and as calm as you please, told him not to cut down on his social life because of her? Shit! He was as disgusted with himself as he was with Gail.

As soon as they arrived, they were escorted into an

examination room. Pleased with her blood pressure, Doc told her to go home and take it easy and to see Dr. Lane for her regularly scheduled appointment.

"What are your plans for today?" he asked, hoping she'd say, "Rest."

Casually dressed, he didn't expect she'd stay in town and shop, but he was concerned she'd overdo it after her exciting day yesterday.

"I'll probably work in my office a while, have a light lunch, and then take a nap." Lucas sighed with relief. "Then Chief and I usually walk down to the stable to see Junebug. She gets lonesome."

"You're not riding her, are you?"

"Of course not. Do you think I'm a complete idiot?"

Lucas cleared his throat. "No, I didn't think you were, but had to ask to make sure. Don't know what's wrong with me lately, but I'm scared to death something will happen to you and the baby."

Her face relaxed. "I promise you, I take carrying this child seriously. I won't do anything to put either of us in danger." She patted his hand. "Try not to worry."

He nodded. "I'm sorry if I'm overbearing."

"It's okay."

He stopped his truck in front of the sheriff's office and jumped out to run around and help her out. When Gail turned to him, her smile was teasing. "Thanks for looking out for me again yesterday. You make a good nurse."

Lucas was ticked off at her cheerful attitude. "You're welcome. I'll come over and plant those bushes for you as soon as Bud removes that yellow tape around the shed."

"That'll be fine." She waved and got in her car. He watched until she'd pulled out, then followed her. When she turned to the road leading home, he honked, waved, and drove on toward the ranch.

~*~

Gail worked in her office for a while and took a nap after lunch. She and Ron agreed she could work from home until she felt well enough to go back to the office. It was easier on her not having to dress up in hose and heels and drive into town every day.

She hadn't been up long. The nursery drew her and she sat in the rocker and picked up her knitting. The yellow blanket, though a little misshapen, was soft to the touch and blended with the colors in the room. She used her toe to set the rocking chair in motion. It creaked, the movement and sounds a comfort to her aching heart. She'd confessed her love for Lucas, yet he'd said nothing. His silence was telling and she couldn't face further rejection.

Tears gathering in her eyes, she sniffed and tried to push thoughts of Lucas from her mind. Unbidden, her gasps turned to sobs. Her body shook as she cradled her abdomen. *Oh God, I'm so sorry for all I've done. Help me, Lord. Let me concentrate on the future, not dwell on the past.*

She closed her eyes and rested her head against the rocker back. The room grew cold and she splayed her hands over her belly as if to keep Samantha warm. Smiling, she took deep calming breaths and slowly exhaled. Peace settled upon her like a blanket, adding warmth. Cigarette smoke tickled her nose. Her eyes snapped open to see a ring of smoke around the chair. She blinked, but the presence around remained.

"Daddy?"

She felt warmth against her hair. *Take heart, baby girl. All will be well.*

~*~

Saturday, Lucas drove over and planted Gail's shrubs. Before he left, he went inside to wash his hands. She leaned against the counter, looking beautiful as always in a pink fleece top and black leggings. "My Lamaze classes start next week and I wonder what you think about me asking your mother to be my coach."

His breath caught in his throat. Oh God, he was dying here. He struggled to keep his voice steady as he turned off the tap and dried his hands. "Why can't I be your coach? I want to be with you when our child is born."

She didn't say anything for a minute. Then her blue eyes locked on his. Did he see a spark of something there? "I wouldn't feel right, Lucas, you sleeping with another woman, being familiar with her body and all. After all, mine isn't attractive anymore. I'd be self-conscious."

He threw the dishtowel against the wall. "That is the most insane notion I've ever heard. Your body is beautiful to me no matter how many stretch marks you get. Yes, Tabitha and I had sex, but I haven't touched her since I learned the truth about Alex."

This woman was going to give him a coronary. He scrubbed his scalp with his hands and struggled for the right words.

"I love you, Gail. I'm sorry for all the bad things that have happened between us. It doesn't matter who's to blame anymore, or who hurt who how many times. I want us to be a family. The longer we're apart, the more likely we'll never get back together.

"I love you, never stopped loving you, and should have told you the night you confessed to me." But she'd made him so damn mad with her attitude about Tabitha and not interfering in his life. He took a deep breath. "I've forgiven you for your behavior with Alex. Please forgive me for turning to Tabitha."

If she didn't want him back, he needed to make a break now.

He touched her face, the skin soft under his fingers. Tears glistened in her eyes and he wanted to hold her but didn't dare take her in his arms. "You know what I want, a life with you and the baby."

~*~

Gail's strict control melted under his intense glare. Finally, the words she'd longed to hear. He loved her *and* the baby. She felt it clear to her toes. Their love was strong enough to get over this crisis.

She stepped into his arms. He grabbed her, pulling her tight against him and it felt so right. "That's what I want, too, Lucas, and I forgive you. I was so foolish for not telling you the truth right away."

He pulled back and looked down at her. His voice hoarse, he asked, "Are you sure? Can we put all of this behind us and learn to trust again?"

Gail had never been surer of anything in her life. She'd learned so much in the past six months. Pride couldn't keep you warm at night and make you smile, and anger and stubbornness only led to greater sorrow. "Yes, Lucas, I'm sure."

~*~

Lucas cradled her closer, as close as he could with her burgeoning belly, and breathed in her delicious scent. "Thank God."

She pulled his head down for her kiss and they were lost in the taste and touch of each other.

Lucas was a starving man, and touching and holding Gail was the nourishment his heart and soul needed. His hands stroked her back, holding her rounded belly against his flat one. "You are so beautiful to me, Gail, lovely." Her lips opened for him and he deepened the kiss, tasting the sweetness he'd missed for so long. He wanted to touch her breasts and belly, feel the changes the baby was making to her body.

"Gail, Gail, I've missed you so—touching you, tasting you. Let me love you." He held his breath and waited for a sign from her.

At her breathless, "Yes, Lucas, it's been too long," he lifted her in his arms and carried her upstairs. He slowly undressed her and reveled in the changes in her body. Her breasts were full and ripe in his hands, a perfect complement to her rounded abdomen. She reached for his shirt and yanked, popping the snaps, and pulled his tee shirt from his jeans. He reached for the hem and tugged them both off at the same time. It didn't take him long to shuck his boots and jeans. He kicked them aside. They touched and stroked until both shook with need and could wait no longer. She stretched out on the bed and reached for him. With arms straight to keep his weight off her, he bent down to kiss her as he eased inside and their moans of pleasure merged. She pushed against him and moving in and out, he stroked her until they both shattered and cried out.

Lucas fell to the bed beside her and she rolled to face him. He gathered her close, and she kissed his shoulder. Tears dropped to his chest and his throat tightened. "Don't cry, sweetheart. We're going to be okay."

She sniffed. "I know, better than okay. I love you, Lucas. I'll never give you reason to doubt me again."

"Oh baby, I should've known something wasn't right from the beginning. If I'd not filed for divorce so soon, you wouldn't have been so defensive and told me the truth." He groaned. "I was wrong to turn to Tabitha, even as mad as I was."

Her head left his chest and she looked into his eyes. "If, if, if... We can't go back, only forward." She twined her fingers in his chest hair and tugged.

"Ouch!"

"Just for the record, I don't share." The smile she flashed him left no doubt who she meant.

"That's over, should never have started." He removed her fingers from his chest and twined them with his. "I'm rather stingy myself, ma'am."

She cocked an eyebrow. "Point taken. Guess that means we're both going to be faithful from this date forward."

"Exactly, love, faithful forever."

Chapter Twenty Three

The afternoon they brought Samantha home from the hospital, Chief met them on the road and escorted them up the drive with happy barks. When Lucas pulled the car to a stop, the dog jumped into the air time and again.

Lucas helped Gail out of the car and handed Samantha to her. Arm around her waist, he escorted her into the house, Chief on their heels. She sat down on the sofa with Samantha on her lap, Lucas beside her, with his arm around her shoulders.

Chief sat patiently until Lucas called him over. "Come on, meet Samantha." The dog looked her over, smelled her from her head to toe, and then licked her arm. "No licking Sam."

Gail patted the sofa and Chief jumped up beside her. He laid his muzzle on her leg, and every once in a while, nuzzled Samantha with his snout.

Samantha woke, making little grunting noises. She puckered up and let out a series of sharp cries. It agitated Chief. He looked from her to Lucas, and when neither moved, yipped.

Laughing, Lucas picked Samantha up and put her to his shoulder. "You're going to be a big help around here, boy."

Gail stood and took the baby from him. "I'll take her upstairs so we can rock while I nurse her."

He placed a kiss on her lips and one to Samantha's forehead. "I'll be fixing us something to eat."

Lucas felt at home in the old farmhouse kitchen. He and Gail had decided to live here and raise Samantha. The house needed some work, but they'd both enjoy doing it. Gail would work from home for a while and they'd get someone to come in full time when she returned to work. Ron had offered Gail a full partnership. They could raise the money and it was what Gail wanted.

Ruth's hysterical condition worsened. The judge sent her to a psychiatric hospital for observation and treatment. If she improved, she'd be remanded to the women's unit in Huntsville, Texas. Not far enough from Stony Creek to suit Lucas, but the judge hadn't asked for his opinion.

After dinner, they sat on the sofa and sipped mugs of hot coffee. Chief refused to leave the nursery so both knew they'd either hear Samantha or Chief when she woke. The room grew chilly and Gail pulled the afghan from the sofa back and draped it over their legs. Lucas put his arm around Gail and dropped his lips to her hair. Out of the corner of his eye, he noticed Chief standing at the top of the stairs, his ruff standing on end. Drifting down the stairs were three smoke rings. They moved toward the front door where they merged, and then passed through the wall to disappear.

He whispered, "Did you see that?"

"I was hoping I hadn't. Is it what I think it is?"

Lucas chuckled and hugged her. "Call me crazy, but I think your daddy just visited his granddaughter. Did I ever tell you about that dream I had?"

Linda LaRoque

About the Author

Linda LaRoque is a Texas girl, but the first time she got on a horse, it tossed her in the road dislocating her right shoulder. Forty years passed before she got on another, but it was older, slower, and she was wiser. Plus, her students looked on and it was important to save face.

A retired teacher who loves West Texas, its flora and fauna, and its people, Linda's stories paint pictures of life, love, and learning set against the raw landscape of ranches and rural communities in Texas and the Midwest. She is a member of RWA, her local Chapter of HOTRWA, NTRWA and Texas Mountain Trail Writers.

Linda writes contemporary western romances, time travel historical romances, women's fiction and futuristic romances.

~ * ~

Visit Linda at these locations:
www.lindalaroque.com
http://www.lindalaroqueauthor.blogspot.com
https://www.facebook.com/linda.laroque
http://www.goodreads.com/author/show/649259.Linda_
LaRoque

Other Books by Linda LaRoque

Contemporary Westerns
Investment of the Heart
When the Ocotillo Bloom

Futuristic
Born in Ice

Time Travel
My Heart Will Find Yours—The Turquoise Legacy
Book 1
Flames on the Sky—The Turquoise Legacy Book 2
A Way Back
Desires of the Heart—novella
A Law of Her Own—novella
A Marshal of Her Own—novella
A Love of His Own—novella
A Time of Their Own—an anthology containing
A Law of Her Own, A Marshal of Her Own,
and A Love of His Own
Birdie's Nest

Women's Fiction
Shattered Vows
Wounded Hearts—novella